UNBEARABLE

AN INHUMAN PROTECTOR ROMANCE
BOOK 5

A. SAMSON

Editor: Anessa Books

Editor: My Brother's Editor

Cover Designer: Rachel Webb

Cover Photo: AuthenticVision/Shutterstock.com

Un·bear·a·ble (ən berəb(ə)l)

Adjective: Not able to be endured or tolerated.

CONTENTS

PROLOGUE

BEING the youngest detective in the Boston Police Department was no walk in the park. Especially as a woman. But Dover had settled into her role on the force without much fanfare.

That was, until today, when she and her partner answered a call early this morning about a body found at one of the local private secondary schools.

The victim was a white male around thirty years of age. He was laid out in the grass of the soccer pitch with his hands resting at his sides. There were no clothes, no driver's license, nothing to identify him. There was nothing about his body to indicate he was homeless or displaced. He appeared healthy and well-kept. He was someone who would soon be missed.

Dover followed her partner closely as he led the preliminary investigation into her first staged murder scene as a detective. It was quickly discovered that the death hadn't taken place at the dump site.

She wasn't new to murder, but in the past, they had usually involved an angry spouse, close friend, or dealer.

Never an unknown. The crime scene techs scoured the area collecting anything and everything. The medical examiner retrieved the body. Still there was nothing.

That was exactly what they discovered when they started trying to put a name with the face. She spent the day harassing the handsome new medical examiner for answers on cause of death.

Fingerprints were run, and the victim's steps traced, only to have everything peter out after tracking him to a bar he'd been in almost twenty-four hours before his death. No one recognized him. No one remembered him. It had been a busy night.

Now, Dover was exhausted. She needed a little down-time before returning to work. The bar down the street would be the perfect place for a break. After all, it was most of the workforce's quitting time. A quick beer and a sandwich would do nicely. Her partner waved her off when she mentioned the idea of them taking a break.

"Go home, Dover," he said. "We'll pick this back up tomorrow. I was heading out myself."

"I just want to organize what we've found. Maybe another hour, but I'm starving. I'll just grab a sandwich." All she wanted was at least an hour to digest the information they had already collected about the victim. She thought best when it was quiet in the office. By the time she was done with her dinner, the office should be empty.

"Suit yourself. See you tomorrow."

She grabbed some cash from her purse and walked out of the building. The day was still sweltering even at seven in the evening.

The summer had barely started, and the city was baking. It promised to be a long summer. August would be absolutely brutal. By the time she reached the bar, she had sweat running down her back. She grabbed several bar napkins and swiped at her face.

"Can I get whatever you have on tap," she told the bartender as she slid onto an empty barstool. "Bring me a roast beef as is while you're at it." The beer arrived icy cold. She took a long sip.

Pulling out her phone, she mindlessly scrolled through her emails until her sandwich arrived. Her stomach growled just smelling the beef when the bartender slid the plate in front of her. She was going to enjoy this.

Dover saw the two men the moment they entered the bar. Actually she had noticed the rental car they'd sat in as she walked toward the bar earlier. There hadn't been any reason to question why there were two men sitting in a car in the sweltering summer heat. People did strange things all the time.

Now, though, they had walked inside. The smaller man headed toward the restrooms, while the giant with him found a booth in the corner.

There was something about them that didn't sit well with her. She couldn't put her finger on it, but they screamed trouble. The smaller man looked tame enough, but the other one—she wasn't so sure. His size, ponytail, and scowl made the hair on the back of her neck stand on end.

The one returned from the restroom shortly and took the seat across from the larger man. Something they passed between them had their attention for a few minutes. From what she could see, it looked like a photo.

Then they turned their attention to her. She caught them staring at her back in the mirror behind the bar. Something was definitely going on with those two.

Whatever they wanted, she wasn't interested. Downing the rest of her beer, she tossed some money on the bar and moved toward the door. She was almost to the side alley when they both stepped outside. Looking around, they must have caught a glimpse of her because they started in her direction.

It didn't matter. She'd soon lose them in the narrow maze of the Boston back alleys before she returned to her office. She chose another one and turned down it.

Her brother didn't live far from here, so she'd just head that direction. At the very least, they wouldn't follow her into his building. Pausing for a moment, she heard footsteps not far behind her.

She didn't panic. She never panicked if she could prevent it. Her training taught her to stay calm and handle whatever situation presented itself. Her pace sped up only to be matched by the two men following her. One of the men had even broken into a jog. Well, if she couldn't outrun them, she would do something different.

Turning another corner, she waited. Her legs spread slightly for better balance. Her arms prepared to strike.

She just wished she knew which one would be first, but at least she had the element of surprise. If she could over-power the one, she had a gun to handle the other one. She left it secured in its shoulder holster for now. She wanted both hands free. Listening closely, she waited for the first man to turn the corner into the alley and struck.

Of course, it had to be the behemoth first. She quickly latched onto his arm, spun, and launched him onto the ground over her shoulder. Her gun was pointed at his companion with the first man trapped under her knee in seconds. Then something she hadn't expected happened. It was a first in her career.

The smaller man began to laugh.

"Who are you, and why are you following me?" she

asked, knowing she needed to maintain control of the situation. The other man laughed for several more seconds before he could compose himself enough to say anything.

"Man, you just got your ass handed to you by a woman," he said, shaking his head. "That was epic. Not the first time though."

"Fuck you," the big man growled. "I think she ruptured my pancreas. I could be dying."

"Of embarrassment maybe. She'd have to stab you to rupture your pancreas," the smaller guy answered. "You're such an idiot."

"Shut up! Both of you," Dover yelled over their squabbling. "You have five seconds to tell me who you are, or I'm rupturing both of your pancreases. You chose the wrong woman."

She reached into the inside pocket of her jacket and pulled out a wallet. Flipping it open, she showed them her badge.

"You thought she was a convicted felon?" Small guy started laughing again. "You were following a cop, dumbass. How did you not know she was a cop?"

Dover quickly patted the big man down for weapons before pulling the wallet out of his back pocket. Just for good measure, she slipped a pair of restraints onto his wrist.

"Sweetheart, the last woman that felt me up like that I married," he mumbled with his face to the bricks.

She flipped open the wallet.

"Knox Monroe," she read. "Chicago, Illinois. Forty-three years of age. Damn, are you really six foot seven?" She looked up at the other man. "Toss yours over too, pretty boy."

"Memphis Prescott," he said, fishing his wallet slowly

out of his back pocket. He tossed it to the ground at her feet. "Minnesota. Not nearly as old and normal size."

She checked his license, then slid both wallets into her pocket. "And," she said, motioning for Memphis to keep talking. Knox started to push himself up, but she shoved him back down with her knee.

"And, we really do have a legitimate reason for tailing you," Memphis began. "We have documentation, back in the car, that leads us to believe that...well, we think you might be our sister. Half sister if you want to get technical."

She decided they must be high on something. She had one brother, and he was currently in his apartment. It wouldn't hurt to get a little more information before calling patrol to pick them up.

"Look," he continued. "We're sorry to spring this on you. I suggested we set up a meeting, but he likes to do things his way. We think we're related through a shared male donor."

"Okay, I'll bite. What documentation?" she asked.

"DNA match. Background check," Knox mumbled from the ground. "All legally obtained."

"And how would you legally obtain my DNA?" She moved Knox into a seated position and waved for Memphis to join him. She debated restraining his arms also, but decided if he wasn't a problem yet, he probably wouldn't become one. Besides, she still had her gun.

"We have a brother-in-law who's with the FBI. He has a program on his computer that alerts him to any possible matches that he shares with us," Knox said. "We were following you because when he pulled up the information, there was a sealed juvenile arrest record associated with it. I wanted to see who you were before we made contact."

"You didn't tell me any of that," Memphis answered.

"I didn't tell you Flint called to tell me his mom is now dating Detective Moore either. So sue me," Knox snarled.

"Really? That's good, I think."

"Did you know his name is Aaron?" Knox asked.

"No. How did we not know what the man's first name was? Did you?" Memphis asked. "Seems like something we should have known. Well, I'm happy for them, anyway."

"Do you always talk this much?" she asked, returning her gun to the holster. No one would blather on like that if they intended her harm. She didn't think so anyway. She pulled out her knife and cut the restraints from Knox's hands.

"He does," Knox said, nodding at Memphis.

"Show me these DNA tests," she said. Memphis pulled Knox off the ground. "And I'm not the one with the arrest record. That's my brother. He's also not a felon. He just boosted a car when he was a teenager."

"There's a brother?" Memphis asked. He met Knox's eyes in confusion.

"A twin actually. I was on the way back to my office when I noticed you following me, but I think we should continue this with him," she answered. "We should go back to your car and get this documentation. We can review it at his place. If what you claim is true, he'll need to know too." She motioned for them to start down the alley.

"Knee?" Memphis asked when Knox limped forward.

"It's fine. Just needs some ice."

"Did you know anything about a brother?" Memphis looped his arm around Knox so he could use him as a crutch. Knox threw his arm over his shoulder. Dover could not understand what was happening. It was like she had arrived in the Twilight Zone.

"There was nothing about a brother. It doesn't make

sense. They wouldn't have the same DNA since they're fraternal twins," Knox said. "I'm going to need my money back from Paul. Private detective, my ass."

"You had me followed by a private detective?" She couldn't believe someone would do that. Even more disturbing was that she'd never noticed.

"Not me. He did," Memphis said. "I wouldn't get too excited. Guy sounds like a real Sam Spade." He smirked.

"More like Frank Drebin." Knox snorted.

"How old are you?" Memphis gave him a feigned look of disgust.

"Greer likes old British crime shows. I haven't touched the remote in over a year." They reached the car, and Memphis pulled the messenger bag from the back seat.

"Let's go. And who's Greer?" she asked.

"Wife," Knox answered. So they weren't your typical stalkers. "She's back in Chicago."

They followed her back down the alley while she tried to puzzle out the DNA results. They reached her brother's apartment building, and she handed the test back to Memphis. Pulling out a key, she opened the door. Her brother, Fox, had given her one when he moved in just in case.

"Let's go, old man," she heard Memphis say behind her on the stairs. He managed to drag Knox up the two flights. She didn't bother to wait for them but left the door open to the apartment figuring they would find it eventually. With any luck, she would have just enough time to warn her brother before they arrived.

CHAPTER 1

FOX TRUDGED up the stairs of his apartment building. It had been a long day at work. Fires had just seemed to erupt everywhere. Not actual fires, the metaphorical ones.

The three-story in Revere the team was tearing back to the studs was demanding more of his attention than it should. The house had become a broken record with one problem after another. That meant he couldn't get to the new build in Brookline as often as he should.

With one of his regular clients chomping to begin his townhome remodel in Cambridge, Fox didn't know how he would ever get any time off. The driving back and forth between sites alone was enough to drive him crazy. His boss kept assuring him that everyone wanted him to oversee their projects.

He knew he was good at his job, but that didn't mean they needed to assign him to all of them. There were two other site supervisors who were perfectly capable. Not as good, but still capable.

He didn't know if it was just his imagination, but the

stairs to his apartment seemed to get longer every time he climbed them. There should be just enough time to get in the shower before his sister came banging on his door. His girlfriend would show up not long after that. Then he would get to enjoy the two women sneering at each other the rest of the evening.

Fox really wished his sister would just leave well enough alone. This relationship was hard enough without her in the middle of it. But Dover had been watching over him for the last forty-one years. She truly believed that being born sixteen minutes earlier meant she got to interfere in everything where he was concerned.

He left his boots by the front door, threw his clothes in the hamper and stepped into the shower. He didn't do much of the heavy labor anymore at the job sites, but he still seemed to get just as dirty.

The water finally ran clean, and he stepped out to dry off. He pulled on a pair of sweats and a T-shirt before heading for the kitchen. He had just turned the oven on when he heard the door open. That would be Dover.

"Hey," she said, walking into the kitchen. "I need some ice. You got any plastic bags?"

"You know where they are," he answered. "Hand me that casserole dish on the top shelf of the fridge while you're over there." He slid it into the oven when she set it on the counter.

"Come into the living room with me. There are some people I want you to meet." She stood with the bag of ice. He shook his head when she walked out of the room just expecting him to follow. He did just that and found two men sitting on his couch. One was nursing a swollen knee. Dover tossed the bag of ice to him.

"This is my brother, Fox," she said. She didn't introduce either one of the strangers. She had always been a little rough around the edges.

"What happened?" he asked. He pulled over a chair from the table for the man to rest his leg on.

"Your sister beat him up," the other man said.

"Mmm," he acknowledged. "I believe that."

"Fox, these two claim they're related to us," Dover said, settling in a chair across from them.

"Really?" he said. "I guess it's possible. We don't really know anything about our biological parents. The Addamses adopted us while we were still in the hospital."

Now that he looked a little closer, he noticed they had the same eyes that both men did. Usually, he wouldn't think anything about that, except they had green eyes that almost glowed. He had never seen anyone else with eyes like that—except his sister.

"Are you going to give them our bank codes and Social Security numbers too?" Dover asked. His sister's voice rang in his mind. What had started as a parlor trick when they were young had developed into something neither of them could explain.

"Aren't you even a little bit curious?" he asked, looking at her.

"And if they're running some elaborate con game? What if they're just some thugs Brooke's ex hired to kill you?"

"Then they would have killed me by now." Fox rolled his eyes and turned back to their guests. "What proof do you have?" he asked out loud.

"This is Knox's DNA profile," one of the men said, laying down a piece of paper. "This one is mine."

Fox looked at the papers. Knox Monroe was the big guy

with the bum knee, and Memphis Prescott was the other one.

"This one is yours," he added, placing another paper on the table.

They began to discuss what they did and who the rest of their party was, but Fox had tuned out. He pulled the three pieces of paper to him and studied them. He had no idea how to read them. He could see there were areas where all three tests matched.

"So, if you're right, we'd be number five and six," Fox said, interrupting something Memphis was saying about more siblings. Was that right? He had heard something about a red-headed sister and a college-age brother during the explanation.

Memphis opened his mouth to say something more when the door opened.

Brooke stopped in the doorway and took a perusal of the room. Her gaze was almost flirty with the two men on the couch. When it fell on Fox, her gaze turned into a smile. With Dover, her glare became glacial. Fox stood to greet her, but she ignored him. She was still trying to win the stare-off between her and Dover.

"We should go," Memphis said, standing. "We'll just leave those for you to study. Come on, Knox." He heaved the large man to his feet and returned the chair to the table. "It was nice to meet everyone. Ma'am," he added to Brooke, half dragging Knox into the hallway.

"How was your day?" Fox asked, giving Brooke a quick kiss on the cheek. "Where's Ethan?"

"He's with his dad tonight," she answered.

Fox tried not to flinch. Ethan's dad was a notorious drug dealer who worked up in Lowell. Fox hated it when she left the little boy with his father. He worried that Ethan wouldn't come home one day because he was in the morgue.

"Doesn't he have school tomorrow?" Fox asked.

"Hey, where's Ethan?" Dover asked, walking back inside from the hallway.

"None of your business," Brooke answered.

"With his dad," Fox said at the same time.

"You left him with that crackhead?" Dover asked. "Are you fucking stupid?"

"Don't you come into this apartment and start telling me who I can and can't leave my son with," Brooke seethed.

It was the same all the time. Fox watched the back and forth until he couldn't take it anymore. Taking a deep breath, he closed his eyes and focused on the small amount of calm still left in the room.

Soon both women seemed to have the fight siphoned right out of them. They wouldn't apologize and make up, but at least they weren't screaming at each other still. The yelling wouldn't change the circumstances. Ethan was still going to be gone.

"I'm going home," Dover suddenly announced. "Can I see you in the hall?" She didn't wait to see if Fox would agree. She grabbed him by the front of the shirt and dragged him through the door. Pulling the door closed behind them, she started smacking Fox in the chest. "Stop fucking doing that," she said.

"Doing what?" He wasn't stupid. They both know what he was doing.

"Being a dick."

"How is diffusing the situation before you come to blows being a dick? Why do you keep fighting with her? It does nothing but make this worse. You know why I can't change anything."

Dover took a deep breath this time before patting on his chest. "I know. How long do you think you can keep this up?"

"I don't know. I don't see any other option right now," he answered.

Her hand dropped. She studied his face before shaking her head.

"I'm sorry. I know how hard this is. Please be careful. When I look at you, you're very blue, and she all but glows red. I don't want to get a call saying she finally killed you," Dover said.

"I will be. I promise," he added when she scrunched her eyebrows at him. She kissed his cheek and started down the hallway. "Hey, what about those guys? Memphis and Knox?"

"I gave them one of my cards. Said to call if they wanted to talk more," she said over her shoulder. "I'll be surprised if we hear from them again, but if so, I'll get to the bottom of it."

He would be surprised if they heard from them again too. It would be interesting, however, to find they had a whole passel of brothers and sisters out there.

"Why do you let her come over here?" Brooke demanded the second he stepped back into the apartment. She had taken off her work clothes and stood in just her underwear.

"She's my sister. I can't just forbid her from coming over. It wouldn't work anyway. You know how she is."

Brooke pouted for a few minutes. "Well, I don't like it," she said.

"I know. I'm sorry."

Her pout morphed into a sexy smile. "Maybe Daddy should come make it up to me." Why had he ever found that appealing? It had even been a major turn-on at one time. Now it just made his stomach turn.

But he would do whatever she wanted to guarantee she didn't run off with Ethan again. That week had been the worst of his life. He had spent sleepless nights wondering what was happening to the little boy.

His mother had been known to leave him in motel rooms alone while she went out partying. There was even a story about Ethan being asleep in the bedroom while her ex and his buddies did lines in the living room.

She pulled him to her and tugged his T-shirt off over his head. Her hand smoothed its way down his body and pushed its way inside his sweats. Her mouth turned down in a pout again at finding him flaccid. Not to be easily discouraged, she dropped to her knees.

Fox closed his eyes when she began to stroke him. There was a time when just looking at her made him hard. That was before he realized that the sexy exterior hid a mind full of venom.

"That's better," she said, pushing back to her feet. "Now come make me scream." Taking his hand, she led him into the bedroom.

Making her scream wasn't hard. He swore from the first time that she exaggerated every orgasm like she was starring in some porn movie. Most of the time, he even had to place a hand over her mouth to keep her from waking Ethan up. She always sunk her teeth into his palm.

But if it kept her satisfied and Ethan here, he was willing to do whatever she wanted. He didn't know how he got into this mess. He just needed to keep going until he could come up with a better plan.

Blessedly, she always fell asleep after he fucked her. It gave him time to himself to catch up on work emails or his reading. She snored next to him as he sat propped against the headboard.

He didn't have many urgent emails, which gave him the chance to catch up on the thriller he'd picked up at the bookstore last week. It was just starting to get good when his phone vibrated on the table next to him. Checking it, he found a text from Brooke's sister.

Bailey: Ethan threw up. I just picked him up. Thought you'd like to know he's safe.

Brooke and Bailey were like two sides of a coin. Brooke was rail thin with a sugary sweetness to those she deemed worthy and viciousness to those she didn't. Bailey, on the other hand, was curvier, smart, and kind to everyone—even Brooke. She was in the same boat as Fox when it came to Ethan.

Fox: Thanks. I'll be able to sleep now. Is he okay? Do you need me to come to get him?

Bailey: He's fine. I think it was just the junk food he had for dinner.

Fox: I have to check on a few things before I can pick him up tomorrow. Is that a problem?

Bailey: None whatsoever. We'll be just fine. See you tomorrow.

Fox set his phone back on the nightstand. Thank God Bailey lived just south of Lowell, close enough to swoop in and take the little boy. He wouldn't have to worry about Ethan for the rest of the night. His aunt loved him without reservation. She also worked from home as some kind of computer person. She had tried to explain once what she did, but it went right over Fox's head.

He turned out the light and laid his head back on the

pillow. Just knowing Ethan was being taken care of made his eyes droop. It also didn't escape his notice that whenever he thought about Bailey, he seemed to smile a little more. He needed to shut whatever was causing that down. The last thing he needed was dreaming about one sister while fucking the other.

CHAPTER 2

FOX PUSHED through the front door of the diner. Ethan held tight to his hand. He had explained to the little boy that they were meeting someone new for lunch. Ethan danced around next to him looking through the diner. He rarely met anyone he didn't instantly take too. Fox suspected Knox might be the first exception.

Dover was supposed to have been here too. She called him that morning asking him to go for her. She had been called back into the station. He wondered what could be so urgent on a Saturday that it required her to go in on her day off. She hadn't had time to fill him in before ringing off.

He spotted Memphis and Knox as soon as he stepped inside. Knox was hard to miss. They sat together in a booth toward the back. Memphis waved at him. Fox looked down at Ethan. Was this really a good plan? He knew nothing about these men. Was he risking Ethan getting hurt? Ethan grinned back up at him.

"You'll behave?" Fox asked. Ethan nodded vigorously at him. "Okay, then let's go see what they want." They wove through the diner to the booth. Fox waited for Ethan to climb on the seat and slide over. "Do you want a booster seat?" This time Ethan shook his head. Fox slid in next to him.

"Hi," Ethan greeted the strangers.

"Hi back," Memphis said with a smile.

"I'm Efan," he announced. Standing so he could lean over the table, he stuck out his hand. Fox had been working with him on manners. He had taught Ethan to shake hands when introduced. Now, he just had to teach him how to pronounce his name.

"Very nice to meet you, Ethan. I'm Memphis," Memphis said, shaking Ethan's hand.

"I'm Efan," he said, turning to Knox.

"Knox," the big man said. His hand dwarfed Ethan's hand.

"It rhymes with Fox," Ethan said excitedly. "Fox and Knox," he added, doing a little dance on the seat. Fox noticed the corners of Knox's mouth twitch up.

"You're very smart," Memphis said with an easy grin. "How old are you, Ethan?"

"I'm four," he announced proudly.

"Ethan, you need to sit down, please," Fox said.

"Okay, Mr. Fox," Ethan answered before plopping down in the seat.

"Mr. Fox?" Knox asked.

"I read him the children's book. He's called me that ever since."

Both men looked at him with amusement on their faces. Was there really a chance they could be his brothers? He wished Dover had come. She was much better at reading people. All he could tell was that there was no hostility or sadness directed at him. Dover would be able to read exactly how they felt.

"Can I have pancakes?" Ethan asked. Fox hadn't noticed the waitress standing next to him.

"You want pancakes for lunch?" he asked. Ethan nodded his head.

"That sounds good," Knox answered before Fox could. "I'll have the same. Bacon?" he asked, looking at Ethan.

"Yep," Ethan responded. He beamed when Knox winked at him.

"I'll just have the same," Fox said, handing their menus to her.

"Far be it from me to rock the boat," Memphis added.

"You're not in a boat," Ethan giggled. Memphis laughed with him. Ethan pulled his farm animals out of his backpack and set them on the table.

"So is he yours?" Knox asked as Memphis helped the boy set his farm up.

"He's my girlfriend's son," Fox answered. "But he's lived with me for a year. He feels like mine." He tried to think of something more to say. This was unbearably awkward. Even if they were related to him, he didn't know them.

"I have a daughter who's almost Ethan's age," Memphis said. He was holding a cow in one hand and a goat in the other.

"She should come over," Ethan exclaimed. "We could play together."

"I bet she'd like that," Memphis answered. "Maybe next time."

"I have two," Knox said. "Kids. I have two of them," he added as if he had to explain. "A son and a daughter. They're twins."

"Like Fox and Aunt Dover?" Ethan asked.

"Yeah, but they're still little. I don't think they'd be much fun to play with yet," Knox said.

"That's okay," Ethan assured him.

"I think that's what threw us when we met you," Knox continued. "We had information on your sister. We had no idea you even existed. Dover said the DNA match was most likely yours. Somehow, our guy followed the wrong twin."

"Yeah, I was." He paused to look at Ethan. "Umm."

"Don't worry about it," Memphis said. "It's not any of our business anyway."

"It was a misunderstanding, but fortunately my records were sealed when I turned eighteen. Never did that again." The food arrived sparing him from any more questions. He could tell Knox wanted to know more. The incident had certainly gotten his attention. There was no way he was sharing with them.

Fox put the farm animals back in the backpack and cut up Ethan's pancakes. He added syrup. Ethan, like always, argued for more. Fox put just a touch more on his pancakes. Just the act of winning the argument always seemed to appease Ethan. The boy never seemed to care that he had maybe half a teaspoon added.

"Hey, sorry I'm late," Dover said, walking up to the table.

"I thought you had a work thing," Fox said.

"It's all good." She waved him off. "Hey there, little man. What've you got?"

"Pancakes," Ethan said, his mouth full. Dover reached across the table and stole a piece of bacon off his plate. "Hey."

"Here, you can have one of mine," Fox said. "Remember to finish the bite in your mouth before speaking next time."

"Okay," Ethan agreed, his mouth still full of pancakes. Fox laughed. He really was crazy about this kid.

"*So what is really happening at work?*" he asked, turning toward his sister.

"*I told you it's fine.*" She stopped chewing to scowl at him. "*I promise. Just some paperwork problem.*"

"You know it's considered rude to whisper, right?" Memphis said. "This seems somehow worse."

"What are you talking about?" Dover tried playing clueless. Fox knew these two men were too perceptive for that.

"Do you think you're the only ones to inherit some sort of something extra?" Knox said.

"*What color is he?*"

"*I can't quite tell. He's always sort of shimmering between orange and red. Like a fire. The other one, though, just hovers between blue and yellow.*"

"Seriously?" Knox growled.

"I'm going to clean Ethan up. Then we're headed to pet some animals." Fox stood. Ethan scooted out of the booth behind him.

"Are you coming, Aunt Dover? Can Aunt Bailey come too?" Ethan asked.

"Maybe later, squirt. I need to talk to Memphis and Knox first," she answered.

"Okay, bye," he said with a wave at the table.

"Fox," Dover called after him.

"I know," he answered, walking toward the bathrooms, Ethan in tow.

⸺

"One of these days he's going to get in trouble hanging

around with Bailey Sullivan," Dover said. "Do you know how I know?"

Both Knox and Memphis shook their heads.

"Because every time he gets around her, he glows pink." They looked back at her with confusion. "You see, he's made the mistake of falling in love with his girlfriend's sister."

"And you know this because he glows pink?" Memphis asked.

"Right. Does that make sense?" she said.

"No," Knox responded. "Let's pretend I'm an idiot, and you have to spell it out for me."

Dover chose not to comment on that. She knew better than to think either one of these men was an idiot. She debated how much she wanted to share with them. The DNA test she studied last night looked legitimate. That didn't mean she bought into the idea of a bunch of extra siblings roaming the earth.

She was still debating when Knox turned to search the diner. Not finding whatever he was looking for, he faced her. Holding his hands together, he rubbed them in a circular motion. She jumped when he moved them apart to show her a small fireball dancing in his hand. He quickly closed his hand over it before anyone else noticed.

"Your turn," he said to Memphis.

"How am I supposed to do that?" Memphis responded. Knox just stared at him. "Fine. Move," he added. Knox moved out of the booth and let Memphis up. "Watch where I was sitting. I'm not doing this for long." He looked around the diner for a minute until he spotted the sign for the restrooms.

Dover sat looking at his empty seat after he disappeared

inside the men's room. Suddenly, the seat wasn't empty. Memphis, or a facsimile of him, sat looking back at her.

Then, just as quickly as he appeared, he faded away. The cocky ass even had the tenacity to grin at her as he did it. She couldn't help it if her mouth hung open like a fish. It was remarkable. Memphis returned to his seat moments later.

"We've shown you ours. Time to show us yours," Knox said.

She debated for a few more minutes before giving in. She just prayed this didn't blow up in her face. Or worse, in Fox's face. He had much more to lose than she did.

"Fine," she said with a sigh. "Telepathy isn't the only thing we can do." She stopped.

"I get it," Memphis said. "If what I can do reaches the wrong people, it would be very bad for me too. I promise you can trust us."

"I can see emotions," she said in a rush. She split a look between both men. Neither one seemed that surprised. She guessed after being able to transport yourself holographically or forming fire with your hands, nothing else much surprised them.

"It shows up through colors. There's a sort of glow that emanates from each person," she said. "For example, Knox shimmers between red and orange. It normally means he's either angry, excited, or horny."

The men looked at each other and then shrugged.

"Sounds about right," Knox said.

"My guess is," she said, shaking her head. "Knox's ability to produce fire messes with my ability to pinpoint his exact mood.

"No, you got it pretty close," Memphis said. "What about me?"

"You're usually blue like Fox. There's a contented calmness in both of you. He only turns pink when he's near Bailey. Even on his worst days with Brooke, he never loses his temper. Which brings me to his thing."

"It differs from you?" Memphis asked.

"Yeah. Fox is more powerful than I am. He can actually control emotions."

"How does he do that?" Knox said.

"We're not sure. It began about the time he turned thirteen. Mine started the year before."

"That makes sense," Memphis agreed. "We've discovered that most of our gifts manifested themselves around puberty. Most of us learned how to control them soon after. Flint is still trying to rein his in."

"I've never learned how to shut mine off. It's why I wear sunglasses most of the time. They help diffuse the colors." Dover picked at Fox's half-eaten food. She didn't understand how any of this mattered in the end. Fine, they obviously were all connected. But what did it mean?

"So if Fox is so hung up on this Bailey person, why doesn't he just dump Brooke for her?" Knox finally asked.

"That's a complicated question," she answered. "How much time do you have?"

"I guess until my plane leaves on Monday," Memphis answered. "Knox has even longer if necessary."

"Then settle in, this might take a while."

CHAPTER 3

BAILEY WATCHED Fox from a relatively hidden spot under one of the tall trees near the entrance to the petting zoo. She knew he brought Ethan here most Saturdays when he was free.

She drank him in. The shaggy brown hair that always hung a little too long. The luminous green eyes that saw right into her soul. And then there was the body that wouldn't stop. He had muscles that came directly from working in a labor-intensive job. No need for him to hit the gym.

For an entire long year, she had lusted after Fox Addams. But he was her sister's boyfriend. It wasn't right to want what your sister had.

She knew it could never be anything more than friendship between them. But that didn't stop her dreams from being filled with him. If only she had met him first. However, her sister would have already stolen him away by now. She believed in the sister code. Her sister did not.

As if he could sense she was watching him, his eyes rose

from where they were watching Ethan pet a goat to hers under the tree. She'd been busted.

It wasn't her worst offense. She had once been caught staring at the front of his swimsuit at the beginning of summer. He had grinned, and she had burned a color similar to a firetruck. It was humiliating. It wasn't like she was fifteen anymore. She was almost thirty for fuck's sake.

He leaned over to Ethan, said something in his ear, then turned to saunter toward her. She should be mortified after being caught spying on him. All she was, though, was sad time couldn't slow down.

It seemed a shame not to have more time to appreciate how his strong thighs propelled him forward. How his pecs bunched as his arms swung at his sides. The dimples that always appeared when he smiled.

"Hey," he said, reaching her. He turned so he could keep an eye on Ethan. "What are you up to?"

"Oh, nothing. I was just driving by and noticed your truck in the parking lot." That wasn't a total lie. She had noticed his truck, but only after driving all the way to the park.

"Come join us," he said.

"What if Brooke shows up?"

"Brooke never comes here," he answered. "She claims the smell upsets her allergies. Come on." He took her hand and pulled her out from under the tree.

She made it a point to never touch him if possible. It made her body tingle all over when she did. Her heart rate would also accelerate to the point of explosion status. Lately, it had become harder to avoid it. Like now.

He gave her no warning, just grabbed her hand. He even interlaced their fingers together like lovers. She giggled at the thought.

"Are you okay?" he asked, looking back at her.

"Yes. Just a tickle in my throat." She made a big deal out of clearing her throat to prove it. Because almost thirty-year-old women did not giggle at their sister's boyfriend holding their hand. She just needed to keep telling herself that.

"Mmm," he said with a smile.

"Aunt Bailey," Ethan squealed. *Dodged that bullet,* she thought, pulling her hand from his. "Come meet the baby goat." She exchanged Fox's cool, rough hand for Ethan's sweaty, small one. "Its name is Buttercup."

"It is?" she asked. Turning to look at Fox over her shoulder, she mouthed "save me." He just smiled as she was dragged into the pen. She was then dragged through the pen with the rabbits, the one with the calves, and finally the one with llamas. They were Ethan's favorite and her least favorite.

"Hey, sport. You pet the llamas, and Aunt Bailey and I will be right over there on the bench," Fox finally said, pulling her out of the pen.

"Thank you," she said, sitting down.

"Still not a llama fan?"

"Still not really a barnyard animal fan."

"Fair," he answered, his eyes still glued to Ethan. She admired how protective he was of her nephew. If he was like this as only the boyfriend, how would he act if Ethan was his? In the short time she had known him, she had had brief glimpses of how hard he worked to protect everyone within his sphere. "Not a lot of barnyard animals around growing up in Everett, huh?"

"No, not really." They stood in silence for a moment watching Ethan sit on the ground with a tiny goat on his lap. "I can make an exception though where Ethan is concerned."

For the briefest moment, he turned to smile at her. It took her breath away. He was handsome anyway, but it was a whole other level when he smiled.

"Thanks again for picking him up last night."

"It's no problem." They lapsed back into silence again. It was always awkward with Fox. She felt like they were right on the verge of saying something important, but neither ever did. There was no question what held them back. It was always the elephant in the room when they were alone together. Brooke. "I should probably go."

"Oh. Yeah, okay. We should too. It looks like Ethan might have fallen asleep on that llama. Hold on, and we'll walk you to your car." She watched as he walked over and hauled the little boy into his arms. "I think all the stimulation made him crash." He laughed and the sound rolled through her body like a tidal wave.

"Looks like your job here is complete." They reached the parking lot, and she unlocked her car.

"You're good, then?"

"Yeah, thanks." She slid into the driver's side.

"Okay. Be safe." There was a moment when she swore he lingered in her door before closing it. But then the moment was over, and all she could do was head home.

When her gaze ventured to the rearview mirror at the entrance, she found him still standing with Ethan in his arms watching her drive away. She sighed and exited to the left.

━━

"Where have you been?" Brooke hissed when he stepped into the apartment.

"It's Saturday, we went to the petting zoo," Fox

answered quietly. Stepping around her, he walked into the second bedroom and laid Ethan on his bed. He pulled a blanket over him before returning to the living room.

"You've been with her, haven't you? I can smell her on you."

"You can't smell anything but the petting zoo because I haven't been with anyone." It was the same argument he had every weekend. Brooke accused him of having an affair at least once a week if not more. If it wasn't one of his clients or a coworker's wife, it was her sister.

"Was she there?"

"Who."

"You know who. Bailey?"

"I picked Ethan up from her house this morning, remember? If you'd stop letting your ex take Ethan, we wouldn't have to do this every other weekend."

"Do not tell me what I can and can't do with my son," she said, shoving him in the chest.

"I'm not," he answered, stepping back. "I just wish you'd consider what goes on in that house."

"Jimmy would never hurt Ethan."

"Maybe not, but it's not Jimmy I'm worried about. It's the rest of his crew that hangs out at his house."

"At least he's not screwing my sister."

"I'm not screwing your sister. Jesus!" He ran his hand through his hair. It was always the same. She went on the attack, and he spent his energy trying to defend himself.

"Calm down," he mumbled. All the fight suddenly went out of her. If he couldn't use the gift he was born with to de-escalate the situation, then what good was it?

"Anyway," she said with a giggle as if nothing had happened. "I'm going out with some friends tonight. You'll need to watch Ethan since he was supposed to be at his dad's tonight."

"That's fine." At this point, he would much rather spend his evening with a four-year-old than the boy's mother.

"I'd better get ready. We're going to do dinner then hit some new bar we've heard about." She kissed him on the cheek. "Don't wait up." With another laugh, she walked into the bedroom. The door closed behind her, and Fox sank onto the couch. Trying to calm her down always took a lot out of him.

"How do I look?"

He was flipping channels on the television when she reemerged half an hour later. She spun around in the doorway. He would like to say that her skirt was way too short and her shirt way too translucent.

"You look as beautiful as always," he said instead.

"Good answer." She pushed off the doorframe and walked to him. Straddling his legs, she slid forward until she was flush against him. "Maybe you should stay up."

Fox was saved from coming up with a response by the buzzer to the building going off. "I swear if that's your sister..."

"It's not Dover, she's at work."

"Never stopped her before."

He was in the process of easing her off his lap when there was a knock on the door. That was odd. How would someone get to their door without being buzzed in? A quick check through the peephole was all he needed to get the answer. He pulled open the door.

"How did you get in?"

"Charm," Knox said, pointing at Memphis. "Brawn," he added, pointing at himself. "It's a lethal combination." In other words, they had talked their way in. Fox rolled his eyes as he opened the door wider.

"Oh, hi," Brooke said, turning on the charm herself. "What brings you boys by?"

"We just wanted one last chance to answer any questions for Fox before we headed out of town," Memphis answered. "I've got a farm call on Monday, so I have to fly home tomorrow," he added, turning to Fox. "I know yesterday was a lot, and we didn't really get a chance to talk at the diner this morning. We just hoped you were free this evening."

"He's babysitting," Brooke answered before he could. "I'm going out with some friends. Fox is such a doll for babysitting for me so I can spend time with them. Being a single mom is so overwhelming."

Fox saw Knox raise an eyebrow before Memphis stepped back in. "We met Ethan this morning. Such a good kid. You must be doing it right."

"Thanks," she answered with a flip of her hair. "I try. Well, I'm off." She pulled Fox to her and placed a languid kiss on his mouth before pulling away. "You boys try and behave."

Her hand grazed Memphis's chest on the way out the door. Knox's eyebrows almost disappeared into his hairline this time which was impressive since he wore his hair pulled back tight in a ponytail.

"She's a lot," Knox said after the door closed with a resounding click.

"Careful," Fox warned. Knox held his hands up in surrender.

"Where is Ethan anyway?" Memphis asked.

"He's asleep. I should probably wake him pretty soon,

or I'll never get him back to sleep tonight. Do you guys want a beer?"

"Sure."

Fox walked into the small kitchen and pulled three beers out of the refrigerator. He handed two out before sitting back on the couch again.

Knox and Memphis each took a seat, one on the couch and the other in one of the chairs. No one said anything as they settled in and cracked open the beer. After a long swallow, Memphis cleared his throat.

"Have you thought of anything else you'd like to ask us? We'll be happy to answer any questions you have. We might also have a few of our own. I guess the one we really want to answer to is—"

"What the fuck is going on here?" Knox asked, growing impatient with Memphis. "Dover said there's another sister in play."

CHAPTER 4

BROOKE WALKED down the steps of the apartment building and turned right at the sidewalk. There were several catcalls as she moved through the neighborhood. She put up with it often, but she didn't mind since she knew she looked hot. She wasn't shallow, it was just a fact. Her sister might have gotten all the brains, but she got the looks. She would take that offering any day.

She moved across the street to wait at the T station. It was such a pain to get to the best bars since Fox insisted they move from their old neighborhood to this slightly nicer one.

He thought her son needed better options for preschool. Why should she have to uproot her life for Ethan? One preschool was as good as the next. Besides, this neighborhood was too far from the best nightlife and too close to his sister.

She tapped her foot with impatience until the train pulled up. She could have insisted on Fox lending her his truck to get there, but parking was always a nightmare. Besides, she didn't want him to know where she was. She wasn't positive if he could track where the truck went, but she wasn't taking any chances.

She stepped into the train car and looked around. A man who looked college-aged slid across the seat so she would have the place next to him.

She sat down and crossed one leg over the other, rewarding him with a generous view of her thigh. He barely took his gaze off of it until she stood as the train pulled up at her stop. It would be nothing to go home with him. That sounded so boring in her head though. No, she was looking for something more exciting.

The bar where she headed was two blocks over from the T station. She threw her purse over her shoulder and headed that way. She knew the moment she entered the door that it was going to be a good night. The music was thumping, and the place was packed with people.

There was an empty seat next to a reasonably good-looking man at the bar, so she slid onto it.

"Hi," he offered. "You waiting for someone?" Not very original, but that didn't bother her.

"I was supposed to meet a girlfriend here, but she just texted me and said she had to stay home with her sick kid. I guess I should just head back home. It's a shame really, we were looking forward to catching up. I haven't seen her since college."

"Oh, what college?"

"BU, of course. Is there any other?"

"That's where I went!" he exclaimed. He was almost too easy. She could tell the difference between a Boston College, Boston University, and Harvard man just by the way they dressed. This guy even had a Terriers tattoo on his forearm.

"Oh my gosh, no!" she answered. She had never

attended college a day in her life, but he didn't need to know that. Rule one when picking up a man was to find something in common with them—or at least pretend to.

"You have to let me buy you a drink."

"Maybe just one." She smiled at him as he grinned back. "I'll just have whatever you're having." He motioned to the bartender who set two bottles of Guinness in front of them. He held his beer up to tap against hers. She obliged before taking a dainty sip. Without a doubt, she could drink this guy under the table, but she needed her wits about her tonight.

"Live around here?" he asked, setting his beer on the bar.

"Yeah, not too far. You?"

"I'm just here on business. I headed back to Hartford after college."

She supposed he was trying to impress her, but every good Massachusetts native agreed on one simple fact. Everywhere else sucked. No one in their right mind from Boston would be impressed by that.

"That's impressive. What do you do in Hartford?" she asked, batting her eyelashes. It was cliché but worked every time.

"I work for an enviromental law firm."

"Wow, that must be so fulfilling. Helping the enviroment and everything." She had no idea what that was, but it didn't matter. Men were all the same. She laid her hand on his arm for emphasis. It had the desired effect. She could see the lust in his gaze as he let it linger on her body.

Turning to face him, she let her legs fall slightly open. She almost laughed when his eyes grew wide. "You must be important if they sent you here all by yourself."

"I'm actually here with one of the senior partners, but he's back at the hotel. Claims he's too old for the bar scene."

"How could anyone be too old for this?" She leaned a little closer as she lowered her voice. It created a much more intimate experience, and she wanted all the intimacy she could force on his mind.

"That's what I said, but he begged off anyway. As long as I'm in the lobby tomorrow in time to go to the airport, he doesn't care what I do." She brushed her breasts against his arm as she leaned in again to listen.

"I bet he's a good boss." The second rule was to make sure he wasn't in the bar with anyone. Who would notice if he left with someone? How long before they wondered where he was? She wasn't worried about a wife, however. She would be back in the city.

"He's not bad. I've had worse."

"I know what you mean. The man I work for now is a real piece of work. One of those who still believes it's fine to cop a feel when he's near you. You know what I mean?"

"That's awful. You should report him to HR."

"Maybe I should," she said, her brows pulled into a thoughtful frown as if putting serious thought into it. "Thanks, I think you're right. I'll do that first thing on Monday."

She watched as he puffed his chest out a little. Men liked a woman who came across as too stupid to figure out things on their own. She'd learned that early in her life.

"I'm glad I sat down next to you when my friend couldn't make it," she added.

"Me too. Let me get us another round." He motioned for the bartender again. "What do you think, shall we be bold?" She shrugged. "Let's have a round of whiskey shots to go along with our beer." The bartender nodded and moved back down the bar.

"If I didn't know better, I'd say you're trying to get me drunk." She squeezed his biceps this time. He immediately tried to flex it.

"Just trying to show you a good time, since you were stood up," he answered. "I'm sorry you missed your friend, just not too sorry."

The bartender returned with fresh beer and whiskey in shot glasses. She used the moment of distraction to slide her nearly full beer down the bar before picking up the fresh one. As much as she would like to drink herself into oblivion, she didn't dare.

They tapped glasses before she took another sip. This time she drank the whiskey knowing he would notice if it went untouched.

"Have you ever tried a boilermaker?" she asked. "I had a friend in college who used to drink them."

"Why not? I say, what happens in Boston stays in Boston." When his beer was finished, he ordered them each a boilermaker. There was no way she planned on finishing it, but he should be hammered soon.

She watched as the shot glass was dropped in the glass of draft beer. He tilted it to his lips as she cheered him on. He finished it in one long draw.

"That was incredible," she said, pretending to sway against him. Her hand landed on his upper thigh as she steadied herself. It was obvious by the bulge straining the front of his slacks, that he was into her, even after all the alcohol. She placed her lips next to his ear to whisper. "I need to go to the ladies. Don't run off."

She turned to the back of the room and walked away.

There was no reason to check if he was watching her, she knew he would be.

She pushed inside the restroom even though she didn't have to go. She did anyway since she was already there. After washing her hands, she checked her makeup in the mirror and then stepped back out.

Just as she thought he would be, he was leaning against the wall in the dark hallway. All of these guys were exactly the same. As predictable as snow in February.

"Hi," he said again. She would roll her eyes, but then she'd have to start all over again.

"Hi," she responded, stepping up to him.

"Come here often?" He gave her a goofy grin, so she giggled like an idiot. Then he was pulling her against him, and his lips were on hers.

He spun her against the wall before he was back on her. Her head smacked the wall, but he didn't seem to notice. At no point had he asked if she was okay with what he was doing. She would kick him in the groin just for good measure, but she had something better in mind for him.

"Not here," she moaned when his hands ran under her skirt to grip her ass. "If they catch us, I'll get kicked out, and I like this place." She stuck out her bottom lip when he pulled back to see if she was serious. "Come on, I know where the back door is."

Taking his hand, she pulled him down the hallway and around a corner. At the back, past the offices, was a crash door without a working alarm. She pressed through it, drawing him out behind her. The moment the door slammed behind them, he had her back pressed against the rough brick wall.

His hand ran under her shirt to pinch her nipple to a hard point. She would cry out, but she could hold out a little longer. "Damn, you're sexy," he moaned in her mouth. His breath smelled like a distillery, and he tasted like dirty socks.

He was too busy pawing her like a horny teenager to realize that she hadn't responded in kind. Pulling her knee up to his hip, he pressed his length against her in a grinding motion.

Just when she thought she couldn't take any more, he pulled back in shock before his eyes rolled back in his head. His body went soft, and he slumped into a set of arms behind him. A hypodermic syringe was yanked from his neck. She bent over to check if he was still breathing. He was...unfortunately for him.

"About damn time you showed up," she snarled, standing back up.

"I was enjoying the show. Were you not?" the deep voice said. A dark gaze stared over the top of the unconscious man directly into her soul. "Help me get him to the car."

"Why do I have to help?" she whined. She knew the tone would get her punished later. At least she was hoping it would.

"Because if you keep insisting on these big ones, it's the least you can do."

With a snort, she tucked the man's arm over her shoulder. The car wasn't far down the alley, just enough to be out of sight. By the time they reached it, she had broken into a sweat. They rolled the man into the trunk with a grunt.

"Now I'm all sticky," she complained. He grabbed her by the throat and thrust her against the car. His eyes blazed as he pressed his mouth to hers. This man she kissed back like her life depended on it. Maybe it did. Somehow, she could never get enough of him.

"Get in the car, little bitch," he hissed, turning her loose. He wrenched open the car door, and she scrambled to get inside as quickly as she could. The door slammed. He crossed in front of the hood and slid in next to her.

With a smile that would scare the most stalwart of men, he turned the key in the ignition. They pulled out of the alley and headed toward the warehouses along the water.

Brooke couldn't help the excitement building inside her. It was the same every time she met him behind a pub with an easy mark. This was a good one she knew. He would reward her well for this find.

Her body burned with the thought of what he would do to her. The game had just begun. Now the ball was in his court.

CHAPTER 5

DOVER STOOD STARING down at the ground. She knew the basic facts of what she was looking at. Or at least as much as the medical examiner would share with her. Male. Caucasian. Approximate age between thirty-five and forty-five. Estimated time of death was between ten and midnight.

What the basic facts didn't tell her was how he died or why he was discovered dead on the field hockey pitch of an exclusive private high school. She looked at the impressive fence surrounding the school. How would he even get here, or how would someone place him here?

"Are you done, Detective?" the medical examiner asked from the other side of the body.

"No identification at all?"

"None that we found. I doubt the kids who found him rolled him either." Her gaze shot up to meet his smirk. Sean Ryan, one of the medical examiners for the City of Boston, stood with his arms folded over his muscled chest. His arms almost split the sleeves of his shirt. Better looking than any medical examiner had the right to be.

"Autopsy?" she asked, ignoring the deep brown eyes studying her.

"Let's say one this afternoon. I know you'll be on my ass if I don't rush it."

As much as she wanted to comment on other things she could do with his ass, she resisted. This was a crime scene, and she was a professional.

"I'll be there."

"I'll save you a seat then." With a wink, he turned his attention back to the body. His assistants moved in to ease the body into a bag for transportation to his office.

She stepped out of the makeshift tent to organize the search of the grounds. As much as she was certain no one at the school had anything to do with it, she had to follow procedure.

"Do you want me to handle the school while you find out who he was?" Danny asked. Danny had been her partner from the first day she reported as a detective. He was fifteen years older than her and kept joking about moving to cold cases. The idea of doing this without Danny's experience to fall back on made her shiver with apprehension.

"Sounds good. I need to deal with something for a couple of minutes anyway. I'll start looking for missing persons and meet you at the autopsy at one." With a nod, Danny walked toward the door to the school while she looked over at the thing that needed to be dealt with. Standing at the fence with the rest of the curious was a giant man with bright green eyes and a ponytail.

"What are you doing here?" she growled when she reached the fence.

"Looking for you," he growled back. She nodded for

him to follow her down the fence line until they were away from the onlookers.

"How did you find me?"

"Memphis."

"How?" She held her hand up when he started to answer. "You know what, never mind. Why are you looking for me?"

"Come on, Dover. I flew all the way up here to meet you. Surely you can spare a little more than one quick breakfast. Memphis and I went to Fox's apartment last night. His girlfriend was out with friends. I don't get a good feeling about her. I want to make sure y'all are all right before I go home. I have an open-ended plane ticket. I can always change it."

"Fine," she said after considering him for several beats. "But I don't have time right now. Come by later tonight." She pulled her notebook out of her pocket and wrote her address down. Tearing the page out, she passed it to him. "I've got to go. I have a dead guy to identify."

"See you this evening."

"Yay," she mumbled, walking quickly toward her car. Reaching for the door, she remembered she had ridden with Danny, and he still had the keys in his pocket. "Hey," she yelled at Knox's back.

"What?" he yelled back.

"Give me a ride back to the office?"

"Yeah, come on. Little sisters are such a pain in the ass."

"Fuck you. I'll take the bus."

"Get in," he said with a grin. He pointed a fob at a small car halfway down the street. With a sigh, she met him by the passenger door. "Are you always so uptight?" he asked when they were both inside. How he found room to drive, she had no idea.

"Only around men who show up claiming to be my long-lost family."

"Fair." He pulled out into traffic. "At least I haven't asked for money yet."

"Don't bother. No one gets rich on a cop's salary."

"Nor a math teacher's salary," he answered with a hearty laugh. "We'll just have to be satisfied being the poor relations." They drove for a block in silence. "Speaking of, what is up with that medical examiner? The women on my side of the fence were starting to swoon."

"How is that speaking of? Speaking of what?"

"Speaking of relations. Relationships. Get it?"

"Not really."

"I'm just saying I'm glad my wife isn't here. I don't think I can compete with that."

"Definitely not."

"Hey," he growled. When he gave her a gentle shove, she had to force down her laugh.

"Don't make me kick your ass...again."

"Next time, I'm setting you on fire. Consider yourself warned." This time she couldn't hold in the laugh that bubbled up. How was it possible this man was slowly growing on her?

"This is me," she said. Knox pulled up to the curb so she could get out. "About seven. Bring food." She slammed the car door closed before he could answer and walked into the police station.

Getting through security always took longer than she thought it should. But then, better safe than sorry she guessed. Her first stop was the coffee station in the break room.

Contrary to popular belief, the coffee was pretty decent. It was also free, which made any coffee better.

Dumping powdered cream and sugar in it, she carried it to her office.

A wiggle of the mouse brought her computer to life. There were plenty of emails in her inbox, but nothing about the fingerprints she'd sent over.

She pulled up the NCIC (National Crime Information Center) database and input all of the information on the victim. At least everything she had right now: height, weight, approximate age, hair color, race, sex. Anything else about the man would have to wait for Sean to share with her.

While she waited for the autopsy, she pulled a new notebook down. It would be the start of everything they knew about the death.

Her initial notes were the first thing added to the book. She also printed off the crime scene photos the moment they hit her inbox. Each one was added to the book. She even drew a crude diagram of the area surrounding the body. No one would accuse her of being an artist, but it wasn't half bad. She slid it into one of the page protectors.

The phone on her desk rang, and she snatched it up. "Homicide, Addams."

"Can you come to the morgue right now, Detective?" Sean asked.

"I thought you said one?"

"There's something you need to see."

"Okay, I'll be there in twenty." She hung up. Taking a minute to text the change of plans to Danny, she chugged her coffee. She tossed the cup and picked up her keys. With any luck, the traffic would be light this time of day. The medical examiner's office sat in the middle of the Boston University Medical Campus. There was always road construction or congestion, no matter what time of day.

The drive took her twenty-five minutes to go the thirteen miles. Finding parking took another ten. Sean was waiting in his office when she finally arrived. Per normal, he looked cool and perfectly coiffed to her hot and sweaty. He stood when she knocked on the doorframe.

"You said you had something to show me?" she asked.

"Follow me." He led her through the offices to the basement where examinations were performed. She nodded to several of the other doctors she knew as they approached a table with various things neatly bagged and labeled. Sean stopped and picked up one of the bags. "Take a look at this," he said, handing it to her.

She flipped the small, clear bag over in her hand. Inside was a medallion strung on a black piece of leather cord. The medallion itself was silver without much wear. She guessed, like the first one, this medal could be found anywhere. They'd still search for where it was bought anyway.

"It's like the one our last guy had only different," she noticed.

"I'd guess it's also a religious medal, but which saint I have no idea," Sean answered. "I thought I'd leave that to you guys."

"They have to mean something, I just don't know what."

"Here's the weird thing. About a month ago, Detective Bianchi had a body in here that had a similar medallion to your two. Might be a coincidence, but then..." He shrugged.

"Yeah, thanks." Her mind reeled with questions. She needed to find Bianchi. What were the chances of three deceased bodies being found with nothing but a religious medallion in a month? "Any idea where he was found?"

"Don't remember. I do remember, though, that it was a homicide. His tongue was removed." She looked up at him sharply. "I'll know more after the autopsy this afternoon," he said, holding his hands up before she could argue that he start it now.

"Okay, I'll go find Bianchi." She turned to leave, and Sean snatched the bag from her hand.

"This still goes to trace," he said.

"I'll be back at one."

"Looking forward to it." She let the door swish closed behind her as she walked back out into the hallway. If she hurried, she would have time to catch the other detective, catch up with Danny, and grab a sandwich before she had to be back. She shook her head to clear her mind. The dead had no auras surrounding them anymore. All she saw was gray space.

Sean, however, glowed with the most beautiful blue-green light. It reminded her of the aurora borealis she saw pictures of in books. It made her want to pack her bag and fly to Norway every time. She could just imagine gazing up at him from her bed, the glow surrounding them. She shook her head again. Back to the murder.

"Bianchi!" she said, walking into the detective's office twenty minutes later.

"How you doing, girly?" he responded. Dominic Bianchi had to be pushing sixty if he was a day. Word around the office was that he could have risen all the way to the top, except he liked what he did. His father and grandfather had been detectives in the Boston PD It was in his blood. "What can I do for you?"

"Sean Ryan at the ME's office was telling me you caught a murder with some similarities to one I pulled today. Had a medallion around his neck? A religious one?"

"A St. Matthew medal," he answered. "You should go to church more. Learn your saints."

"My parents were Protestants, so it wouldn't do any good. What can you tell me about your victim?"

"Let's see." He pulled a folder off a stack on his desk and flipped it open. "Name was George Goodwin from Buffalo, New York. In town on business. Worked for a bank. Mid-thirties, fit, middle class, white."

"No leads on the suspect?"

"Not yet. Still looking, but I'm not feeling confident we'll find who did it."

"Can I get a copy of what you have?"

"Yeah, I'll send it over to you."

"Perfect, thanks, Bianchi."

"No problem. Let me know if you find anything I missed."

"I doubt that," she said, leaving his office. She found Danny sitting at his desk in their office down the hall. "You're back early."

"Nobody saw anything. The custodian managed to get the scene locked down before most of the kids got there. He and the principal checked that the guy was dead, locked down the field, and called us. No one recognized him from his photo," he answered. "I was just typing up my notes."

"I might have something."

Danny stopped typing and turned to face her. They shared an office large enough for both desks, a filing cabinet, and a large whiteboard. It wasn't spacious, but it worked. "ME's office called. They found a St. Francis medal hanging around his neck. It's like our first guy, only his was a St. Bernadette. It also seems Bianchi had a case that was similar about a month ago. He's sending it over." She sat at her desk and checked her email.

"Christ. I thought two were bad, but now you're saying

there are at least three? You think there might be even more?" he asked.

"Don't know yet. Seems worth a look though." She printed a picture of the medal from the other crime scene and taped it to the whiteboard.

"Their vic have a name?"

"Yeah." She leaned back over her desk and printed out a photo. Taping it to the board, she wrote the name "George Goodwin." "It might be nothing, but I thought I'd check."

Returning to her desk, she downloaded the preliminary medical examiner's report. She printed a picture of their victim and added it to the board. Under it, she wrote "John Doe." At least they had been able to identify the first victim, Trent Alleman.

"We need to find out who this guy is," Danny said. He returned to typing his notes but paused. "By the way, how did you score an autopsy this fast? It usually takes a day or two of waiting."

"I guess Sean thought it was a high priority."

"Uh-huh." He smirked before turning back to his computer. She ignored the implication and the fact that her face grew hot. Instead, she started pouring over missing person reports. Someone had to be missing him.

CHAPTER 6

DOVER WAS FLIPPING through shows on her television that evening when her phone buzzed. Pulling up an app, she stared at the face at the other end of the line.

She debated ignoring him for a few minutes before he scowled at the small camera next to the exterior door of her apartment building. She doubted ignoring him would in any way deter him from coming upstairs, so she pressed the button to unlock the door.

"I brought food," he said a few minutes later when she opened her door.

"And a duffel bag?" she added as he pushed his way past her.

"I thought I'd stick around for a couple more days."

She watched as Knox crossed to her kitchen island and started unloading bags of food. Letting the door slam closed, she stomped after him.

"So you thought what, you'd stay here instead of a hotel?" she snapped. She looked over the selection of food. "No pizza?"

"Why would I buy pizza in Boston? I live in Chicago,

remember. Might as well have carved up some cardboard to eat." He took the plate she pulled out of a cabinet and helped himself to a heaping spoonful of shepherd's pie. "Your pub food, however, is pretty solid."

"Yeah, it is. Our Italian is fucking amazing too."

"Tomorrow night," he answered.

She begrudgingly filled her plate with food and followed him to the table. He had already opened two beers he'd pulled from one of the bags. "You can't just force your way in here," she said around mouthfuls. "Sharing a biological sperm donor does not make us siblings."

"Technically, it does."

"In name only. Are you this aggressive with Memphis?"

"I save the worst for him." He took a long swig from his bottle. "I haven't even tried to set you on fire yet."

"You're just scared I'll kick your ass again."

"Pfft. I teach high school. Nothing scares me anymore."

They lapsed into silence as they finished eating. She tried glaring at him, but he ignored her, so she gave up. She put the leftovers away while he loaded the dishwasher. They took their seats in her living room, her staring at the television and him staring at her.

"What?" she finally asked.

"Memphis and I dropped in on Fox last night."

"Okay. So?"

"So, we're worried about him. His girlfriend's moods flip like a bad penny."

"Why is that your problem?"

Knox blew out a breath and ran his hand through his hair. His gaze landed back on her. It was the same one she saw every morning in the mirror. "Damn, you're prickly."

"Prickly?"

"Yes, prickly. Ready to take offense and generally difficult," he snarled. "It's our problem because he's our brother. We don't walk away when one of us isn't okay."

"I just don't understand why it matters to you. Especially now after forty years."

"Because it took me years to put this family together, and I'm not walking away. So stop fucking arguing. I'm here now, and I'm not leaving until this is settled. If you want to try to push us away, that's fine. Doesn't mean we'll let you, though."

Dover sighed. She took a few minutes sizing Knox up before rejecting the idea of trying to physically toss him from her apartment. Last time she took him down, she had the element of surprise on her side. This time, however, he had his guard up. Brothers were a pain in the ass. All of them, apparently.

"I'm pretty sure she's seeing someone behind his back," she said. She might as well cave. He obviously wasn't going anywhere. "Fox suspects so too, although he won't admit it."

"What makes you think that?"

"I've been there when she's getting ready to go out with her 'friends.' Her aura slowly morphs to black. I only see that in violent offenders. It makes me stress out about Fox and Ethan's safety. If she was just having an affair, I would usually see yellow. But the hues I see can go either direction. Just because you glow yellow doesn't mean deception. It could mean you're cheerful. Black though? It's a bad sign."

"That sounds confusing."

"It is. Red is very hard too. My boss glows red, but so do a lot of the people I arrest. It's either confidence or aggression. Anyway, I think it's more than just an affair. I just don't know what."

"Have you tried following her when she goes out?" Knox asked.

"She knows me, and I can't ask any of the plain clothes guys to do it without bringing in the police. If it is just cheating, I'd be laughed out of the office."

"Okay, let me work on it. She knows me too, and I don't exactly blend into the crowd. I know a guy, though, who's pretty good at following people. Makes a decent living from doing it. Let me get him on it. In the meantime, one of those bags has cannoli from Mike's if you're interested."

"If I'm interested," she mumbled, rolling her eyes. She snatched the bag off the counter and returned to her seat. Halfway through the first cannoli, Knox took the bag from her. "I have killed for less," she teased.

"I'm willing to take the chance," he answered. They sat in silence as they blazed through several cannoli each. Finally, Knox took a long pull on his beer before turning to face her again. "So what's the deal with the dead guy at the school?"

"I can't discuss an ongoing investigation," she answered, licking her fingers clean.

"Yeah, yeah. Who am I going to tell? I don't know anyone around here. Besides, I have government clearance."

"How?" she asked, then reconsidered. "You know what, never mind. Here's what I can tell you. We think this is at least number three. They're all successful businessmen or professionals. We haven't put a name to number three, but based on his haircut, manicure, and lack of calluses on his hands, we're thinking he's the same.

"All of them have been killed somewhere else and posed at a private school in the city. They're all strangled with something like a belt, and they've all been wearing a

Catholic medallion of a saint. That part isn't public, so if you leak it, I'll rip you apart."

"You might want to see someone about your violent tendencies." She glared at him, but he just smirked. "Do you have any idea who it is?"

"Not yet. I will though, if I can hang onto the case."

"Someone taking it over?"

"I'm sure the boss will want someone more senior than me to run with it. The feds will be brought in soon, I'd guess. You know how they like a good serial killer. The autopsy today turned up nothing. Body was completely clean—no fingerprints, blood trace, nothing."

"Do you want me to poke around and see if I find out anything?"

"Poke around how?"

"I have connections," he answered. "State Department, FBI, Houston welding union, several cities I've been asked not to return to."

"You know when you say things like that, I almost think I could grow to like you."

———

Bailey was bent over her computer hunting for where the code had broken on her current project when she heard her doorbell ring. She debated for a moment ignoring it. She hated to be interrupted when she was on the hunt for that tiny mistake in a long string of computer code. The bell rang for a second time, so she got up and walked to her front door.

"Hi," Fox said when she opened it. "I was checking on a job a couple of blocks over and thought you might like to go for lunch. If you're busy, though, I'd understand."

"No," she barked. "No, that sounds nice," she tried again a little less aggressively. "Let me just go find some socks and shoes. Come in, I'll just be a moment."

Leaving the door open for him, she raced back upstairs to see what she could do with her current condition in the few minutes she had.

Since Bailey worked from home, she didn't always dress to go out. Quickly, she traded out her ratty workout shorts for a nice pair. A simple T-shirt would have to do for now. Grabbing her sandals from the closet, she headed back downstairs. Fox had moved into the living room, so she took the extra minutes to throw her hair into a ponytail.

"Sorry, I'm almost ready." She hopped around the entry trying to pull her shoes on.

"You're good."

"I thought you worked mostly on the south side," she said.

"Yeah, well, my boss has me running all over town now. You'll have to pick lunch. I'm not up on food this side of the city."

"Sure, no problem." She followed him outside where he opened the door of his truck for her. She slid into the passenger side and watched as he walked around the hood. She took a moment to look around the truck. It was the first time she had ever been inside the work truck. She took a deep breath of the smell of his cologne.

"Doing okay?" he asked.

"Yeah, good." She worried for a minute he had caught her sniffing the seats.

"It's already so damn hot out, I'm afraid the truck doesn't take long to heat up."

"No, it's not bad." She let out a breath in relief. "This is the first summer I've had air conditioning anyway. I'm used to the hot."

"That's right. I remember Brooke saying something about you having air conditioning installed last year."

He started the ignition, and they pulled away from the curb. She guided him across the suburb to a small Italian restaurant. He found a place in the back of the restaurant and pulled the truck in.

She met him at the back of the truck before he could come around to open her door. There was no reason for her sister's boyfriend to work that hard at tending to her.

"This place makes a great parmesan," she said as they walked to the door.

"Veal, chicken, or eggplant?"

"Any of them. You just can't make a bad choice." They were escorted to a table toward the back of the restaurant. Fox held her chair until she was settled at the table.

"I'll have water," he said. She doubled the order, and they picked up their menus. "I think I'll take your advice and order the chicken parm."

"So, how is Brooke?" she asked after they placed their order. As much as she hated to bring up her sister, it seemed wrong not to. She needed a reminder that this wasn't a date.

"Good, I guess."

"Ethan?"

"Ethan's great," he answered with more enthusiasm. "He got his own library card the other day. Brought home a massive stack of books. He thinks he's all that now." Fox's face lit with a smile that made her knees weak. It was a good thing she was already sitting down, or she would have melted to the floor.

"I love when he stays with me," she agreed. "I let him pick out the movie we watch in the evening. It always involves a dragon." They both smile at each other. Then Fox sobered.

"I worry about him," he said. "If you had to take Ethan and run, would you? If he was in danger?"

"Of course. Why?" He was starting to worry her. "What's happened?"

"Nothing yet, but Brooke has been acting more erratic lately. I just need to know that you'll be willing to do whatever you have to for Ethan." He stopped talking when the waitress arrived. They lapsed into silence.

"You're scaring me, Fox," she finally whispered.

"I'm scared too." He sighed and looked up at her. "It's not fair, you know."

"What's not fair?"

"That Ethan's not yours. That I didn't meet you first."

Bailey felt her head swim at his words. She had felt the same way so many times. Why did her thankless sister get the best things in life? Not that she didn't have a good life, but Ethan and Fox deserved better.

"Fox—" She didn't know what she wanted to say, but she didn't get the chance.

"I know," he admitted. "I've stepped way outside the line."

"You can't help how you feel."

"But I can keep from saying it out loud." His gaze moved around the room until they settled back on her. "It doesn't matter anyway. I'm with Brooke, and Ethan needs me. What I want isn't important."

CHAPTER 7

FOX SAT outside the preschool Ethan attended. The text had said simply that Brooke would be home late and to pick up Ethan. He had left work early to drive back across town in time to be there when the bell rang. Climbing out of his truck, he joined the other adults milling around the gate to the school. Moments later the bell rang, and teachers marched their students to the gate.

Ethan ran toward him waving a paper in his small hand. "Fox, look!" he yelled. He was caught by the teacher at the gate and told to wait like everyone else.

Fox hid his grin at the boy's rampant enthusiasm and his sudden dismay. When it was finally his turn, the teacher checked his driver's license before releasing Ethan to him. He appreciated her diligence.

"Look what I drawed," Ethan said, happiness once again etched on his face.

"Look at what I drew," he corrected, taking the paper.

"Drewed. It's you, me, and Momma. Do you like it?"

"I love it. Can we put it on the fridge when we get home?"

"Yeah. Oh, and I drewed Uncle Knox one too, and Uncle Memphis one." Fox debated trying to explain that they weren't his uncles but decided it could wait a little longer. So far, they were the only uncles in his life. He could do worse than Knox and Memphis.

"That's really nice. We'll send your pictures to them."

They walked to the truck where Fox pulled the booster car seat out of his toolbox in the bed. Ethan waited patiently while he was securely belted into the passenger seat. His small backpack and lunch box were deposited on the floor at his feet.

"Where's Momma?" he asked when Fox reached for the ignition.

"She had to work late." The text had said nothing about what she was doing. He had tried calling her, but it went straight to voicemail. It wasn't the first time that she had gone out without so much as an explanation.

What bothered him was it was happening more and more. He wanted to confide his fears to Bailey, that Brooke was seeing someone else, but he had already crossed a line by admitting he wished things were different.

"Can we have pizza?" the small voice broke into his thoughts.

"Sure, buddy."

"Can we invite Aunt Dover?"

"We can ask. She might still be at work, though." He pulled over in the parking lot, fished out his phone and texted his sister. She agreed to come almost immediately. "She said she'll meet us there."

"Yay!" Ethan cheered. Fox wondered how someone produced by two toxic people could have such a sweet, loving spirit. It was one more reminder why he couldn't simply walk away from Brooke no matter how much he wanted to.

They arrived at the small pizza restaurant first and found a booth near the back. He ordered them both water while they waited. It wasn't the best pizza in town, but there was a small arcade in a room off the main dining room that Ethan loved. After eating, Fox would let him play a few games before going home.

Ten minutes later, Dover pushed through the front door followed by the giant. She stomped over to their table and slid into the opposite side of the booth. Knox wedged himself beside her.

"I thought you were heading home?" Fox asked.

"Decided I'd hang around for a few more days instead. See Boston," Knox replied.

"So you're like a bad penny."

"More like gum you can't get off the bottom of your shoe," Dover groused.

"Your sister is very bitchy," Knox said, rolling his eyes.

"She grows on you," Fox answered.

"Like fungus," he agreed.

"Speaking of, where's Brooke?" Dover asked.

"Momma is working," Ethan answered. Fox made quotations with his fingers.

"Where does she work?" Knox asked.

"At a spa not far from Ethan's preschool. She's a massage therapist. It's how we met. I pulled a couple of muscles in my back on a job and went in to see if they could be worked out. Brooke was my therapist. She gave me her number before I left. I called the next day." He was interrupted when the waitress arrived.

"When did they move in?" Knox asked after they placed their order.

"Probably three or four months later."

"Way too fast if you ask me," Dover added.

"I don't know. Greer and I weren't even together when we started living together, but that's a whole other story," Knox said. "If you mentioned how much 'work' she seems to be doing do you think something would happen? Something unpleasant?" He looked at Ethan who sat across from him coloring on a paper menu.

"I can't risk it. Sometimes the...outburst has to be contained," Fox answered. "I just wish I knew what was going on. I don't want anyone put in harm's way."

"I have someone coming who can find out more about what's going on. And before you mind-meld me," Knox said, holding up his hands, palms out. "It's our brother-in-law. He's very good at poking around unnoticed. He'll be here tomorrow."

"No one asked for you to interfere," Fox challenged.

"I've already tried," Dover responded. "You might as well give up. He's all 'family this' and 'family that.' It can't hurt though. Guy's apparently a fed."

"Great, that's just what I need," Fox snarled.

"Look, maybe she's just...'working' on someone else. If it's something more, though, you need to know," Knox argued.

"Do you get in the middle of everyone's business?" Fox asked. "You do this to Memphis?"

"Hey, I'm the reason Memphis even met Thayer, same for Dex and Tyler. Flint and Willow, however, were all them. I just made sure they kept living. So, yes, I do this to everyone I give two shits about." Ethan's head bobbed up, his eyes wide. "Sorry, little man. I'll put money in the swear jar when I get home."

"You have a swear jar?" Ethan asked, his eyes still wide.

"I do. I think it's funding our next vacation."

"Can we get a swear jar?" he asked, looking at Fox.

"Thanks." Fox scowled at Knox.

"See, your life is already better with me in it." Knox smirked back.

━━━

Brooke placed the cash through the door in the glass separating her from the cabbie. She stepped out onto the curb and closed the back door.

"Are you sure you'll be okay down here?" the cabbie asked.

"I'm fine," she answered and stepped back against the building.

"Suit yourself," he said with a shrug and drove away.

This was always the part she hated. You never knew who was along the waterfront after hours. It wasn't dark yet, but that didn't deter the drug dealers.

She had been propositioned several times as she'd walked the two blocks. This time she just got a catcall for her efforts. She teetered down a road never meant for five-inch heels.

Reaching the heavy metal door, she pressed the buzzer on the wall. A few minutes later the door was rolled back, and a strong hand jerked her roughly inside. It was dark except for a work light hanging over the door. Her eyes struggled to adjust before he had her by the arm and was dragging her through the darkness.

She guessed she should be used to this by now. It wasn't the first time he had insisted she meet him at the warehouse. Her heart would race whenever she got the text to meet him. The flesh on her body would tingle the second she stepped inside the immense space.

He pulled her past the crates into his office and straight to the back wall.

"Turn around," he snarled. She pouted but followed his instructions, turning her back to the wall. Somewhere on the wall he had a lock installed that opened a secret room. She heard the sound of stone scraping against cement, and her heart began to race. This was her favorite part of the game.

"Come on," he said stepping inside the room. She turned around and followed. The door closed behind her.

Her gaze immediately fell on the back wall. She took in the intricacy of the mural first. He explained that it was the school crest where he had attended high school. It was an almost lifelike rendering of an eagle.

But, unlike most eagle mascots, this one looked like it was flying right at you. The talons reached out in front of it, like it would swoop you up in them. It sent a chill up her spine every time she entered the room.

There was a motto written in Latin underneath the eagle that she muttered to herself. He had told her what it meant several times, but she never could remember. The only word that had stuck with her was the word pietas— piety.

Her gaze roamed over the rest of the wall. The driver's licenses, ticket stubs, car keys, money. There were even several cell phones attached to the wall. Anything they found in the men's pockets.

It was amazing what people carried with them. The silver-haired attorney had a pocket full of condoms. She wondered how lucky he'd thought he was getting that night. Turns out, not lucky at all.

"Do you see it?" he asks, slipping up behind her. His hand snaked around her throat, and she gasped. "Halfway down on the left," he whispered. His other hand clamped on her breast. She felt the wetness soak her panties. "Do. You. See. It?" he asked once again. She quickly nodded her head.

He pressed against her as he moved her closer to the security badge of the bank executive. There was a second photo of the moment he died and one of the man laid out on the pitch at the private school.

Spread around the pictures was breath spray, a poker chip, and a photo of his family. She wished she could pick the ones who weren't just looking to cheat on their wives while they were in town on business. The kids in the picture would be better off without him, she reasoned.

She felt her dress pushed up over her ass. His hand snaked over the globes of her ass until they wrapped in the string of her barely there panties. With one twist, they were yanked away from her body. A moan slipped out from between her teeth. She was inches from the photos of her last mark when he entered her in one harsh stroke. She would have screamed, but she could no longer draw a full breath.

Her arms stretched in front of her until they felt the wall to keep from falling forward. She knew he would punish her if she toppled against it. There was a part of her that craved that punishment more than anything. His praise for her being obedient was an even more powerful drug, so she pushed back as he railed into her. His hand around her throat tightened until she had to struggle to remain conscious.

"Finish me," he hissed. She felt a sharp slap against her backside that pushed her body to orgasm. It was exactly how he had been training her. All she wanted was to please him, and she knew exactly what he needed. He froze behind her as he pumped his seed inside. He never wore a condom. It was a good thing she had taken care of any chance of getting pregnant again when Ethan was born.

He slid out and slumped into a desk chair. She turned to make sure he was happy to find his pants still open. Dropping to her knees, she crawled across the rough cement floor to him.

"Fucking hell," he snarled when she reached for him. "Give me a minute." She sat back on her heels and waited. "You'll never believe what happened today." He laughed, and her heart soared. "My parents are having their town-house remodeled and awarded the work to the group your boyfriend works for.

"Do you know what that means?" he continued. She looked up waiting for him to explain it to her. "It means it's time I meet your boyfriend. Don't you think?"

"If you think so," she mumbled.

"We can arrange to run into each other at dinner one night. I'm sure he'll invite me to sit with you. Would you like that demanding pussy to be fingered under the table while we're all getting to know each other like friends?"

"Yes, please."

"That's a good girl. Maybe I can fuck you in the bath-room between courses. You'll still feel me on you when you go home with him. Would you like that, my little dove?"

"Very much," she answered. She wasn't sure about any of this, but she knew it was better to give him what he wanted. The last thing she wanted to do was wind up on the machine behind the glass at the other end of the room.

"Then put those pretty lips to work, and I'll see what I

can do." He sat back with his legs spread as her head dipped toward him.

CHAPTER 8

DOVER STOOD outside of the police department with her arms crossed. She should be inside working on the latest case instead of waiting for Knox and the brother-in-law he wanted to introduce to her.

She checked the watch on her wrist once again. They had two more minutes, then she was returning inside. She was turning to open the door when a car pulled into a visitor's parking space.

Knox unfolded from the driver's side of the car, and another man climbed out of the passenger's side. "All I'm saying is there's no reason to honk so much," Knox complained.

"There is when you drive like an old lady from out of town. Hi," he said, turning to Dover. "I'm Dex."

"The FBI guy, right?" she asked.

"That's right, but I'm here unofficially," he added, holding his palms out. "Just helping out family."

"You were at the Washington Bureau, but you're now in Houston? What happened there?" Knox had given her a confusing introduction to her new family before bed last night. She still didn't quite have everyone straight.

"Fell in love while busting up a major human trafficking outfit."

"Gets you every time," Knox chipped in.

"You'll be following my brother's psycho girlfriend to see where she's going?" She waited for Dex to nod before turning to Knox. "I still don't like this."

"I'll just gather information," Dex said, cutting Knox off before he could say anything to piss her off. "What you do with it, we'll leave up to you." He glared at Knox until he nodded. "Is that good with you?"

She studied him trying to make up her mind. Unlike Knox whose aura shimmered in orange and reds like a fire, Dex was surrounded by a cool blue. There wasn't any deception in him as far as she could tell. If he screwed her over though, federal agent or not, she'd cut him off at the knees.

"Fox can't know," she said.

"I promise no one will know I'm there, and Knox won't tell him. That will be up to you," Dex assured her.

"I'm not sure what we'll do even if we find out she's screwing around. Fox will never leave Ethan if he can prevent it. The only way Ethan would be safe is in Bailey's custody, but I don't see that happening," she said. "Just don't fuck this up."

"Damn, she is related to Tyler," Dex pointed out. "Is that what binds us, our attraction to hard-headed women?"

"Without a doubt," Knox agreed. "If they're not related directly, they're put directly in our paths."

"Oh, fuck off," she responded, turning to return to her desk, but she was laughing as she entered the building. Her "extended family" was starting to grow on her, and that pissed her off for sure. Still, if she had to have a bunch of extra siblings thrust on her in her forties, these weren't so bad.

"Everything okay?" Danny asked when she arrived at her office.

"Yeah, just dealing with family bullshit."

"The new brother?"

"And a brother-in-law apparently. They're coming out of the woodwork."

"It'd freak me out to have all these siblings suddenly appear."

"That's the thing that worries me," she said digging through the box on her desk. "There's like a big age gap between the youngest two. Does that mean there's a bunch more out there we don't know about yet."

"Could be. Guy wasn't shooting blanks for sure."

"No, he wasn't." She searched her desk for a moment. "Hey, what do you think about moving this to one of the incident rooms so we can spread out?"

"Good idea. I think I just stumbled across another one out in Cambridge."

"No shit?"

"Same MO."

Dover picked up a box from her desk and walked out into the hallway. There had to be at least one free incident room. If this kept going, they would have a task force by the end of the day.

Danny grabbed another box and followed her. They found a room no one was using and moved into it. Turning on the lights, she began building case files on the magnetic whiteboards at the front of the room.

She barely noticed as a fourth case was added to the boards. The more she worked, the more it looked like the cases were similar. She finally stepped back to take a look, and Danny whistled low beside her.

"You need to take this to the boss," he said. "I'll go see if anything new has popped up from our search." She took a few more minutes after he left to get her facts straight. It had to be the same person doing this. What did they say? Three or more done by the same person was a serial killer. Though, she knew from her training that wasn't always the case. With one last look at the boards, she left the room.

"How's it going, Leah? Has he got a sec?" Dover asked the captain's administrative assistant when she reached the office.

"Ask him yourself," she answered. Leah had the tendency to be snarky which was probably why Dover had always liked her.

"Hey, Cap, can I talk to you?" she asked, sticking her head in the chief's office. He motioned her into his office without looking up. She waited patiently until he finished what he was doing.

"What can I help you with, Detective?" he asked.

"I think we might have a serial killer, sir." Damn, that wasn't how she wanted to start the conversation. With all the facts swimming through her head, though, that was the first thing that popped out. He arched an eyebrow at her. "I mean, I think we've found a link between our cases and another. Two others actually."

He sat back in his seat and waved his arm for her to continue.

"All four were successful men. They were all strangled by something like a belt, and the ME found a religious medallion on each one. A St. Matthew, St. Francis, St. Christopher, and St. Bernadette" she continued.

"St. Bernadette? That's unusual."

"Yes, sir. They were all left on private school properties arranged on their backs with no clothes or personal effects. Sean, uh, the medical examiner is positive they were killed elsewhere. Danny and I set it up in Evidence-2 if you would like to see what we have."

The chief stood and followed Dover down the hall to the other end of the offices. There were already several other detectives in the room when they arrived. She let him study the boards for a minute before stepping up to them.

"The first is Ian Moore from Minneapolis here on business. He was found in Cambridge three months ago. This," she said, pointing to the next picture of a handsome smiling man, "is George Goodwin from Buffalo. Dom is working that case and can speak more on it. This is who we found last week. Trent Alleman who worked at Mass Gen and was found here in Roxbury."

"We just got confirmation from dentals on the latest victim," Danny said, handing her a piece of paper. She wrote Jack Dawson above the photos from the morgue. She would add a photo of him alive as soon as possible. It was important to remember that these were men with lives and people who loved them, not just some body on a slab.

"Mr. Dawson was from Hartford. Looks like he was here on business too," she added. "He was reported missing by his boss when he didn't turn up to head to the airport the next day. He was also found stripped of clothing with a St. Francis's medal around his neck. We should know more when the lab gets back to us with their report."

She looked over the report for any other details she needed to voice. Finding none, she looked up at the chief waiting to see what he would say.

"It looks like you might be right, Detective. See what else you can find. Touch base with Cambridge. We'll need a copy of their files," he said. "You'll be point on this. Are you good with that, Danny?"

"Yes, sir."

"Good. Dom, Kyle, shift your load to someone else. I assume you'll want to be in on this." He turned once again to face her. "I'll expect a full report tomorrow morning." With a nod, he left the room. Those who remained turned their gazes on her awaiting instruction.

"Okay, Dom, do you want to keep working on the Goodwin case. Danny, contact Buffalo and see if they can send someone to interview the boss. I'll contact Cambridge and have them send over their files. We might have the detectives on that case brought over for a while. We'll meet back at about four. Sound good?"

She watched as the other detectives got to work. If they could just connect the dots on the cases, maybe it would lead them closer to their killer. She knew Danny would get to work tracing Dawson's whereabouts during his trip to Boston. Now to convince another district to turn over their case.

She returned to her office and put in the request for the case file from Cambridge. Danny reported that Buffalo PD was sending someone to the law office to interview Dawson's boss. She doubted he could shed much light on what happened, but with any luck, he could tell them where Dawson was going that night.

"Hope I'm not interrupting," Sean said, walking into the office. "I thought you'd want the final autopsy findings as soon as possible." He crossed the room and dropped into the side chair next to her desk. "I emailed you a copy, but here are the hard copies of everything."

Dover snatched the copies from his hand and began pouring over them.

"Nothing new to report. He was strangled by some sort of belt. I don't think it was done manually because there are no defense wounds. I did find a small needle mark on his neck, but whatever he was given doesn't show up on the toxicology report. My thought is he was kept alive for a while before death. At least twelve hours if GHB was used."

"Thanks, Sean." He was sitting close enough for her to catch the scent of cedarwood. It took all of her concentration not to lean into it. She mentally shook her head. There was no way she could develop a crush on the medical examiner during an open investigation of this magnitude. It was completely unprofessional. Not to mention ridiculous.

"Alleman and Dawson were very similar except for the medals. I pulled Bianchi's case back out and reviewed it also. It's definitely the same MO down to the same size strap used in your case. I didn't notice anything the other ME missed. If you'd like me to, I can read over the Cambridge case when it arrives. Just let me know."

"That would be great. I'll forward it as soon as it shows up." He smiled, and she couldn't help but smile back.

"Yeah, there's no special treatment there," Danny mumbled once Sean left.

"Strictly professional."

"Then why are you still grinning like a fool?"

Dover scowled. Snatching up the autopsy, she stomped out of their office. She needed to add the latest notes to the boards in the incident room anyway.

She wondered if Danny was right though. *Was it possible Sean was interested?* She shoved the high school crush thoughts to the back of her mind. Uncapping the dry-erase marker, she began updating the case boards.

Dom had been filling in the timeline for the Goodwin.

He had last been seen at a bar in Southie in the company of a blonde woman. That was interesting. It wasn't far from where they had traced Alleman's last whereabouts to. She needed those files from Cambridge, now.

"Hey, Danny?" she said, stepping back into the office. "Do we have a list of all the Southie bars?"

"Should." He pounded on his computer for a minute until the printer started to hum. "That's a pretty big list," he added, nodding at the printer. "What are you thinking?"

"Bianchi's vic was last seen at a Southie bar with a blonde. It's worth a shot. Alleman was also seen in Southie. Maybe that's his hunting ground. Do we have a better photo of Dawson yet?"

"Just came in." He handed her a photo of a young man smiling for the camera. Her heart hurt for the family who would never get to see that smile again.

"Can you hold it down, while I go see what I can find?" She checked her watch. "Everything should be open, but not too crowded yet."

"Go on. I'll call you if anything comes up."

"Thanks, Danny." She took the list off the printer and headed out.

CHAPTER 9

"THANKS FOR WATCHING HIM," Fox said, ushering Ethan into Bailey's house.

"It's no problem. There's a snack on the table if you want it," she answered. Ethan ran into the kitchen without even saying goodbye.

"It's just, I have to go in tomorrow, and I don't know what Brooke is doing. I feel better if he's here."

"We'll be fine. Don't worry about it." Her hand landed on his arm, and the feeling of fire shot up it. "Would you like to come in for some cheesy bread? I made extra."

He should say no. He should walk away, but there was something about her that kept pulling him closer. There was no doubt that whatever was between them wouldn't end well. How could it when you fell for your girlfriend's sister?

"Sounds great," he said, stepping inside. He followed her to the kitchen where Ethan was just finishing his snack.

"Can I go outside, Aunt Bailey?" he asked.

"Of course, sweetie." She opened the back door, and he shot into the yard. They watched through the windows as he jumped on one of the swings on the playscape. "It's too hot to leave the door open, but we can see him from in here. He should be fine." She flitted around the kitchen preparing plates of bread and pouring two glasses of lemonade.

"I was supposed to be off, but I have to meet the boss tomorrow at some townhouse in Beacon Hill. I guess some rich guy is remodeling his place. I'll come get him when I'm done."

"Don't worry about it, you know I love when Ethan is here. Brooke is good with this?" She took a sip of her lemonade.

"I didn't ask her."

"Fox."

"I know. But you know she would have pitched a fit. It's better to ask for forgiveness than permission when it comes to Brooke." He could feel her gaze on him as he watched Ethan run around the backyard kicking a ball.

"Still." He frowned, and she let the subject drop. "Is your other brother still in town?"

"Yeah. Would you believe he's crashing at Dover's place?"

"I bet that's like throwing fuel on a fire. They haven't killed each other yet?"

"Not as far as I know." He chuckled. "We should be able to see the explosion from here when it happens, though."

"It's so crazy to think you had more siblings out there all this time."

"Yeah." They ate the cheese bread in silence. "I like your kitchen," Fox finally said. "Yellow is always a good choice. Makes the room feel bigger."

"It's my favorite color. I can't imagine not having a

yellow kitchen. I painted it as soon as I moved in." They lapsed back into silence again.

"Well, I should be going," he said, standing. "I'll just say goodbye to Ethan." He slipped into the backyard. "I've got to go, little man. You be good for Aunt Bailey, and I'll be back to get you tomorrow." Ethan ran over to hug him. "Have fun." Ethan ran back to the swings, so Fox returned inside. The food and glasses had been cleared from the table.

"Be careful getting home," Bailey said, leading him back through the house. She stopped next to the front door but didn't open it.

"I will," he answered quietly, standing in front of her. His hand was on the door, but he didn't want to open it either. Just one more moment with her. It was all he would ever get, but he would take anything. Leaning forward slightly, he took in the scent of her shampoo. Citrus, always citrus. It was seared into his memory like it was a part of him.

She looked up at him, her eyes smoldering. He took a quick glance at her lips, free of the heavy lipstick her sister wore. It would take nothing to lean a little farther until their lips brushed. But before he gave in, he stood straight again and turned the doorknob.

"Thanks again," he said and walked outside. He didn't even glance back at the house as he drove away.

By the time he made it back across town, he had pushed his feelings for Bailey away. Brooke would be home by now. He needed to be ready to head that cyclone off. He found parking near the building and climbed up the stairs.

"Where have you been?" Brooke demanded the second he walked into his apartment.

"I thought we could use a night out, so I took Ethan to your sister's house."

"Without asking me?"

"I wanted to surprise you. I thought we could dress up and try the new fish place downtown." He didn't wait for her to rage out of control. His gaze met hers, and he focused on calming her down.

"That sounds good. Just give me a little bit to get ready," she said, swaying on her feet slightly. She hurried into the bedroom, and Fox slumped onto the couch. He had put the plan together earlier when he found out he had to work the next day. He didn't trust Brooke not to go out and leave Ethan in the apartment on his own.

When they'd first met, she had doted on her son. Fox had only seen the side of Brooke that she wanted him to. She was beautiful, fun, and a good mother.

After they had been kicked out of their apartment and moved in with him, he began to see a much different Brooke. She was still beautiful, but she spent most of her time either fighting with him or going out. Ethan barely mattered at all.

"You'd better get changed, silly," she said, walking out of the bedroom. She was wearing a short blue dress that barely covered her ass. Her high heels could double as a weapon. This was the Brooke he remembered from before. He might have altered her mood a little too much.

"I need to run through the shower. Give me twenty max." He walked into the bathroom shedding clothes.

The reservation wasn't until seven thirty, but he knew Brooke would want to do some window shopping before then. Even knowing she was buzzing around the bedroom hunting for accessories for her outfit, he couldn't stop his mind from moving to Bailey. His hand automatically moved to caress his hardening length.

"Are you doing something naughty in here?" Brooke asked playfully, stepping into the bathroom.

"No," he answered. His hand moved to press against the wall of the shower. He turned his back to her.

"I can join you if you want," she teased.

"No, don't do that. You already look perfect. I don't want you to have to start over again." In truth, he was having a hard time convincing his mind to let go of the images of Bailey he had just been envisioning. Being with one sister while fantasizing about the other was undoing him piece by piece. "Wait until we get home. Then I'll help you out of that dress with my teeth."

"Can't wait," she purred. He breathed a sigh of relief when she left the room. Turning off the water, he stepped out and grabbed his towel. Tonight was already shaping up to be agony. He wrapped the towel around his waist.

Staring into the mirror over the sink, he studied his face. He couldn't see any way out of the situation with Brooke. He had willingly traded his happiness for a small boy.

He stepped into the shared closet. He pulled on a gray pair of slacks and a white dress shirt. It would complement Brooke's dress without calling any attention away from her. He knew how much she enjoyed being the center of attention everywhere they went. Not his of course, just everyone else's attention.

"Are you ready?" he asked, walking into the living room.

"What do you think?" Her mood was already shifting. He knew he couldn't alter it forever. If he could, then they would all be living happily as a family.

With Brooke though, it seemed like her good humor lasted a little less every time. There might even come a day in the near future where he couldn't control it any longer. Then what?

"We'll take the truck tonight," he said, ignoring her comment. All he had was his work truck. It made parking in the city a real nightmare. "I don't want this beauty sitting on a dirty train seat." He held out his hand to her. She finally relented and took it. "We'll even do valet." He saw her eyes light up. She loved putting on airs. He just didn't want to hunt for a parking space downtown on Friday night.

They found the restaurant easily. Fox pulled into the valet line. Brooke exited the car like a movie star when the man opened the door for her. She waited just long enough for Fox to join her before marching her way into the restaurant. The host showed them to the bar until their table was ready. Fox couldn't convince her that they were too early.

"I'll have a whiskey sour," she said when the bartender found them seated at the bar.

"Just club soda with a twist. Thank you," Fox added. "This is nice."

"It's not bad. We might come back." He caught himself before he rolled his eyes. She was just a working-class girl from Newton. What would she know about upscale dining? The bartender set their drinks on the bar. She took a sip of hers. "Heavy on the whiskey. It just went up another point."

"Glad it meets your standards." She shot him a glare. He simply held up his drink to clink against hers until she relented. "The fish is supposed to be first class."

"We'll see."

Fox's phone buzzed in his pocket. "They're ready to seat us." He took both of their drinks and followed her to the host stand.

They were shown to their table quickly. Brooke was

seated by the host while Fox set her drink in front of her. She took another long drag before picking up her menu.

━━━

If they'd been paying better attention, they would have noticed the man who followed them from the bar to the dining room. He now sat in a dark booth just far enough from them that he couldn't quite hear what they said to each other. Fox wouldn't have known him even if he saw the man, so he had no reason to pay attention to another diner.

Brooke, however, had missed him also. She would know him instantly. She had sent him a text the moment she went into the bedroom to dress.

Looking around for him would only serve to alert Fox that something was going on, so she didn't dare. Gooseflesh rose on her arms just knowing he was somewhere in the restaurant watching.

"Are you cold?" Fox asked. He slid his jacket off and slid it around her shoulders.

"I think there's a slight draft on my side is all."

"Do we need to trade sides?"

"No, I'll be fine. I think I'll have the salad."

"You don't want fish?" he asked.

"I'll just have a bite of yours. You don't expect me to look like this by bingeing on a giant slab of meat, do you?"

"I think you'd be gorgeous no matter what size you are."

"That's ridiculous," she stated. Her gaze swept the room carefully hoping to get a glance of him. "I'll just have a bite of yours."

"Whatever you want to do." He always gave in too

easily. She might enjoy his company more if he ever fought back. It was so easy to get what she wanted.

Her lover didn't roll over so easily. He took what he wanted from her which made her want to give him everything. Maybe she already had. She had offered to leave Fox several times, but he said to stay. He liked the game they were playing.

"I guess it'll be a no to dessert then?" Fox asked.

"That's later, remember." She gave him a quick wink. At least he was skilled at some things. He didn't make her blood boil, but he could force more than one orgasm out of her.

No matter what she was told, if Fox got where he couldn't even do that, she was gone. She would simply gather up Ethan and disappear from the apartment. There were plenty of places to hide in a city like Boston.

"May I take your order?" the server asked from the side of the table.

"I'll have the Caesar with anchovies and another one of these," she answered, shaking her glass.

"I'll take the salmon. Baked potato and green beans. Just water for now. Thank you," Fox added. The server left, and Fox leaned back in his chair. He smiled at her. She matched the smile, but it wasn't meant for him.

Her mind was on the man hidden somewhere in the very restaurant she sat in across from her boyfriend. A tendril of excitement threaded its way up her spine at the thought. With any luck, he would summon her tomorrow and give her what she really craved. She just had to wait until then.

CHAPTER 10

FOX PULLED into the parking lot of his office. His boss had texted him early that morning to ask him to stop by before heading out to check on his jobs.

He hadn't slept well last night, and his head ached slightly. He chalked it up to worrying about his current relationship situation. The dinner had been okay, but Brooke seemed distracted most of the night.

"Hey, Maeve," he said, stepping into the office foyer. "Boss said he wanted to see me?"

The office wasn't anything fancy. All the company needed was someone to answer the phones and file paperwork. His boss sat in an office behind her desk working on bids.

All the billing was done at the main headquarters in a building out in Wellesley. He'd only been there a couple of times and always felt underdressed. It's where their clients met with the developers.

"Sure thing. Have a seat, and I'll let him know you're here."

Fox smiled to himself. Maeve had the most Bostonian

accent he had ever heard. His was tempered by growing up in Maine. Once when she had too much to drink at the company Christmas party, he couldn't understand her at all. He took a seat on the old leather couch in the corner to wait.

"Do you need a cup?" It came out cuhp.

"I had two this morning. That should do me," he answered. He pulled out his phone and began to scroll through his email.

"Addams," his boss bellowed from his office. Fox jumped hard enough he dropped his phone. He had just scooped it off the floor when his boss appeared at the door. "You've got a request."

"A request?"

"Yeah, that rich lady in Beacon Hill is waiting for you. Guess you did her friend's place. She's an important client. We play our cards right, they own rental property all over town. Make sure you don't fuck it up. Here's the address." Fox took a piece of paper from his hand. "Just do the measurements and stuff for the bid. Some designer is supposed to meet you there with the mock-ups."

"Sure. What time do I need to be there?" Fox asked.

"You should just make it if you leave now," his boss answered, checking his watch.

"Guess I'll head that way then. See you later, Maeve."

"Sure thing, kid," she answered.

He punched the address into the GPS app on his phone on his way to the truck. Snapping his phone into the holder, he pulled out of the parking lot heading across town.

He racked his brain for who could have recommended him. Most people don't even bother to learn his name, much less refer him to someone else. Usually, he's just another nameless face in a group of workers.

The traffic was not on his side, so he pulled up to an

austere-looking townhome five minutes past when he was supposed to have been there. He quickly grabbed his notebook and tape measure before jumping out of the truck.

At least he managed to find a place to park not too far away. When he reached the door, an anxious-looking woman pulled it open before he could knock.

"Traffic?" she asked.

"Yeah, sorry."

"I'm Heidi with The Ossman Design Group," she said, sticking out her hand.

"Fox Addams." They shook hands, and she turned to lead him through the house. They met a tall, slim older woman standing just inside the main living room.

"Mrs. Anderson, this is the contractor. He's here to take measurements for the proposal." She nodded but didn't offer her hand. "And this is her son, Edmund." He did offer his hand. "This is Fox Addams."

"Fox as in the furry red dog creature?" the man asked with a sneer.

"Actually, my name is short for Foxworth, like the town in Maine."

"How creative," the man said drolly. "Mother asked me to be here—for safety, of course."

Fox wondered if it was really to watch the valuables.

"To be honest," Edmund continued quieter, "I'm not sure she felt she would be able to answer any questions you might have. She's usually drunk by this time of the day."

Fox took a step back in surprise. Why would anyone tell a complete stranger that? He heard Heidi giggle uncomfortably and turned to follow her.

They silently climbed a set of stairs to the second floor with three bedrooms on it. Each had an en suite bath that she wanted remodeled. He flopped open his notebook and began taking notes as Heidi described what needed done to each room.

Edmund stood near watching every move with a look of interest. "How long have you been wielding a hammer?" he asked while Fox kneeled to look in a low cabinet.

"I've been working construction since high school." He pulled his measuring tape off his belt. "I've been a supervisor for about six years now."

"No interest in moving up?"

Fox chose to ignore the question rather than answer it. What he really wanted to do was shove Edmund out a window. That was frowned upon though, so he continued to add figures to his rough sketch. The guy bothered him. He didn't feel like he was a direct threat, but there was just something about him that didn't sit right.

"I think I have everything I need for these three bedrooms and baths. What else?" he asked.

"The primary bedroom suite takes up the third floor," Heidi answered, leading him to more stairs.

They stopped at a pair of double doors on the third floor that she threw open. Edmund pushed past them and flopped on the bed. He placed his head on his hand like he was posing for a modeling job—except he was no model.

Edmund was as average as men came. He was around five foot ten with light brown hair and eyes. His features were more round than angular. The extra thirty pounds he carried didn't help him either. He had, however, perfected the bored, pampered look.

Fox glanced at him before turning back toward Heidi as she explained the changes to be done to the room. He could feel eyes trained on him as he moved around the room with his tape measure and notebook. When they moved to the en suite bath, Edmund moved to lean against the doorjamb.

"All right. No changes to the first floor?" Fox asked.

"They decided that will be phase two," Heidi answered.

"I do have one more thing," Edmund said as he glided back across the bedroom. "I didn't talk to you about it, Heidi, but I'm sure Mother won't mind." They followed him from the room. He turned and smiled at Fox. "Just up the stairs at the end of the hallway. Why don't you wait here," he said to Heidi before disappearing up a narrow stairwell behind a door.

"Call 9-1-1 if I don't return," Fox murmured to her. She bit back a smile as he moved toward the stairs. He found Edmund standing in a large attic surrounded by boxes and a Christmas garland hanging from the rafters. "What were you thinking?"

"Can you make this into a private lounge? A mancave, if you will."

"Maybe. Let me take a look around, and I'll let you know." Fox moved around the room taking measurements and checking specification requirements to convert the room. Edmund followed on his heels.

"Most mancaves are in basements or garages," Fox continued. "You have good clearance up here. It's going to depend on the insulation and if permits will allow. Do you want us to add this to the current project bid or as an addendum?"

"You can add it. I'm certainly not paying for it," Edmund answered. He took a step closer to Fox, so they were almost touching. "I mean, it will be mine someday. There's no telling what I can get up to up here." His hand grazed down Fox's arm so slightly, he wondered if it was simply his imagination for a moment.

"Okay. I need to get back to the office so I can start on

the work." He turned back to the steps and climbed down quickly. He found Heidi anxiously pacing the hallway.

"You had me worried," she whispered.

"You weren't the only one," he agreed. They quieted as Edmund joined them. Fox followed Heidi down to the main floor where they found Mrs. Anderson. After thanking her, they left through the front door. Edmund followed them out the door, preventing Fox from saying anything more.

Fox took his copy of the plans from Heidi and climbed in his truck. As he turned the corner at the end of the block, he glanced in his rearview mirror. Edmund still watched with a smile on his face.

He decided instead of driving straight back to the office, he would check on one of the other sites since he wasn't far. The boss wouldn't get around to crunching the numbers for this job until later in the week anyway. There was no reason to hurry back. He wove through town and circled the area several times before he found parking down the street.

Flipping open his notebook, he started to review what progress he could expect when he toured the building site. It was a full remodel on an old office building. A group of attorneys had bought it and wanted it turned into a multi-use building.

It was old enough to require a refit of all electrical and plumbing, not to mention bringing the bathrooms up to code. He had assigned one of the better foremen to the project, though, so he wasn't worried.

He jumped at the tap on his window. Looking up, he found soft brown eyes looking back at him. He quickly rolled the window down.

"Hey, I thought this was your truck," Bailey said.

"What are you doing here?"

"I had a doctor's appointment across the street. I

noticed you parked here when I came out. Have you had lunch yet? There's a cute little diner around the corner."

"No. Lunch sounds good." He rolled back up the window and opened his door. She took a step back to let him out. "Is everything okay? With the doctor?"

"Yeah, just my yearly physical," she answered.

"Sorry, it's none of my business." He motioned for her to lead the way.

"It's fine. Nothing to report."

"You would report though if something was wrong, right?" Her gaze met his as she waited at the crosswalk. He could feel the warmth in his cheeks. "I mean if you needed help or anything." A smile stretched across her lips. "You can just ask if you do. Please tell me to stop talking."

She laughed and placed her hand on his forearm. "I like when you talk. Also, thank you." She removed her hand, and he had to fight not to pull it back to where it had rested. Everywhere she touched, he could feel his skin tingle. He knew he couldn't cross that line, but he wanted to rip it to shreds and march across it.

"This is it," she continued when they stopped in front of a quintessential Boston diner. It had a bar in a U-shape in the middle of the room with booths around the outside. He was willing to wager they made a hell of a breakfast omelet. He'd keep that in mind next time he was up here. Bailey weaved through the room until she found an empty booth in the back.

"What's good here?" It was like a repeat performance of the last time they had lunch.

"I've only eaten here once before. I don't remember what I had, but I remember it was good. I think you're safe with whatever you choose."

She dipped her head to study the menu while he

studied her. She had dressed up for the doctor. A floral print dress with a V-neck accentuated her assets perfectly. For a moment, he found himself jealous of the doctor.

"So, this doctor. He an old guy?"

She looked up from the menu with a smile. "He's happily married with kids and grandkids," she answered. "Why?"

"Just making conversation."

"Conversation, huh?"

"Yeah, might be in the market for a new doctor."

"Are you? In the market for a new doctor?" she teased.

"Not really. No." He found his smile matching hers. That was the thing about Bailey, he never felt anything but happiness from her. It was another world from Brooke, and it was becoming a problem. "Though, you never know. How old did you say?"

She laughed, and in that moment, all was right with his world.

CHAPTER 11

"BURNING THE MIDNIGHT OIL?" Knox said, stepping into the incident room. Dover had been standing at the front of the room staring at the boards for the last half hour. Everyone else had already headed home. There wasn't anything more they could do today, but she just couldn't bear to leave. There had to be more, if she could just see it.

"How did you get up here?" she asked without turning around.

"Charm," he answered. "Works every time."

"My credentials might have had a little something to do with it too," another voice said. This time she turned around to find her brother-in-law, a GQ-worthy man with cheekbones that could cut glass standing next to Knox.

"Should have known it was the G-man brother-in-law," she said.

"That sounds ominous. You know you shouldn't believe everything he tells you."

"I've figured that out, yeah. What I don't understand is why he thought we needed a fed just to follow my brother's no-account girlfriend around. I mean, I don't think she's deadly."

"You don't know that. Besides, I'm just trying to keep it in the family. He could use some time away from our sister anyway. A sort of impromptu vacation." She noticed the smirk Dex fired at Knox.

Somehow, she doubted anything involving Knox turned out to be a vacation. From the stories he had been telling her, death and destruction followed in his path.

"Don't let the fancy clothes fool you, he's good at his job," he continued.

"You're going to spoil me being this nice," Dex said, smoothing away the nonexistent wrinkles in his starched polo shirt.

"Saved my ass a time or two also."

"Now you're just gushing."

Dover watched as the two men sparred good-naturedly. She wondered if the entire family was nuts or if she had just drawn the crazy ones. It made her curious to see what the rest of her siblings were like.

"Looks like you've got your work cut out for you," Dex said, motioning to the whiteboards.

"Yeah, we could use a break," she agreed. "No one remembers seeing these guys downtown, but the bar scene gets pretty hectic on the weekends. There's something here, I just can't see it."

"Do you mind telling me what you do have? Sometimes it helps me to talk through the evidence."

"Sure, it's worth a try. Death was by manual strangulation with some sort of belt. All of the victims were staged at private school athletic fields," she said. "A religious medal on each body. All the bodies were nude."

"The St. Matthew medal is interesting. There's a lot to

unpack. Does he crave power? Control? Are they sexually motivated?"

"Sean...I mean, the medical examiner found no trace of sexual assault."

"Okay, I would wager there is a sexual element somewhere though. What does the private school mean? Is there a socioeconomic meaning?" Dover watched as Dex trolled over the boards expressing his thoughts. "Did he attend one of the schools. Is he Catholic, or is that a red herring?"

"One of the schools is Episcopal, so I don't think he's necessarily Catholic," she said.

"I know St. Matthew is the patron saint of the money lenders. I have quite a few of my students who are on scholarship. They're brilliant, they just don't have the funds," Knox said, taking a seat.

"That's true. Did something happen to him at a private school? Was he bullied? He's comfortable moving around them. I assume there's not great CCTV coverage of the fields."

"Not really. Danny sent what we could get to tech, but they haven't found anything."

"It's a good guess he didn't start with these three. He had to have worked up to this. So what was his first kill? I would look through records for any other offenses within the private school community."

"Already on that. I have records being pulled for up to thirty years previous. I don't think there will be many, and most incidents are dealt with internally to save the families public scrutiny."

"Yeah, I don't know if that will pop much, but it's worth trying. How did he get the bodies into the dump sites?"

"It looks like he has keys or is very good at working padlocks. I can't imagine any of the school employees opening the gates after hours for him. We haven't found any employees that have all the schools in common either. We're trying to run the kids to see if any of them overlap. All three schools are fighting that, citing privacy issues."

"How busy are the areas the schools are in?"

"Very. One is even near a hospital with people coming and going all the time."

"Interesting. So he's very sure of himself. Any drugs found in their systems?"

"Nothing. Not even an aspirin in their stomachs. The medical examiner did find a puncture mark in the necks of all the men."

"So he's keeping them long enough for anything to process out of their systems." Dex stopped and studied the boards for a long time. Dover opened her mouth several times to say something but thought better of it. Finally, he shook his head and turned to her. "I'm sure you're fine without my interference."

"I'm good with any thoughts you have."

"Well—" Knox started.

"Not you," she shot back. Dex rolled his eyes, but she noticed he did it with a slight smile.

"Why don't you give me your profile of him first?"

She took a deep breath before starting. "White male, twenty-five to thirty-five. I'm going to say he comes from a wealthy family, but that's up in the air if Knox is right, and he had been on scholarship. I think he knows these schools too, so he's from this area.

"All of these men seem to be in successful careers according to what we've discovered. They were all either making six figures or had the potential to soon. All of their supervisors sang their praises.

"I wonder if he is working alone. It would help if

anyone at the bars they were at remembered them. We did have one remember a blonde woman, but that's not much to go on. They just seem to disappear after that until they turn up on a sports field."

"Why is he angry with these men or type of men?" Dex mumbled. "I think you're going in the right direction, you just have to figure out what picture he's painting. I would leave it until tomorrow. Come back in when you've had a chance to sleep on it."

"I agree with Dex," Knox added. "How about something to eat followed by a good night's rest. You'll be ready for tomorrow."

"Are you needing a bed too?" she asked, giving in. She really could use some sleep.

"A bed? Don't tell me he's staying with you," Dex said with a laugh. "I've got a room, but thanks." They followed her into the hallway.

"That's good because all I have left is a couch. Let me grab my stuff, and we can go." She disappeared into her office. After pulling her purse from her desk drawer, she closed the door on the way out. "Where are we eating?"

"Some place quiet," Knox answered. "I figured we could fill Dex in on Fox while we eat."

"Sounds good. Follow me." She led them through the building and outside. She debated for a minute questioning the desk sergeant about letting them in, but decided she was too tired to bother. Besides, she was sure she would have let a man with an FBI badge and those cheekbones in the door too.

She led them to a pub between the police department and her apartment. Knox had quickly acquired a taste for Irish pub food, so she knew he would approve of her choice. Pulling into a parking space, she climbed out of her car and met them at the door. The hostess took them to a table at the back away from the late-night bar crowd.

"I had a thought on the way over here," she said when they settled in a booth. "Would you mind coming in tomorrow and reading through the files. Just see if there's anything we missed. We've all looked at it so many times now, I worry about what we're overlooking."

"I'd be happy to. First, though, I want to hear how you got the drop on this guy," Dex answered pointing at Knox.

"What? Like it's hard?" She laughed when Knox scowled.

"I wouldn't say she got the drop on me. Memphis was dragging his feet again, or I wouldn't have been looking over my shoulder."

"That's not what I saw," she added. "Memphis isn't the one who barreled around that corner. In his defense, he didn't know what he was walking into."

"I would have paid good money to see that," Dex said.

"I didn't know he had a bum knee, or I would have gone a little easier on him. I will next time."

"Please, don't do me any favors," Knox grumbled. "Her brother is much nicer."

"Harsh," she argued. "Anyway, about Fox. I still don't know if I buy into the idea of following Brooke. Even if she's cheating on him, he'll never break up with her. It would mean losing Ethan. He would never stand for that."

"But you agreed the best case would be for Bailey to get custody of Ethan, then Fox would be free to leave her," Knox pointed out.

"Yeah, but how do we do that?"

"Leave it to me. In the meantime, Dex can find out what's happening."

"Honestly, I'm not sure how this will help anything either," Dex admitted.

"I just want to know what she's about before we take a chance on having to identify Fox's body at the morgue," Knox said. "Don't look at me like that," he added when Dover scowled. "Something's going on with her. I'm pretty good at recognizing when something isn't right now."

"He's not wrong," Dex added. "Knox said she works at a spa during the day?"

"Yeah, it's not too far from where they live and the precinct," she agreed.

"Then I'll come to your office for as long as you need me this week, and in the evenings, Knox and I can check out your brother's girlfriend. No harm, no foul. We just need to know when she's going out," Dex said.

"I'll tell Fox that the next time Brooke goes out to let me know so I can come hang. Even if I have to cancel, at least we'll know she's out of the apartment," she added.

"Like I said before, we'll give you everything we learn, and you can decide what to do with it," Knox promised.

"It just feels weird. Did you stalk any of the other siblings like you are us?" she asked.

"He did taser Memphis and tie him to a chair," Dex said. "Flint, our youngest brother, found us. Since he was still a college kid, Knox was nicer to him. Tyler he met while she was still in high school. She was the only sister. There's also the fact that she's stronger than all of us put together and can break him in half, so no on that front. I think he just likes jacking with Memphis the most."

"Friggin' hell. Why does he even talk to you?"

"It's the charm," Knox answered with a grin.

"Sure, that must be it," she said with a smirk.

"Hey, I did introduce him to his wife."

"Actually, Memphis rescued Thayer from a root cellar after she'd been abducted and used for an extortion scheme. I was the agent on that case," Dex added.

"Well, that just sucked all of the romance out of it," Knox teased.

"Memphis almost died," Dex continued. "There was nothing romantic about it. Glad they wound up together in the end. Oh, Knox also burned Memphis's house to the ground. But," he said, raising his hand when Knox opened his mouth to protest, "he was trying to save him from getting gunned down."

"Why do I feel there's a lot more to my new family than I previously thought?" she asked.

"A lot more. That doesn't even cover how his wife was kidnapped by a Houston gang to be sold into slavery or how she was entrapped in New Orleans by a crime boss. As I've learned in the short time I've known this family, there is a lot more than meets the eye. How much time do you have?"

CHAPTER 12

BROOKE STEPPED onto the sidewalk with a singular purpose. Her instructions said to take the T to a relatively new bar downtown. She supposed it was full of young businessmen trying to impress each other and anything in a skirt as well. A shiver raced down her spine at the thought of a new hunting ground.

That's what he called it. She didn't think of what she was about to do so much as hunting as retribution. The last man had a tan that didn't include where his wedding band normally sat. His wife was probably better off without him. That's what she told herself anyway. What did she care? Men were all the same.

The same catcalls reached her as she crossed to the station, same leers hit her as she found a seat, and the same brushes slid across her as she hunted for a seat at the bar. It wasn't long before her first free drink was set in front of her. A cranberry vodka.

"No, thank you," she said, sliding it back across to the bartender. "I'll take an old-fashioned with whiskey."

She spun around in her seat to take in the atmosphere

while the bartender mixed her new drink. It wasn't bad as far as bars went. They had managed to keep an old-world feel while still appealing to the younger crowd. She picked up her drink and took a sip while watching the growing crowd. There were plenty of young, successful looking men to pick from.

"Didn't have you pegged for a whiskey gal," a man said, sliding onto the stool next to her. His accent labeled him as a visitor to Boston right off the bat.

"So you placed the pink fizzy water order?" she asked.

"Guilty." He smiled at her with an "aww shucks" look on his face. This one wouldn't even be a challenge. "I like a woman who can hold her whiskey, though."

"Then you won't mind buying me another." She gave him her best smile. "You don't sound like you're from around here."

"Oklahoma. I'm just in town for a convention."

"Really? I don't think I've ever met anyone from Oklahoma. What convention?"

"It's for casino managers. I'm Cody," he said, holding out his hand.

"Cassie," she answered, holding his hand just a little too long. First rule of picking up men in a bar: never give them your real name. "How long are you in town for?"

"Just the weekend, then it's back home. Do you live around here?"

"Not far. How do you like Boston?"

"It's getting better by the minute."

She laughed and lightly slapped his chest. The bartender sat another round of drinks in front of them. Keeping her gaze on him, she took a sip through the stir straw. Then she let her gaze drop. Based on the bulge in his nicely pressed jeans, he was definitely interested in her.

She was debating how long she had to keep the banter up before enticing him down the hallway toward the bathroom when she felt her phone vibrate.

"Hello?" she said, holding a finger up to him. Her heart started to pound at the voice on the other end.

"Make up an excuse to leave. Go out the back," the voice said.

"Oh no," she gushed, pulling just enough disappointment on her face. "I'm so sorry. This is the babysitter. Apparently, my kid just puked all over her. I'm going to have to run home."

"That's—" Cody began running his hand through his hair. "No, of course. I'll see you around sometime." She would have laughed at how fast he managed to fade back into the crowd, except the voice was still on the end of the phone.

"Put your earbud in and leave. I'll give you instructions as you go."

She fished her earbuds from her purse and placed one in her ear. She then dropped her phone in her purse still connected. Noticing that Cody had dropped some cash on the bar before beating a hasty exit, she stood and moved toward the bathroom. When she reached the back, she slipped out the back door.

"Turn left down the alleyway," the voice continued. Her heels sounded like machine gun fire as she clacked down the pavement. No doubt she was the only one who could hear them over the din of the city. She raised on to her toes just in case anyway. "Now right and pick up the pace. You're being followed."

She turned the corner and moved into a light jog. It took all of her concentration not to look back over her shoulder.

He continued to give her instructions as she wove through downtown. Her feet were aching.

"When you reach the next street, step inside the first door on your right." She hurried forward until she saw a metal doorway. Quickly, her hand pulled on the handle. To her amazement, it was unlocked. Silently, she stepped inside the dark building. A hand clasped around her mouth, and she was pulled against a hard chest.

"Shhh," he hissed against her ear. A hand she could barely see turned the dead bolt, sealing them both inside. He continued to hold his hand over his mouth as they listened intently. The door jiggled twice before whoever was outside moved on. Slowly, his hand dropped from her mouth.

"How did you know someone was following me?" she asked.

"I have eyes everywhere. You need to start paying more attention."

"Who was it?"

"I'm not sure. I don't think he was one of Boston's finest. Why would someone be following you?" He spun her around and pressed her against the brick wall. "Have you been talking?"

"No. I promise I haven't said anything." The brick was rough and bit into her bare shoulders. Her panties became wet when a strong hand clamped around her throat and began to squeeze. She grabbed at the arm. "Please," she gasped. "I would never say anything. I love you too much, Edmund."

"What do you mean you lost her?" Dover asked.

"I mean I've never seen anyone rabbit like that," Dex answered. He gave up trying to pick back up her trail after half an hour.

Knox had been waiting around the corner of the bar in the car and had joined the chase when Dex called him. They found Dover heating up last night's leftovers when they returned to her apartment. She had just gotten home from work.

"Why would she bolt?"

"I don't know. She was at the bar flirting with some guy when she got a phone call. Two minutes later, she disappeared out the back door. I booked it after her while calling Knox. We chased her through several back alleys before she just vanished."

"Did she make you?"

"No, I don't think so. I was on the other side of the bar, and she never looked my way."

"Did she see Knox?"

"I didn't pull up until I was sure they were inside," Knox answered. "I was a block away and didn't leave the car until Dex called. I trucked it around back, but I never saw her."

"What about the guy she was talking to? Do you think he made you?"

"No, he was just some eager stooge trying to have a good time. He's out the price of two expensive cocktails for his efforts. He also hurried on to other fish when she got the phone call. Whatever she said to him did the trick," Dex said.

"I wonder if she went home?"

"Text Fox and ask."

"I can't just ask if Brooke is home. He'd know something is up.

"Well, I can," Knox said pulling his phone from his pocket. He pressed a button and held it to his ear. "Hey, man, what's up?" Dover leaned closer as she waited. "Oh yeah, just you and little man then?"

"I knew it," she hissed. Knox waved her away.

"Yeah, I could eat some shitty Boston pizza. I'll be over in a few." Knox hung up and looked at Dover. "Well, now I have to go hang out. Brooke didn't go home." He stood and stomped to the door. "I'll be back later." The door slammed behind him.

"What are you thinking?" she asked, noticing Dex staring up at the ceiling deep in thought.

"I don't know, but that was weird. I would have expected her to flirt half the evening with that guy. I could even see sex at some point, but just to run? I don't know. And who was on the other end of the phone call?"

"Who knows. It's more than I can deal with right now. Between whatever mess my brother is in and the private school bodies, I'm burning the candle at both ends. Maybe I just turn Knox loose on my brother. It doesn't look like he's going home anytime soon anyway."

"Might not be a bad idea. He's pretty much a bulldog when it comes to getting to the bottom of a problem. It drives you crazy at the time but usually turns out all right."

"Can I ask you something?" she asked after studying him a few minutes. "How are you okay with all of this? The superpowers thing, the continuous hunt for family?"

"Well," he began, "I've been around this crew for a while. I knew there was something different about Knox and Memphis from the beginning. Memphis was too good at finding people. Even better than I am. Not to brag, but I'm damn good. And things kept catching on fire around Knox."

"What about Tyler's strength? That didn't intimidate you?"

"I wouldn't be much of a man if one of the best things about my wife intimidated me. When I fell in love with Tyler, I knew that not only did I have to fully embrace how different she was, but also her crazy family. We have an unwritten rule. We take care of each other at all costs. I think Knox is on his fourth or fifth life by now doing just that."

"I've never told anyone I date about my ability to see emotions," she said. "It's a stupid power, and I'm afraid they'll just think there's something wrong with me."

"The right man won't. He'll see how incredible you are."

"Thanks, Dad."

"Anytime, kid." He laughed. "Now, I should head out. I could use some sleep. I'm not used to staying out this late anymore." He stood and walked to the door. "Still want me to meet you at the office again tomorrow? See if anything new pops up?"

"Yeah, that would be great." He opened the door and stepped into the hallway. She waited until the door was closed behind him before smiling. At least the brother-in-law wasn't irritating. She could survive him.

She took her bowl to the sink before heading toward the bedroom. Tomorrow promised to be another long, frustrating day. The search for where the medallions had been bought turned up too many options to trace. Nothing in the school records looked promising. He could very well be in there, they just didn't know who he was.

Like she thought would happen, none of the schools were copping to any reports of harassment. Everyone with a key to the facilities had clean records and alibis for the time of death for each victim. Hours of tape from the bars just proved that they were popular places that really needed to update their equipment.

She brushed her teeth and cleaned her face while running through the evidence in her head. A headache was beginning to form behind her eyes. What she needed was a distraction. Her mind flitted across the thought of the sexy medical examiner before she pushed it aside. The newest Ruth Ware thriller would have to do.

Falling into bed, she picked up the book and began to read. Five minutes in, she realized she had read the same paragraph three times. It was too good of a book to miss. Placing it on her nightstand, she turned off the light. Knox still hadn't returned from her brother's house, but she couldn't keep her eyes open anymore to wait for him. Slowly, she drifted off into another restless night.

CHAPTER 13

FOX PULLED up to the curb in front of the multi-storied townhome in Beacon Hill. It was the last place he wanted to be. He was meeting both Heidi and his top renovation contractor to make sure everyone was on the same page before they began tearing everything out.

He grabbed his notebook and stepped out of his truck to meet Heidi where she waited on the sidewalk.

"Thanks for taking the job," she said as he approached. There hadn't been a choice. His boss had returned a bid in record time, and the Andersons had signed it that same day.

"Joey should be here in a second. He's our best renovation expert, especially for these older homes." As if Fox had summoned him with just his words, a matching work truck pulled up behind his.

"Joey, this is Heidi," he continued when the man met them in front of the house. "She's the designer on this project, so we'll be working closely with her to make sure everything is to the homeowner's expectations."

"Good to meet you, Heidi," Joey said, stretching out his hand.

"Very nice to meet you too," she said, taking his hand. "Shall we?" She led the men to the front door that was opened by Edmund. Fox fought the resigned sigh that threatened at the man's appearance.

"Who's this?" Edmund demanded.

"This is Joey," Fox answered. "He's our expert in custom remodels of these historic homes."

"I thought you were going to do it." Edmund scowled at him, barely giving the other man a glance.

"I'm just the supervisor. Joey is the real talent. All I do is make sure he has what he needs and that the work runs on time."

"Hmm, we'll see about that," Edmund snarled before whipping his phone out of his back pocket and stomping into the other room.

"Okay, well, let me show you the tradesman entrance off the driveway," Heidi said, leading them through the house.

"I've arranged for a roll off to be set up tomorrow. Is it good in the driveway?" Joey asked.

"Yes. Mrs. Anderson has left for a spa in the Berkshires for the duration, and Mr. Anderson is in Europe this time of year on business. Edmund will be in and out, but he lives elsewhere. Work can't begin before eight in the morning and must end at five in the evening."

"That won't be a problem," Fox began when his phone rang in his pocket. "Go ahead, I'll catch up on the second floor." He answered his phone as they disappeared upstairs. "Yes, sir?"

"I just got a phone call from the Andersons' son insisting that you were being uncooperative," his boss said.

"I'm not sure how."

"Look, I don't like that kid any more than the next man,

but that family has the potential to send a lot of work our way. If he wants you with a hammer in your hand, that's what you'll need to do. You can check in with your other jobs when you have time. They can always call if there's a problem, or do I need to assign someone else to your other projects?"

"No, sir. I've got it." He wasn't about to let one of the other guys swoop in and take the commissions he had worked so hard to negotiate. With any luck, he could start looking at a small house with a yard for Ethan to play in somewhere outside of Boston.

"Good man," he heard before the line went dead. With a sigh, he pocketed the phone. Turning back to the stairs, he found Edmund leaning against the newel post with a smirk on his face.

"Everything all right?" he asked.

"Everything's good," Fox answered before brushing past him. He climbed the stairs in a few strides and joined the others. "Looks like I'm joining your team for a while." Joey gave him a confused look for a moment before his features straightened back out. Fox assumed that meant Edmund was now standing behind him.

"Glad to have you." Joey patted him on the back before following Heidi to the next room.

"Yes, Foxworth, so very glad to have you onboard," Edmund said.

"Hey, guys," he called without acknowledging Edmund. "I'm going to kick off so I can check the other projects. Are you good?"

"We've got this," Joey said, sticking his head back out of a bedroom. "I'll see you at eight."

"Yeah, eight." Fox spun around and almost raced back down the stairs. He was through the house in a matter of seconds. Closing the front door behind him, he breathed a sigh of relief.

He had just made it to his truck when he saw the front door swing back open. Edmund stood on the threshold with a smile. Something about it made a chill run down his spine.

He threw his truck in gear and raced away from the curb. There was no real direction in mind as long as he got away. Spending the next several weeks in that house was going to be miserable. Edmund had to have a job. He couldn't possibly hang around all day. Could he?

He had worked in several of the large houses in the area, especially when he was starting out. None of those residents had even taken notice of him.

Fox was on the north side of the city before he realized it. He pulled over in front of the house he kept finding himself drawn back to every time. There was no reason for him to be parked here.

The sensible thing to do would be to head over to the one project he had on this side of town, but his sense of self-preservation seemed to be failing him more and more lately.

He was still debating what to do, when the front door opened and the one person he longed to see waved at him. It would be rude to drive away now he reasoned. Turning off the engine, he slowly slid from the driver's seat.

"Perfect timing," Bailey called. "I was just making some lunch. Care to join?"

"I would," he answered. She led him through the house to the kitchen in the back. Never did she question why he kept showing up unannounced. She simply motioned at him to take a seat while she moved back behind the island.

"I hope turkey is okay. If not, I have peanut butter and jelly."

"No, turkey is perfect." He watched as she layered on

meat, cheese, and plenty of vegetables on the sandwiches. "Mayo, please." She smiled at him before smearing a healthy amount of the spread on his sandwich. When she set the plate in front of him it included a pasta salad, fruit, and chips. "This is better than any sandwich shop. Thank you."

"Anytime."

They ate in silence for several minutes, but he could feel her watching him. No doubt she wondered what brought him to her doorstep this time. If he was being honest with himself, there really wasn't a reason other than he just wanted to see her. He had to tell her something, though.

"I've had the strangest day," he finally said.

"Oh? Strange how?"

"We're redoing this house in Boston, and the homeowner's son is just creepy."

"How old is he?" Bailey picked up a chip and popped it in her mouth before her gaze landed on his.

"Around my age, I'd guess. He's just always there saying weird shit. Like, when I did the measurements for the bid, he just followed me around even though the designer was there. I'm sure it's just my imagination, but I can't help being weirded out. He makes my skin crawl."

He watched as she slowly sucked the salt from the chip off her fingers. *How did eating chips become so damn sexy?* He moved his gaze back down to his plate to break the spell.

"I doubt it's your imagination. If my gut tells me that something seems weird, it probably is. Maybe he has a crush on you." He looked up, and she winked. "I get it. Guy like you, wielding a hammer, all sweaty and such. What's not to like?"

"Yeah, okay." He laughed. It was either laugh the

comment off or throw her on the table and eat that pussy like a starving man. Laughing seemed like a safer option to him.

She had no idea what she did to him every time she talked like that. It felt a little beyond innocent flirting and a little dirty since he was with her sister. Still, he didn't mind. Not at all.

"I made brownies," she said, letting the subject slide. She stood and scooped up his plate.

"What sane man says no to a brownie?"

"Well, I'd hate to deny you your sanity."

"I hate to deny you anything." Her hands froze as she scooped some of the brownies onto a plate. Her soft brown gaze met his, and he swore he could see longing in them if only for a moment before she continued to plate the brownies. "I'm sorry," he mumbled.

"Don't be sorry," she said, joining him again at the table. "I feel the same."

"Shit." He sat back in his chair and ran a hand through his hair. "What do we do about this?"

"I don't know, Fox. But we can't risk Ethan. If Brooke knew you were here, she would take him away from both of us, and we're the only stable thing that little boy has in his life."

"You're right." He scooped two brownies from the plate and stood. "I just don't know how much longer I can keep pretending I want to be with her. I don't know how much longer I can keep my hands off you." He heard the small gasp she let out. "Somehow, I'll figure this all out. I'll find a way for us to be together with Ethan. If that's what you want, that is."

"It is," she admitted. "But, until then, we can't be together. We can't even be seen together as friends. This," she added motioning vaguely at the table, "can't continue. It won't end well. You have to understand."

She stood to walk him to the door. Before she could step away from the table, he took her face in both of his hands and peered into her eyes.

"I understand, but don't think for even an instant that I like it." He brushed his lips softly against hers. He was walking down the hall away from her before it had even sunk in that he had kissed her.

"Thank you, Bailey," he said, stopping at the door. His back was to her, but he knew she heard every word. "For the lunch." He paused before adding, "And for being so damn good. For being the safe haven in this hurricane."

He was out the door before he could change his mind. His feet took him to his work truck, but his heart stayed behind. If only for a moment, he had glimpsed what normal felt like. He knew what her sweet lips tasted like. It wasn't enough, but it would have to do for now.

―――

Bailey stood just inside her front door and watched as Fox pulled away from the curb. The kiss had been so fleeting that, for a moment, she could almost pretend it never happened. But then it would flood her senses once again. It hadn't been carnal by any means, but it had still been perfect.

She felt the same angst, yearning, and need from him in that moment that she felt all the time. It was wrong on so many levels. He was her sister's boyfriend. There was a code for sisters and their boyfriends.

Then again, when had Brooke ever considered her when she'd made a decision? If they hadn't been six years apart in school, she was positive her sister would have stolen every boyfriend she had.

A close friend she could bounce all of her feelings off of would have been a welcome thing right then. Working from home, though, didn't help when it came to making friends. She never saw her work colleagues since they all worked remote like herself. College was long enough ago that she had lost touch with those friends.

"Maybe it's time to get a dog." She shook her head when she realized she had been standing in her doorway for at least the last fifteen minutes staring down the road. "Good grief, Bailey." She stepped back inside and closed the door. "The dog doesn't sound like too bad of an idea, though. At least I won't just be talking to myself."

Climbing the stairs to her office, she tried to put all thoughts of Fox out of her mind. It would be an impossible task. She knew that kiss would feature heavily in her dreams both at night and during the day.

She already had a problem with dreaming about him most nights. Most of them were rather X-rated, which meant her vibrator was getting a workout. Now she could add him to her days too. Earning a living was becoming harder every time she saw him. How did she work when she was too busy staring into space imagining what could be?

She slumped into her office chair with a sigh. A couple of more hours of work, and then she could start scrolling for a dog. Her computer came to life with a swipe of her mouse. Soon she was knee deep in code again.

In the back of her mind though was a nagging thought. *What if she gave in? What if next time she kissed him back? What if they did more than kiss?* Brooke didn't need to know, not yet anyway. Not until they could come up with a plan that didn't harm Ethan.

Opening a new document, she typed "Fox plan" at the top. She would come up with a catchy name later. She then skipped a line and typed "1."

After several minutes of watching the cursor blink, she closed the document. She wasn't clever enough for a plan that complicated. Brooke would be. She sighed again and turned back to work. It felt like they were all racing toward a collision, and she couldn't see how it would end well.

That dog looked better and better by the second. At least when it all blew up in her face, she would have company to commiserate with her. She shoved the thoughts of Fox deep down and focused on the three screens in front of her. Without realizing it, she had pulled up dog rescues in the area on one of them. She might as well check while she was there.

CHAPTER 14

DOVER FOUND Dex sitting in the incident room early the next morning. He was staring at the boards at the front of the room. He seemed to be especially riveted on the board with the first victim on it. She took a sip from her takeaway coffee and crossed the room to him.

"I keep coming back to the blonde with the first victim," he said as she approached. "Have they not found her at any of the other bars before the other two disappeared?"

"Not yet, but she may have learned to stay out of camera range."

"True."

"Sean said he thinks it would have taken a lot of force to strangle the victims, though, so we've ruled it most likely a male suspect," she said. "I mean, the medical examiner."

"You can say Sean." Dex smiled over at her. "You're not fooling us. Don't worry," he continued when she opened her mouth to protest. "We can keep a secret. Although I can't guarantee Knox won't put him through his paces."

"Speaking of, where is Knox?"

"He said something about a drug buy in Lowell. I don't

know. He was talking to some DEA guy on the phone yesterday."

She debated asking more but decided she didn't want to know. The only thing that she knew about the drug trade up north was that Brooke's ex-husband was wrapped up in it. As much as she knew she should protest Knox getting involved in that, she couldn't. One less bad influence in Ethan's life, the better.

"Do you think there's a chance it's a team?" he asked.

"Like a man and woman team killing men?"

"It's uncommon, but not unheard of. Bernardo and Homolka, Starkweather and Fugate."

"Bonnie and Clyde. I guess it could be. I'm not ruling anything out," she said. "So, she picks a target based on certain parameters and lures him from a random bar?"

"I doubt they're random. We need to see what all the bars have in common. The one I was in the other day had a hallway to the bathrooms and a back door at the end of that hallway. I doubt a woman without some sort of training could subdue any of these men once outside."

"Okay. Even if she could, someone might notice a struggle. Hence the needle marks Sean found. So you don't just think the bars are random, that they're part of the MO?"

"Maybe. They can't just drug them outside the front door. I bet the victims are lured out a back door to a waiting car. The one door without a camera. Which means they have to do reconnaissance on the bar in advance. We already know they're killed somewhere other than where they're dumped."

Dex sat back in his chair. His eyes were so intently focused on the evidence boards that Dover waited until he was ready to speak again.

"I think it has to be a man and woman team," he finally

continued. "Two of the victims were married, so the chance they were lured away for a same sex encounter isn't too high. I guess anything is possible though. Except I can't get past the blonde woman."

"I'll add it to the board," Dover said, standing. She walked to the farthest board and drew a line under their profile of the male suspect. "Female."

"I'd say close to his age or a little younger. All of the victims are white, so I feel safe saying she is also."

"What do you think are her motivations?" Dover asked.

"I'm not sure we can even guess. I'd say she's been groomed most likely. Maybe a submissive character to his dominant? Whatever it is, he gives her something she craves or thinks she does. There is a chance though that she's as twisted as he is or even the main aggressor."

They sat in silence again studying the boards, each lost in their own thoughts. She noticed more information had been added to Ian Moore. He had been a young pilot from the Minneapolis area on a layover. When he was found, he had been wearing a St. Christopher's medal. Everything else was similar to the other victims.

He had strangulation marks made by some kind of a strap or belt. There were no personal effects on the body. The only reason they had identified him so quickly, according to the report, was because he failed to show up for his scheduled flight the next morning. She pulled out her phone and looked up St. Christopher.

"St. Christopher is the patron saint of travelers," she said.

"So, we have a pilot with the traveler saint, an environmental attorney with the nature saint, a doctor with a saint of the sick, and a banker with the saint of money lenders. They make sense, but what's the point?"

"I don't know, but we need a break soon. Someone who sees him dumping the next body or remembers something at the bars. Danny is still combing through old case files looking for any more of them that match. He can't have just started out this good at killing."

"No, that's unlikely. There will be some lesser crimes. Assault or something. There's one more thing you might try." He stops until her gaze meets his. "You might have to do a press conference."

Later that afternoon, Dover found herself standing next to her captain in front of a bank of microphones and cameras. Her boss agreed that a press conference was necessary as soon as possible before even more speculation about the deaths circulated. All of the larger Boston stations were in attendance. She even recognized several of the reporters.

"Good afternoon," the press liaison began. "Captain Bradford would like to say a few words before turning this press conference over to lead Detective Addams. Please hold any questions for after."

Dover watched her boss step up to the microphones. She knew he was speaking, but she had tuned him out as she went over what she needed to say in her head. This would be her first press conference where she had to speak. She had stood in the background in several, but never at the front.

The captain stepped back and nodded to her. Wiping her hands on her slacks, she stepped forward.

"On June seventh, at approximately seven twenty-five in the morning, Detective Gallagher and I were called to a homicide at a local private school. The victim, Trent Alleman, had been strangled and left on the soccer pitch.

"The following week, Jack Dawson was discovered strangled and dumped in a similar manner. During the course of this investigation it came to our attention that two other homicides matched the MO of both Mr. Alleman's and Mr. Dawson's murders.

"We have provided photos of each victim in your press packet. We are asking the public to look at the photos closely. Each man was last seen at a bar in the Boston area. If you have any information or saw any of them on the dates of their disappearances, please call."

She followed up by giving the phone number of the new hotline being set up back at the office. She also repeated the dates each man was last seen before stopping.

A cacophony of questions immediately flew at her. Both she and the captain did their best to answer them all. Finally, the press officer stepped forward and brought the conference to a close.

They didn't mention the name of the bars the victims were last seen in. Hopefully, they wouldn't become overwhelmed with false leads from bars not involved. And no one wanted to be the cause of lost business when people found out a serial killer had been prowling a particular pub.

Dover followed the rest of the team back inside the police station. She split off to check on the call room that was now staffed by several junior officers. The phones would start ringing soon after the five o'clock news. For now, they were sipping on sodas from the vending machine and talking to each other. There would be no time for that soon.

"Did you catch the news conference?" she asked, walking into her office.

"I did," Dex answered. He was sitting on the other side

of her desk looking through a file. "I just got an interesting phone call."

"Addams," the captain said, sticking his head in the office. "You and Tanaka come with me." He walked off without waiting for them. Dex stood and followed Dover into the hallway.

"What did you do?" she whispered.

"Probably has to do with the phone call I just got." They walked past the captain's assistant into his office. They both took a chair when motioned to.

"I'm sure you already know," Captain Bradford began by looking at Dex. "I've been on the phone with your boss down in Texas. Figured since you're already up on the case it would be much easier to simply have you temporarily reassigned here for now."

He turned to address Dover. "It's time to pull some help in from the feds on this. I've also been on the phone with the Boston office making sure we don't ruffle any feathers. They're going to send over a couple of juniors to help with support."

"Yes, sir," she answered.

"You're still in charge of this investigation," he continued, splitting a look between them. "He's just here for assistance. Understand?"

"Yes, sir," she said again.

"Of course, whatever I can do to help the investigation," Dex said, rising from his seat.

"Be prepared for a briefing tomorrow morning at nine," Captain Bradford said before dismissing them by returning his focus to the papers on his desk.

"Yes, sir." She couldn't think of anything else to say.

"So what do you need from me?" Dex asked when they walked back into her office.

"Dex has been added to the investigation," she said to bring Danny up to speed.

"Sweet. Welcome aboard, officially," he answered. "By the way, we got another one."

"Shit," she swore. "Where? When?"

"Quincy. Before the one in Cambridge." He handed her the paperwork just pulled from the printer. "I've already requested the files be sent over. Here's what we have for now."

They followed her into the incident room. Taking the dry erase marker, she began to add to the boards. The man had been named Terrence Oldman, and he was a civil engineer at a local firm. The rest was very similar to what they'd already seen. He was strangled by some sort of strap, dumped in the commons of a private high school, and had nothing on that identified him.

The only thing different was that Terrence Oldman was wearing a St. Patrick's medal. It was what flagged the murder. "St. Patrick, patron saint of engineers," Dex said before she could look it up on the phone herself.

"It looks like it was six months before the murder of Ian Moore in Cambridge," she added.

"I'm expanding the search to the surrounding counties," Danny said. "When I'm done, I'll run it through everywhere else."

"I can run it through our databases and see if anything hits," Dex said.

"Do that, and I'll go brief the captain about the latest victim."

"Quincy said the files should be here before end of shift," Danny informed her before leaving for their office.

"I'll set up in the back of the room and see what I can pull up. As soon as the files show up, I'll try to get last known whereabouts from Danny. We can hit that location as soon as possible." Dex moved to a table at the back of the room and pulled his laptop out of a messenger bag.

Dover studied the printed pages one last time before returning them to Danny to organize in the book. She walked to the captain's office for the third time that day to fill him in on the latest case so he wouldn't be surprised at the briefing the next morning. She reached the office and was waved in before she could even speak.

"Sir?" she said, knocking on the doorjamb.

"I'm afraid to ask," he said after looking up.

"We found an earlier case. About a month before the Cambridge one. This one was found in Quincy," she said.

"You'd better have a seat," he answered with a sigh. "Tell me there's something in the file that will break this wide open."

"I hope so, sir. They're sending the files over now. Unfortunately, preliminary looks like they have pretty much what we have. I'll have the ME's office pull their records also. Maybe Sean can find something."

"Sean?"

"Yes, sir. He's the medical examiner working with us on these cases."

"What happened to Otis?"

"He retired about three months ago and moved to Florida. Sean Ryan is his replacement or at least the new hire."

"Hmm. Let's hope he can spot something no one else has. Thanks for bringing this to me, Detective. I'll hear more about it tomorrow at nine."

"Yes, sir." She stood and walked out of his office. At least one good thing was happening from all of this. She got to make another visit to the medical examiner's office. She could just call him, but where was the fun in that.

CHAPTER 15

BROOKE FELT SOMEWHAT sorry about sacrificing Jack. He was the first man who she felt actually might do some good in the world.

He wasn't very interesting though, droning on about his job as a lawyer. That had counted against him. In the end, Edmund had been thrilled with her pick. Well, maybe not thrilled, but at least satisfied.

Jack had also made a beautiful sacrifice sitting strapped to the wall, completely nude, harnessed to the winch. The St. Francis medal hung around his neck glinted in the light as the belt tightened.

Edmund explained how his contraption worked once, but the physics had been lost on her. All she knew was that the more the men struggled, the tighter the belt got.

He told her a smart man would understand that. The only way to beat it was to remain calm. So far, none of the men had tried to remain calm. It proved that the only man smart enough for this world was Edmund. She wondered vaguely if Fox would beat it. Maybe someday she'd get to find out.

She shivered with the memory of being pressed against the glass separating her from Jack while Edmund pounded into her from behind. Jack continued to cry and beg as he gazed at her naked breasts pressed against the translucent wall. She climaxed as his life slipped from him. It was glorious.

"Mommy?" Ethan's little voice broke into her musings. "Is Daddy coming?"

"Yes, but we can't talk to him," she answered. "Just be quiet and play with your truck."

Her idiot ex-husband had finally been busted with enough methamphetamine and fentanyl to require prison time. They were currently waiting at his bail hearing.

He'd called her from the holding cells to inform her of when the hearing was so she could pay the bail if necessary. He promised to pay her back, but she would be surprised if that happened.

All she knew was that there would be no hope of any more child support if he went to prison. Chances of that happening, based on what he told her, seemed high.

He claimed he had been set up. That the drug taskforce seemed to know exactly when the drugs were in his apartment. Just a couple hours later, and they would have been gone. No doubt in the hands of teenagers out on the street somewhere. Not that she cared. If those brats wanted to fry their brains, what was it to her?

Since she couldn't guarantee she could get back to Boston to pick Ethan up from daycare in time, she'd had to drag him along. Fox was tied up on the townhouse job until late every night, so he was no help and she'd rather do anything than ask her scheming sister to keep him.

It would probably do Ethan good to see what being stupid, like his father, would get him. She didn't care if her ex sold drugs, but he should know better than to get caught. It's why Edmund had her change up the bars she visited. Routine bred familiarity, and familiarity would make you lazy.

If her ex was nothing else, he was lazy. She looked down at her son. He was kneeling on the floor in front of the bench playing with his truck. A soft motor noise escaped his lips.

She wondered if he would turn out to be just like his father. At least he took after her in the looks department. Edmund hated kids. He had made that perfectly clear to her. She wouldn't be taking Ethan with her when she left Fox for Edmund. That was for sure.

Her thoughts were interrupted when the current group of prisoners were ushered out and the next group brought in. Ethan popped his head up just in time to see his father walk through the doors in a white T-shirt, gray scrub pants, and handcuffs. He smiled and waved. His father waved, as much as the cuffs allowed, back.

She had to sit through three cases before it was his turn. All of the cases before him involved drugs, but his sounded the worst.

"This hearing is just to determine if bail will be set and how much, if allowed. James Vargas is charged with possession with intent to distribute. I understand this is his third offense. How does the defendant plead?" the judge said.

"Not guilty," Jimmy answered.

"What does the prosecution say on bail?"

"We ask for remand, your honor," a man said from the other lectern. "This is a repeat offender with no ties to the community. The prosecution plans to ask for the maximum sentence possible."

"Your Honor," Jimmy's attorney responded. "The

defendant has a small child in Boston. He has no wish to flee the area and plans to prove his innocence."

"The defendant is remanded. Next case."

Brooke stood and took Ethan's hand. There was no reason to hang around since Jimmy would be heading right back to holding. At least she didn't have to pay for bail. She wasn't sure how that would work anyway. She had nothing to put up for collateral, nor would Fox lend her the money. She could always have stolen it from him, but this way she didn't have to worry about it.

She was moving to the back of the room toward the exit when her gaze landed on someone she knew. Sitting in the last row in the back corner was Fox's long-lost half brother. She couldn't quite remember his name. She just thought of him as the giant one, as opposed to, the pretty one. Her eyes narrowed as their gazes met.

He didn't look away but continued to glare at her as she continued down the aisle. *Why would he be here?* He must have something to do with this. It was the only explanation as to why he was here.

She pulled Ethan through the door before he recognized the man. He already went on and on about how amazing he was. Her head churned with the possibilities of how he was involved.

Pulling open the back door of her borrowed car, she waited impatiently while Ethan climbed into his car seat. She quickly buckled him in and slammed the door closed. By the time she reached the driver's side, she was positive Fox had something to do with that man being here. *Knox.* That was his name. It rhymed with Fox. The whole family had stupid names.

A thought hit her so hard, she paused with her hand on

the door handle. *Did they all have something to do with Jimmy being busted for possession?*

She jerked the door open and slid into the hot seat. The blast of cold air was a welcome relief once she got the car started. It did nothing to cool her temper though. She needed to get to the bottom of this.

"Momma's going to take you to a friend's house to play. Fox and I need to talk. Undisturbed." She checked the rearview mirror. Ethan was watching her, but he stayed silent.

She raced the car through town, dodging around cars going too slow. The car horn got a workout as she wove through traffic. Finally, she pulled up in front of a walkup in Dorchester.

She unhooked Ethan from his car seat, grabbed his hand, and marched him up the stairs to the stoop. Locating the correct apartment number, she pressed the buzzer. "Yeah?" answered a few seconds later.

"I need you to watch my kid for a couple of hours," she answered.

"Why?"

"Because I didn't report you when you brought yours to work." She heard a door close somewhere upstairs before a face appeared at the glass a few minutes later. The door opened and Brooke pushed Ethan forward. "Just a couple of hours. Here's his backpack," she added, handing over a small dinosaur pack.

"Sure," the woman answered. Brooke turned and walked to the car before her coworker could change her mind. She was going to have it out with Fox about his fucked-up family, and she didn't need Ethan in the way. "Hey," the woman called as Brooke opened the car door. "Am I supposed to feed him supper?"

The car door closed before she could answer. The woman could figure it out on her own. If she wasn't back by dinner, then feed him. It wasn't rocket science. She drove into the nicer neighborhood they lived in and found a parking spot not far from the building.

Fox's apartment was one of the reasons she stuck with him. It was in a decent neighborhood with better neighbors. It just sucked it was so close to his sister's office. It also didn't have an elevator which was ridiculous. That wasn't worth giving up the apartment for though. Sometimes the good outweighed the bad.

She walked in the door to find the place still empty. She had at least an hour before he got home.

It was closer to two hours before Fox arrived home. Brooke jumped up from the couch where she had been stewing over the afternoon. "Where have you been?" she snarled.

"At work," he answered. "I was at the townhome I told you about."

"Sure you weren't in Lowell setting Jimmy up?" She crossed her arms over her chest so he would know how mad she was.

"What are you talking about?" He looked around the living room like he would find the answers hidden somewhere among the furniture. "Where's Ethan?"

"You know exactly what I'm talking about," she said, poking him in the chest with her forefinger for good measure. "I had to spend the afternoon waiting in a courthouse to see if Jimmy would get bail. Guess what? He didn't." Her voice rose in pitch the angrier she became.

"Where's Ethan?" he said louder this time.

"None of your fucking business. Did you set Jimmy up?"

"Brooke, listen to me," he said, taking hold of her arm. "I don't know anything about Jimmy. Tell me where Ethan is."

"If you don't know anything, then why was your overgrown brother in the courtroom? Don't tell me he just happened to be there. I don't believe you." She was yelling.

Fox narrowed his eyes and stared at her. It only made her angrier. She was positive he knew what happened, he just wouldn't tell her.

"Calm down," he said in a soft voice.

"Don't you dare tell me to calm down." He took a step back in surprise. She wondered if he was surprised that she wasn't doing what he wanted for once.

His eyes narrowed once again as if he was trying to mesmerize her. That's when she slapped him. It was hard enough to make him back away, but when he looked back up at her, blood poured from his nose.

"Brooke—" he started.

"No. I know you had something to do with Jimmy being arrested."

"I can find out what happened. Just, please." He reached for her, but she batted his hand away. Blood dripped onto his shirt.

"That's disgusting," she said, stomping to the door.

"Wait." He looked around the living room, then disappeared into the kitchen. He returned shortly with a kitchen towel held up to stop the blood. "Let me make some calls. Then we can go get Ethan."

"How about this," she said, opening the door. She threw her bag over her shoulder and turned back to him. "You call me when you fix things with Jimmy. Then I'll tell you where Ethan is. Until then, I'm going out. Don't wait up."

She stepped through the door and slammed it closed

behind her. Seconds later, she was almost to the stairwell when Fox jerked it back open.

"Brooke," he barked. She turned and stared back at his gaze for a few seconds. He gagged as blood began flowing again. Without a second though, she stomped down the stairs and out the door. She would find a bar to unwind in for a couple of hours.

Crossing the street, she hurried to the T stop. She pulled out her phone and texted her work friend where to find her car before shoving her phone in her purse.

She looked back one last time, relieved to see Fox hadn't followed her. Maybe she would text Edmund when she got to the bar. With the mood she was in, it would be a good night to hunt. It would be even better if she could find someone who had the same features as Fox to lead out the back door of the bar.

There was a smirk on her face as she ignored the stares from several men on the train. None of them held her interest; they never did. Pulling her phone back out of her purse, she sent a quick text to Edmund. Her smirk turned into a smile as the train headed for downtown. Tonight was turning out to be a good one.

She wasn't really that concerned with her ex-husband's illegal activities or his impending sentence. Nothing surprised her when it came to him. She just couldn't abide someone thinking they could interfere in her life.

Whether Fox had anything to do with it or not was immaterial. She would let him stew over Ethan for a while as punishment anyway. Next time, they would all think twice before crossing her.

The T came to a stop not far from one of her favorite bars. She entered and looked around. It was overflowing with young, handsome professionals.

A tall man with brown hair, a well-trimmed beard and mustache, and light-colored eyes smiled at her. It wasn't quite Fox, but then no one else she knew of had green eyes quite like his. He would do though. He would do perfectly.

CHAPTER 16

FOX LISTENED to Brooke's voicemail message for what felt like the hundredth time since she stormed out. "Hi, you've reached my voicemail. Leave a message." He had already left several messages that she hadn't responded to.

He punched the end call button in anger before pulling the key for his sister's apartment out of his pocket. If he couldn't find Ethan, at least he could wail on the person who caused this.

He slid the key into the lock and burst into the apartment. Three sets of eyes turned their gaze on him. Dover was sitting at the table eating something in a bowl, already assessing the situation for a threat.

Dex sat on the couch reading through a file folder. He acted as calm as ever, but ready in case he needed to act.

Fox's main attention, though, was on the large man sitting in an armchair with a book spread open on his crossed leg. Life had been a lot simpler before he came to town. It wasn't necessarily better, but definitely simpler. Now Ethan was missing, Brooke was who knows where, and Knox was to blame.

"Ethan's gone," Fox snarled, his gaze boring a metaphorical hole through his brother's head.

"What do you mean, gone?" Dover asked. She left her dinner half-finished and stood to meet him.

"I mean Brooke has left him somewhere and won't tell me where. What did you do?" he aimed at Knox.

"I didn't do anything. He did it to himself."

"Wait, what happened?" Dover tried again. "Your nose is bleeding."

"Shit." He put his hand over his nose and walked into the kitchen. Grabbing a handful of paper towels, he returned to the living room with them pressed to his face. "I can't get it to stop."

"Were you trying to make her calm down?" Dex asks.

"Yes, but it didn't work this time. Can Memphis find him?"

"Not without something personal of his," Knox answered. Setting his book on the coffee table, he placed his hands on Fox's face and pressed the upper part of his nose with his thumbs. "Hold still," he barked when Fox fought back. He stopped fighting choosing instead to spit the blood that collected in his mouth on Knox's shirt. "Nice."

"Fuck you."

Knox scowled at him but refused to let go of his nose.

"I swear if anything happens to Ethan, I will rip you apart with my own two hands," he continued.

"She's not going to do anything to harm Ethan," Dex said, breaking into the standoff. "She's too smart for that. She knows that's how she controls you." Fox's glare slid to Dex, but the agent ignored it. "Did she give you any clue where he is? Is he at a friend of hers or a relative? Bailey's house maybe?"

"She would never leave him there voluntarily," he answered.

"I'll call Bailey, just to make sure. How about someone from work?" Dover suggested.

"Maybe." *Why is he still here, meddling in our lives?* He continued silently.

He's worried Brooke is up to something that's going to blow back on you. That's why Dex is here too. They tried to follow her one night, and she was a professional at losing them.

"Stop," Knox growled. "Say what you have to say out loud."

"You've been following her?" Fox spit out, shoving Knox away from him. "Why?"

"There's something fucked up about her," Knox began.

"I wasn't talking to you." Fox turned to stare at Dex.

"At first we thought she was just seeing guys on the side," Dex said after clearing his throat. "Now, I'm not so sure. I'm pretty good at following people, but she got a text and rabbited out of the bar she was at. We chased her until she just disappeared through a locked door in one of the buildings near the wharf."

"Her cheating on me doesn't surprise me," Fox said after taking a minute to take in what Dex had said. "I don't know how she would know someone was following her, though, if you were just hanging out in the bar. Are you sure you were following the right person?"

"It was the right person. She was chatting up some cowboy at the bar then suddenly ran. It felt like she was getting instructions from someone, though. It doesn't make sense to run if you're just talking at the bar."

"She's always meeting friends for drinks. I have no doubt she flirts with anyone who looks good and will buy her a drink. But if she thought you were stalking her, wouldn't she just stay in the bar? It would be safer."

"Bailey doesn't have him," Dover said, returning to the living room. She had slipped into the kitchen to make the call right after being called out by Knox. "She's going to try calling Brooke. Maybe she will answer her call or at least text where Ethan is."

They fell silent as they watched Fox pace back and forth across the living room. His stomach was tied in a knot, his mind reeling with all of the bad things that could be happening to the little boy. *When did I get so wrapped up in the welfare of a child?*

Since the moment he moved in with you, Dover answered.

"I can't stand just waiting. I'm going to go see if I can find an after-hours phone number at the salon. Maybe one of her coworkers knows where he is," he said. He scooped up the keys he had tossed on the side table next to the door.

"I'll go with you," Knox said.

"I don't need any more of your help."

"I don't care. I'm going."

Fox studied the determined man for a few minutes before shrugging. He barely heard Dover telling him she would ask patrol to keep a look out as the door closed behind them.

He didn't check to see if Knox was behind him when he stepped into the elevator. Crossing his arms, he leaned against the cool metal as he willed the doors to close.

"We'll find him. In one piece," Knox growled.

"You don't know that."

"True, but I haven't lost one yet, and I don't plan on starting now." Fox had heard a few of the stories from his family's harrowing past. None of that mattered now. He didn't need fairytales—he needed results. He needed Ethan found.

The doors finally opened, and they left the building. Fox's truck was right where he left it, except now it had a parking ticket on it.

"Of course," he mumbled ripping it out from under his windshield wiper. He tossed it in the back seat as he climbed into the truck. By the time the engine roared to life, Knox was riding shotgun. He dropped it into gear and slid into traffic.

The trip through town was driven in silence. He didn't feel like talking, and, he assumed, Knox could tell. That was one thing they had in common—neither one of them liked to chat. There was one other thing he found odd that they had in common.

"Do all of us have green eyes?" he asked.

"So far. Must have been one hell of a dominant trait."

"Do you know anything else about him?"

"Mom has a blurry picture taken at some concert in the '80s, and he stayed with Flint's mom until Flint was about ten. Mom's always been pretty closed mouthed when it comes to him though."

"You have a mom?"

"Yes." Knox looked over at him with a scowl. "Her name is Sunny, and she lives in Kentucky. What of it?"

"Are you always so defensive?"

"Are you?"

"Okay, point taken," Fox answered after a moment of thought. "I guess that must be a dominant gene too."

"Nah. I set Memphis on fire all the time, and he barely flinches. Flint is pretty laid back too. As far as Tyler goes, I never push her buttons since she can break me in half."

"She and Dover should make an interesting pair."

"I'm looking forward to the fireworks, personally."

Fox pulled into the parking lot of an upscale strip mall. There were several boutique shops, a bistro, and the salon on the end. Several of the businesses had already closed for the night, including the one Brooke worked at.

He stepped out of the truck and walked over to the door. With his hands cupped around his eyes, he looked through the glass door. Then he pounded on it with his fist hoping someone was still in back.

"Is there a chance she left him inside?" Knox asked.

"I don't think so. She wouldn't want to get in trouble with the boss. She likes working here." He looked around the front windows for anything with a phone number on it.

"I'll go ask the other shops if they have the owner's number," Knox announced before walking off down the sidewalk. Fox pulled on the front door before heading around to the back of the building. There was nothing in back but a dumpster and a row of metal doors. The only signs indicated that it was for deliveries only.

"Anything?" he asked when he returned to the front to find Knox standing next to the door.

"A couple of names, but no last names or numbers. I also learned they do great highlights, in case I'm interested."

"Shit." They stood next to the salon trying to figure out what to do next. Without at least a last name, Fox had no idea where to look. Both men startled when his phone toned in his back pocket. He jerked it out and pushed accept without really registering who was calling. "Yes?"

"I finally got her to respond," Bailey said. "She sent an address. He's staying with a colleague from the salon named Suzanne. I'm texting it to you now." His phone pinged again, and he held it out to make sure the address came through.

"Can I bring him to you?" Fox asked, pressing the phone back to his ear. "I don't think he should go home until I see how angry Brooke is. I don't need him in the middle of a dangerous domestic situation."

"Of course, just bring him straight here. Please let me know as soon as you have him."

"I will." He hung up his phone and thrust it at Knox. "Route me to that address. I guess he was left with someone she knows from work. Tomorrow, I'm sending something to Memphis, so I don't have to worry about this again."

"Not a bad idea. He has a closet full of bagged stuff from the spouses and kids. The rest of us, those who share the same blood, he can find without anything."

"That sounds better than calming people down. Except, I don't guess I can even do that anymore. I've never had a nosebleed before."

"Memphis got where he threw up every time he came back when we were looking for Thayer. Looked like death by the time that was over. I think it just takes so much brain power. There's nothing to throwing a fireball. I just have to check which way the wind is blowing."

Fox laughed. It felt good to release some of his frustration.

"Now, let's go get Ethan," Knox said.

They climbed back in the truck and drove to an older apartment complex. There was a group of men standing around the entrance and debris spread on the ground. It was obvious that no one was interested in upkeep anymore.

They pulled to the curb in front and shut off the truck. Fox heard Knox climb out behind him as he rounded the truck.

It wasn't until the men backed away that he realized having Knox along might be a good thing after all. He pressed a buzzer at the door and was let in without anyone bothering to answer. They climbed the stairs to the second floor and banged on the door to number four.

The door was opened a few minutes later to a cacophony of noise. Fox counted at least three kids crying, several dogs barking, and the television loud enough to be heard over the din.

"You here for Brooke's kid?" a woman asked.

"Yes, I'm Fox." The woman didn't seem to care as she turned around and hollered down the hallway for Ethan. The boy slid carefully from one of the rooms in back. It took a beat before he realized Fox was walking toward him. Ethan ran into his arms, wrapping himself around him as tight as possible. "Thank you. How much do I owe you?"

"I got you. Let's leave these people in peace," Knox answered, holding out a wad of bills, before the woman could.

He waited at the bottom of the stairs until he was given a sign it was safe to step outside. Another reason it was good to have Knox with him. He carefully pried Ethan from his body to secure him in the booster in the back seat.

"You're going to stay at Aunt Bailey's house tonight after we drop off Uncle Knox. Okay?" He saw the little boy nod his head in the rearview mirror.

His emotions were stretched to their limit having found Ethan in one piece. They almost crumbled completely when he saw Knox reach in the back seat and take Ethan's small hand.

He drove back to Dover's building. It didn't escape his notice that Knox held Ethan's hand the entire way which had to be uncomfortable for the big man. Pulling to the curb, he put the truck in park then turned to Knox.

"Thanks for coming with me."

"Just needed to make sure I didn't have to burn this town to the ground to find him."

Fox felt the corners of his mouth tilt up. Knox winked and eased his hand from Ethan's hand. He nodded as he closed the door.

Fox had no doubt at that moment that his brother would have burned the whole of Boston to the ground if he'd had to. They really were family now, and Fox felt himself begin to accept it. More family in his life didn't feel so bad in the end.

CHAPTER 17

BAILEY WAS PACING on her front porch when Fox pulled up outside. She rushed down the steps to the truck and pulled open the passenger side door. Carefully, she unbuckled a sleeping Ethan from his booster seat in the back.

"Let me help you." She moved aside to let Fox sweep the small boy into his arms. He followed her inside and up the stairs to the bedroom she had designated as Ethan's not long after he was born. Gently, he laid him on the small twin bed and pulled the dinosaur covers over him. Tiptoeing out, they left him to sleep.

"What was she thinking?" Bailey hissed when they reached the kitchen.

"It's a convoluted mess that I think was done in Ethan's best interest ultimately," he answered.

"Well, I'm too wound up to focus on anything else, so lay it out for me." She set a cup of coffee on the table, motioning for him to sit. She added a piece of coffee cake in front of him when he complied.

"Knox went with me to get Ethan tonight," he began when she sat across from him with her coffee. "I dropped him back at Dover's before coming here. He told me on the way back to her apartment that it was decided you needed one less obstacle in the way on your path to be awarded Ethan."

"What?" she asked, startled. He knew that she would take Ethan in a heartbeat, no strings attached but had never harbored any hope she could get him. "What did he do?"

"Seems he watched Jimmy until he was certain the apartment was loaded with drugs from a big delivery. He called the cops with an anonymous tip. They caught Jimmy with enough to charge him with distribution. He'll be going away for quite a while."

She took a long sip of her coffee before speaking. "I mean, I'm not sad he's going away, but how did that lead to Ethan winding up missing?"

"I guess Knox decided to be in court when Jimmy was arraigned. Brooke went to post bail if he was awarded it. She saw him and figured I had something to do with it."

"And Brooke would blow it all out of proportion," she mumbled. "What are you going to do?"

"I don't know. She stormed out and told me not to wait up." They sat in silence while he finished his cake. Her thoughts swirled with possible solutions to this latest problem.

Brooke had always had extreme reactions to anything that inconvenienced her. Still, what did she expect when she'd married Jimmy in the first place? The only good thing to come from that union was Ethan.

"Why would she post his bail money in the first place?" she wondered aloud. Fox simply shrugged. "But then, why let your deadbeat ex keep your kid for the weekend?" She stood to take the empty dishes to the sink. "I don't know why you stay around. You could just move her out, you know. No one would blame you."

"Look," he said, catching her wrist when she reached across the table to collect his plate. "That's not who I am. I don't bail on something just because it gets hard. My only mistake is—" He looked up, catching her gaze. "I met the wrong sister first. I would leave her in a heartbeat if you asked."

She inhaled deeply. Everything in her wanted to tell him to leave her sister. Leave tonight. Just pack his bag and never return to his apartment. She wanted to beg him to stay. He would fill the spaces of her life in the best way.

"But what would happen to Ethan?"

All of her thoughts came crashing down around her at his simple words.

"Maybe your brother is right then."

He opened his mouth to protest, but she held up her hand. The one, anyway, that wasn't bursting into flames where he touched it. "I know his methods weren't the best. But what if I can get Ethan? What if we can be assured he's safe?"

"Then we'd let the chips fall where they may," he answered. His hand slid down her wrist until she felt his long fingers lace through hers. Slowly, he pulled her around the table. Pushing his chair out, he eased her onto his lap. "So what do we do?"

"I think we let your family keep doing whatever it is they're doing."

"And us?" he whispered into her ear.

"You tell me."

"How about if I show you?" His hand left hers to snake up her body and around the nape of her neck. She closed her eyes as his warm lips pressed against hers. This was more than the barely there kiss from last time. This was everything she longed for.

He stood her up without breaking the kiss and repositioned her astride his thighs. The kiss turned into even more as his tongue traced the outline of the seam of her lips.

She couldn't help but think about that tongue on other parts of her body. Working its way down her neck, making her mad as it teased her hardened nipples, making her scream in ecstasy as it circled her clit. A moan slipped from her before she could stop it.

Fox pulled her closer to him. She could feel his hard length pressing against her urgently. It now had her thinking of other ways he could make her scream. His tongue swiped inside her mouth. Throwing caution to the wind, she sucked it between her lips. Suddenly, he sat back and gazed at her.

"Damn it. I would really like to see where this could end up," he growled. Anywhere would work for her. The kitchen table was sturdy enough. She had a nice bed with a practically new mattress. Even the kitchen wall would do. Instead of reading her mind, however, he cleared his throat.

He eased her off his lap until she was standing. His hands lingered on her hips until she was able to regain her balance again. He stood, and she watched as he adjusted a very impressive bulge in the front of his pants. Then, instead of taking her hand again to lead her upstairs, he took a step away.

"I'm sorry," he said. "As much as I want to be in you right now, I just can't. I don't cheat, not even on Brooke."

"No, you're right," she answered, although she didn't give a rat's ass about her sister at this moment. Still, if she found out they had been together, Bailey didn't know what would happen to Ethan. They couldn't take the chance.

"None of this is right." He grabbed his keys from the table and walked to the front door. "But I promise I'll figure this out." He stopped at the door, turning to look at her. Pulling her to him, he leaned over until their foreheads met. "Somehow, this will all work out. You believe me, right?" He nodded which made her nod too.

"I'll come get Ethan tomorrow," he finally said with a heavy sigh. Then he was out the door. She closed it, throwing the dead bolt. Her back pressed against it until she heard his truck pull away.

"I believe you," she said quietly. "I just don't know how."

When she felt more under control, she pushed off the door. She would wait for tomorrow to deal with the kitchen. She turned off lights as she closed up the house. Reaching the second floor, she slipped into Ethan's room.

She had turned one of the spare bedrooms into his long ago. It had everything a little boy would need. The dresser had spare clothes tucked inside, a toybox sat in the corner with everything to keep him entertained, and there were plenty of blankets to make him feel safe.

She chose a clean pair of pajamas from the drawer. Carefully, she changed him into them without waking him.

He was tucked back under the covers with his stuffed animal under his arm when she was done. For a few minutes, she just stood by the window looking around. This was a room a child deserved to grow up in. There was no doubt in her mind that Fox had one for him at his apartment that looked similar.

Maybe if she and Brooke had shared a room like this, her sister would have turned out different. Instead, they had slept on dirty cots shoved into a tiny room in a squalid apartment. Their father had left when Brooke was still a baby. That left her mother, a woman with no interest in providing, to raise them.

For some reason she still didn't understand, they had taken different paths. She had chosen to throw herself into school as a means of escape. Brooke had found men much easier to derive satisfaction from. A computer teacher helped Bailey chart a path to college and where she was now. Brooke seduced the English teacher into giving her what she wanted.

"I promise to do whatever I have to for you," she whispered to the tiny sleeping body under the covers. "No matter what it takes." Moving to his bed, she bent down to kiss his head, then slipped from his room.

Her nightly routine was always the same—teeth, face, hair. Bed would be a welcome relief, although she doubted she would sleep much. There was too much to keep her awake. Not just Ethan, but Fox also.

If he kept kissing her the way he did tonight, there was no telling what she might do. Her sexual frustration had been on high alert from the first time she met him. Now, it was entering atmospheric.

Hadn't they just agreed to stay away from each other? Of course that didn't count in an emergency, and Ethan's safety was always an exception to the rules. She was still lying awake, staring at the ceiling when her phone vibrated. Rolling on her side, she checked the text.

Fox: Made it back.
Bailey: Good. Was she there?
Fox: In bed already asleep. How's Ethan?
Bailey: Fresh pajamas. Sound asleep.

Fox: Thank you. For everything. I don't know when I'll collect him tomorrow.

Bailey: Not a worry. He can stay as long as he needs.

Fox: TY. Sleep well. I wish I was beside you.

Bailey: Me too.

The phone went silent, and she placed it back on her nightstand. She worried about his safety too. He was a big man, capable of taking care of himself, but her sister was more volatile than even he realized. Bailey had spent her entire life walking on eggshells around her.

Rolling over on her side, she swore to put all of it away so she could get some sleep. Ethan deserved a fully alert aunt to make him breakfast in the morning.

One thought did strike her before she drifted to sleep, however. It was time to meet Knox and the rest of the family. She needed to know what he was planning for Brooke. As bad as the fallout would be, if it meant Ethan's safety, she would welcome being a part of the plan.

She would call Dover first thing in the morning and get his phone number. She would insist he meet her and Ethan tomorrow for lunch.

With that settled, in her mind anyway, she let herself relax. The house had fallen silent as the night deepened. She listened for any noise coming from Ethan's room for a second. Hearing nothing, she let her eyes close. If she was lucky, her dreams would be filled with Fox. Tomorrow's problems would wait for tomorrow.

The next morning when she called Knox, he insisted they meet near her house for lunch. She picked a diner that still served pancakes at noon, knowing that would make Ethan happy.

They were early, but they only had to wait a few minutes before a man who, even though she had never met him before, she knew immediately, walked through the door.

"Uncle Knox!" Ethan shouted with an enthusiastic wave. The scowl on Knox's face immediately turned into a grin as he approached their table. Ethan jumped up and threw himself at the large man.

Bailey knew he was taller than Fox from his description, but she wasn't prepared for how much taller. She also wasn't prepared for the piercing green eyes peering back at her. They matched Fox and Dover's exactly.

"You must be Bailey," he said after extracting Ethan from around his neck. His large hand engulfed hers as they shook. "I have to admit I was a little surprised when you said you wanted to meet for lunch. I'm glad you did though."

"Well, after last night, I thought it might be a good decision."

"Ahh," he said before picking his menu up. "I guess this is where you threaten to remove my intestines and use them to hang me?"

"Um, no. I hadn't thought about that. Are you always that dark?" she asked. She might have made a mistake asking him to meet her. But she felt a little better when Ethan looked up at him adoringly, and Knox ruffled his hair. "Do you have any children, Mr. Monroe?"

"Mr. Monroe? Is this a formal meeting? I would have worn a suit if I'd known," he teased. Or at least she thought he was teasing. "How about you call me Knox. I know it's a little confusing with a brother whose name rhymes. I guess Dad didn't think about that."

The waitress appeared at their table, so she had a few minutes to regain her composure while they ordered. This man had managed to unsettle her in a manner of minutes. Still, he had helped track down Ethan the night before. *He couldn't be all bad. Could he?*

"The answer is two," he continued when the waitress walked off.

"What?" For the life of her, she couldn't remember what she'd asked. He smiled at her with amusement. His eyes seemed to dance, something she hadn't seen Fox's eyes do.

"I have two kids. Twins. A boy and a girl, but they're not as old as Ethan." He sat back in his chair with his arms crossed over his chest, waiting. "Go ahead, ask anything. I'll answer what I can."

"Okay, then I have several questions. We'll start with an easy one. Why did it look like Fox's nose was...you know?" Her eyes cut to Ethan. She didn't want him to overhear something he shouldn't. Fortunately, Knox understood what she was asking. It hadn't escaped her notice that Fox's nose had been bleeding, but he didn't have any marks to indicate a fight.

"An easy one, huh?" he mumbled. "How much has he explained about how else we're connected besides sharing a father?"

"What else would there be? Are you in an Irish gang or the Mafia?"

"Nothing like that." He sat studying her long enough that she began to squirm. "Okay, here goes. We all share one other trait besides green eyes. Each one of us inherited a strange ability, for lack of a better word."

"You're talking in riddles," she pointed out.

She watched as Knox looked around at the table next to them. Then he began to rub his hands together. When he pulled them apart, she had just a second to glance at a small ball of fire before he clapped his hands together.

She snatched his hands from across the table and pulled them apart. There were no burn marks although his hands were a little warmer than normal.

"I don't understand," she said.

"We were all born with a different gift. Memphis can find people through some form of teleportation, Tyler is stronger than any man you'll ever meet, and Flint can control water." He wagged his head back and forth. "Well, sort of. Flint's still a work in progress."

"That's not possible," she argued.

"I wouldn't have believed it either until I burned down Mom's shed one day when I was in middle school. There are more things in this world than we can understand. We happen to be a family of one of those things. Fox can calm minds. It's been how he's dealt with your sister, until last night."

The waitress delivered their food, but Bailey had lost her appetite. It was ridiculous to think someone could do something superhuman. That was the stuff of comic books. Still, she had seen the small fire before he put it out.

It would also answer how Fox had managed to stay with Brooke for so long. Longer than any other boyfriend she could remember.

"Next question," he said. She looked up at him. He was cutting up the smiley-face pancake Ethan had insisted on. Her nephew had slowly moved his chair until it butted right up against Knox. She had a choice. She either accepted that not everything was black and white in this world, or she ran screaming with her nephew away from this family.

"You know what, I think I'll save the rest for Fox when I see him," she said. Knox smiled back at her. She knew that he knew she had made her choice.

For better or worse, she would stand by the man who had kept her nephew safe this far. Besides, the thought of having a superhero in her corner wasn't such a bad thought. A whole family of them? Even better.

CHAPTER 18

"SON OF A BITCH," Dover spat as she stood from inspecting the body laid out in the middle of the lacrosse field. She stepped outside the tent surrounding the newest victim and scanned the crowd pressed against the security fence. Each person gawking at the crime scene had an aura of color surrounding them. She studied them all hoping for any indication that the person who killed the man was one of them.

"Son of a bitch," she growled again. Nothing unusual grabbed her notice as she peeled the Tyvek suit off. At least she didn't have to worry about any students staring out the windows. School had been released for the summer at the end of last week. The only way the body was discovered was because a lone security guard happened on it early in the morning doing his rounds.

"Dr. Olmstead, the head of the school, is waiting in his office for you," Danny said walking up to her. "The security guard didn't have much to say. He was pretty shaken up. I sent him with patrol to the office to make a formal statement. Bianchi said he'd handle it."

"Thanks, Danny. I'll go speak to Dr. Olmstead as soon as—" she stopped mid-sentence seeing the medical examiner jogging toward her. "There he is." Even standing in the middle of a crime scene, she felt a rush of adrenaline seeing Sean hurrying toward her.

"Sorry I'm late. Damn car wouldn't start this morning. I had to bike in," Sean said when he reached them.

"Don't you live in—"

"Cambridge, yeah. Hence why I'm late. I'll find you when I'm done." Without looking back, he stepped inside the tent. She noticed the tension ease in the leader of the crime scene collection team. They had been standing around waiting for Sean also having cleared around the area earlier. She left them to hash it out while she spoke to the head of the school.

"Dr. Olmstead?" she asked when she finally found his office.

"Yes. Please, come in," the tall man said with a gesture of his arm. She guessed he was in his mid-fifties, with graying hair and signs of crow's feet at the corners of his eyes. He was also almost vibrating with anxiety. "I can't believe this. We've done everything to make this a safe learning space. How does this happen?"

"Have a seat, Dr. Olmstead," she said with a deep sigh. She sat in one of the chairs across from his desk. After several moments of hesitation, he came around his desk and took the one next to her. She pulled out a notebook from her pocket. "Have you noticed anything unusual? Anyone that looked out of place last week?"

"No. No, I don't think so. No one brought anything odd to my attention."

"Anyone hanging around outside the lacrosse field?"

"No, but the games are always open to the public. The season finished a month ago though."

"Can I show you a photo of the victim to see if you recognize him? Just a close-up of his face," she quickly added when he flinched.

"Of course." She opened her phone and handed it to him. The man in the picture looked more like he was taking a nap. She had cropped out the ugly marks where he had been strangled.

"No, I don't recognize him. He's not any of the staff, and if he's a parent, he's not one I'm familiar with. Do you have his name? I can have the admissions clerk come in and search the database."

"Not yet," she said, taking her phone back. "Do you recognize the names Terrence Oldman, Ian Moore, Jack Dawson, George Goodwin, or Trent Alleman?"

He shook his head.

"Who has access to the field?" she continued.

"Everyone on staff has keys to the building. There's a crash door leading out to the fields."

"Thank you, Dr. Olmstead. That should be all for now. If I have any further questions, I'll contact you." Dover set one of her business cards on the desk. "If you remember anything, no matter how insignificant, please contact me." She stood, and he stood to walk her out. "One of my officers has your security guard's keys. He'll return them as soon as the crime scene is released, and we clear out."

"Yes, okay. Thank you."

She left him watching after her as she walked out the door. Sean had just stepped out of the tent and was taking his Tyvek suit off. He looked as hot as she had felt emerging from the tent earlier.

Actually taking a better look, she realized it wasn't just

the temperature. The sweat made his T-shirt stick to him highlighting every ripple of his torso.

"Your mouth is hanging open," Danny said next to her.

"It is not," she exclaimed, maybe a little too loudly. She heard a rumble of laughter and debated smacking him. That would only draw attention, so she chose to ignore him. She found the medical examiner sexy. Whatever.

"Shut up," she snarled, making Danny laugh even more. The noise must have traveled because Sean looked up and smiled.

"I was just coming to find you," he said, walking toward her. "Looks like he died between ten and midnight. I'll know more this afternoon. He was wearing this." He handed her an evidence bag. Inside was a medallion she had come to dread. Flipping in over, she held it closer to her face.

"We've also got a name," he continued. "Tony Russo. He was in the system. Got sent up for theft. He was on parole."

"I'll head back to the office and see what I can pull up on Mr. Russo," Danny said.

"Yeah, I'll see you," she said distractedly. She barely noticed when her partner disappeared through the far gate. "Is this St. Nicholas?" she finally asked.

"According to Google, yes," Sean answered. "Santa Claus or in this case patron saint of repentant thieves maybe?" She flipped it over several times as she studied it. Then with a frustrated sigh, she looked up at him.

"What do these mean?"

"I have no idea. I'll leave the detection up to you." He gently took it out of her hands. "I can drop this at the lab on the way to the morgue. This guy will get priority when we get him back." He nodded to the men standing next to a gurney, and they entered the tent. A few minutes later they left, awkwardly rolling a body bag across the turf. "I should be ready to start around two."

"Thanks, Sean. I'll see you then." She walked back to the tent to find the crime scene team finishing up. "Anything?" she asked Jillian, the person in charge of the team.

"Not really. We'll put a rush on it though. Sean said he'd drop the medal with the techs when he got back. They can start on it immediately," she answered. Dover liked when the middle-aged woman was assigned to her crime scene. It meant nothing would be missed. She was still model pretty but could also crack a proverbial whip at her team.

"I appreciate it. Something has to break soon. We can't keep coming up empty-handed." Jillian nodded her agreement and turned back to her team. Dover watched for several more minutes before deciding there was nothing more to do here. Danny already had a team doing door-to-door interviews, but so far, nothing had turned up.

With no one left to check on, she walked to the gate. There was a young officer standing in front of it with a snarl on his face. It broke into a smile when she approached. Quickly, he unlocked the gate and ushered her through before locking it back up.

"I've had to keep it locked to discourage the hangers-on," he explained.

"Good idea. Make sure the head of school gets the keys back when the scene is clear."

"Yes, ma'am," he answered, making her feel years older than she was. Ignoring it, she climbed in her car. The drive back to headquarters gave her a chance to think. This made victim number six. The only things they had in common were the method of death, being last seen in a bar, and the medallion each wore.

If they could just catch a break at one of the bars, it might be the lead they needed. She knew Danny would already be calling around hoping to trace his last known location. He would canvass the area where the victim was last seen while she attended his autopsy. Their boss would be waiting for an update as soon as she arrived. It was turning into another long day, and it had only just begun.

Her partner was hanging his phone up when she walked into the office. She watched from where she perched on the corner of his desk as he jotted down several notes. He handed her a file and picked up his notes.

"Anthony Mateo Russo, twenty-five years old. He got in some minor trouble as a juvie. Got sent up for two years for boosting cars as an adult. His parole officer said he was living with his mother while trying to get a job. He thought he had a chance as a mechanic, said he was good with cars," Danny began.

"Obviously."

"I was waiting for you to do the death call. I told the boss we'd bring him up to date when we got back."

"Yeah, I guess we should go." She stood from his desk. He followed her to the car, and they headed across town. "What else did you find?"

"Not much yet. I'm hoping his mother knows where he was going last time she saw him. We might need to ask that before telling her about his death. Dex is waiting to run down video as soon as we have a place."

"Good idea. Are victim services meeting us there?" she asked.

"I told them to wait outside for us. We don't want it to

look like we're rushing the house. Hopefully he was only into cars, but you never know."

They reached a small house in one of the rougher parts of town. It couldn't have been more than a thousand square feet in size with peeling paint and a patched roof. She would bet it was still an object of pride based on the flowerbeds that lined the house. The yard was also clean and neat. She stepped out of the car, meeting Danny on the sidewalk.

"Mrs. Russo," Dover asked when an older woman answered the door. She guessed this must be Tony's grandmother. "I'm Detective Addams, and this is Detective Gallagher. We're with the Boston Police Department. May we come in?"

"Gloria," the woman shouted over her shoulder before turning back to Dover. "Are you here about Tony?"

"Yes, ma'am. May we step inside?" Danny asked. The woman opened the door, and they slipped inside the house. It was as she expected. Neat, warm, and inviting.

"Mom, what's going on?" a woman not much older than Dover asked, stepping into the entrance.

"Ms. Russo?" The woman nodded. "May we sit down?" Wordlessly, she ushered them to a floral couch that had to have come straight out of the seventies. They sat down, and the women took the two armchairs. "When was the last time you saw Tony?" Danny continued.

"Two nights ago. He said he was going out with some friends to a bar in the north end," the younger Ms. Russo said.

"Do you know which bar?"

"Sbarra. He said he might just crash with one of his friends since he had an interview the next morning. Why, what's happened?"

"Can you give me a list of his friends?"

"If you tell me what's happened."

"Ms. Russo," Dover cut in. "I'm so sorry to have to tell you, but we found Tony deceased this morning." She watched as the older woman cried out and clutched the younger's hand.

"Give me your book," the younger woman hissed. Danny handed her his notebook and pen. She hastily scrawled something on it before handing it back. "Those are his friends. Tell me what happened."

"We don't have all of the details yet, but I promise to keep you informed as we get more information. There is a liaison outside who would like to introduce themself. They will make sure to answer any questions you might have. May we have them come inside?" Danny waited for them to nod then got up.

"I'm so sorry for your loss," Dover said again.

"Just tell me you'll find out what happened," the younger woman said. She now had her arm around the older woman as she cried into a handkerchief.

"I will do my very best. That, I promise you."

CHAPTER 19

FOX BENT over the new floorboard he was nailing in place. The Victorian home needed more work in the attic than he had originally thought. Every time he turned around, there was another problem.

He also had the problem of Edmund sitting around watching him as he worked. He had been Edmund's entire focus from the moment he started.

The second story had a team working on the remodel, but the owner's son insisted he handle the attic personally. The space wasn't part of the original remodel when air conditioning was installed. It was the attic after all. He'd set up fans but still poured sweat. Nothing seemed to help.

It was late in the afternoon, and for once, it was just him in the attic. Sweat ran down his body in rivulets. He debated taking his T-shirt off.

Then Edmund showed up with his iced drink and nasty smirk. Something about him gave Fox the creeps. Everything about him gave Fox the creeps. The work was progressing slowly as well because of one specific problem—the man kept asking him questions.

Edmund took a seat in the lawn chair he had dragged up. Fox felt his gaze run over him as he undoubtedly was thinking of the best way to torture him. Finally, he sat his drink on an old box next to him and cleared his throat. Fox braced himself for the onslaught.

"Why do you have to replace those boards? They look fine to me," Edmund asked.

"There's old termite damage. They're too weak for continual foot traffic," he answered. He began another countdown in his head. It felt like the hundredth since the project began, but he knew it was better than losing it on a client. *Did the man never go to a job?* He let his mind focus on ripping out the current board and counting backward from ten.

"Hmm." Edmund always answered with a derisive sounding grunt if the reason Fox did something didn't agree with his observation. Fox would love to leave the floors as is so Edmund would fall through them eventually. Not enough, though, to lose his job over.

"We should go out for a drink sometime." The comment surprised Fox so much, he almost hit his foot with the nail gun. He took a moment to secure the new board in place.

"We have a company policy against socializing with clients. Sorry." He didn't know if that was true, but there was no way he was going out with this man. Even for a friendly beer which he doubted Edmund drank. "Have you picked out what color you want this room?"

"No, that girl—what's her name—is supposed to put together some samples for me to look at." Fox found it interesting that he couldn't remember the name of the woman he'd hit on earlier and who turned him down. What a farce.

"Heidi?"

"Whatever," he answered with a shrug. "Where do you buy your shirts?"

"Oh." Fox looked down at his T-shirt. "Target usually. Sometimes Tractor Supply, if I'm near one."

"Goodness," Edmund laughed. "I don't think I've ever been in a Target. Or to, what did you call it? Tractor something? I will admit, I prefer a more polished look. If I'm going to wear a T-shirt," he added with disdain in his voice. "It's going to be, at the very least, Ralph Lauren." He picked an imaginary speck of dirt from his dress shirt. Fox couldn't think of an appropriate answer, so he didn't say anything.

"Did you go to school to learn how to do that?" Edmund waved dismissively at the floor.

"No, just on the job training. I started at the bottom and worked my way up." Fox was proud of how far he had come at this job. From gopher to supervisor was nothing to sneeze at in the construction industry. He'd begun at eighteen when he moved to Boston with his sister. She went to college while he went to work. He was proud of both of them.

"Yes, I suppose. Not everyone can have a real education after all. We need the rest of you to make the world spin."

Was the guy trying to get under his skin? He hit a new board harder than necessary with the nail gun. If he stopped responding, maybe Edmund would grow bored and drift off.

He walked to the farthest corner from where Edmund sat in his chair to examine the boards. There weren't as many that needed replaced, but it would at least give him a reprieve from the questions. He made a mental note to bring his ear protection tomorrow.

"What do you do for fun, Fox? What gets your motor going when you're not here?" Edmund said a little louder.

"I spend time with my family," he answered.

"Ahh, the little woman and the demon seeds." Fox gave him a hard stare, but Edmund seemed unfazed. "No nights out with the boys?"

"Just work and family."

"No little by-blows running around out there from too much cheap beer at the bar?"

What. The. Actual. Hell?

"I need to go speak to Joey about something. Excuse me," Fox said, laying the nail gun down. If he didn't leave now, he might drive a nail through Edmund's head.

Without waiting for an answer, he headed for the stairs. Unfortunately, Edmund followed him. Fox picked up his pace when he reached the second floor almost running into the foreman when he turned a corner.

"Hey, Fox. How's it coming along up there?" Joey asked.

"Slowly," Edmund answered behind him. Fox barely managed not to roll his eyes. "He's spending a lot of time inspecting the floor."

"Ahh, well he's just one man up there, and it's impor-tant that the floors hold up. When we're finished down here, I can send more up to help him," he said, addressing Edmund before turning back to Fox.

"I don't think he needs more help," Edmund continued. "I just think he needs to focus a little more and move on to more important things."

"I was coming to find you anyway," Joey said after a few minutes looking between the two men. His eyebrows crimped in the middle as he studied Edmund. Fox wasn't sure if his foreman could read minds or not, but he must know that Fox couldn't take much more without breaking.

Edmund was an asshole. "Boss said there's some problem at the Woburn build. He wants you to go check on that."

"Great, good. Can you send up someone to finish replacing the floorboards upstairs? That would help me a lot."

"Sure. You'd better head out though."

With a grateful nod, Fox headed to the back stairs. He left Edmund scowling after him. What that man's problem was with him he couldn't begin to fathom. The sooner this job was over, the better.

He tossed his tool belt into the seat of his truck and jumped in the driver's side. It wasn't even worth returning his gear to the site.

He doubted there was anything wrong with any of his job sites. The foremen were too good to let something get out of hand. Any excuse to get out of there, he welcomed, though.

He'd have to take Joey out for a beer when they were finished to thank him. That he wouldn't mind. At least, this way, he could pick up Ethan before it got too much later.

Deciding it wouldn't hurt to check on the Woburn job site anyway, he pulled into the site parking area after weaving through the north side of the city. He grabbed his hard hat off the back seat and shoved it on his head as he left his truck. The foreman met him in front of the building.

"Heard you were spending your time man-caving an attic for some eccentric," he said as he shook Fox's hand.

"Yeah, but I left early to see how things are going here."

"We're right on schedule. It's been a pretty quiet couple of days. Come on, and I'll show you where we are."

Fox spent the next half hour walking the site with the foreman. The man had been right. Everything was progressing smoothly. After visiting for a few minutes, he returned to his truck. He didn't start the engine though. Instead, he sat contemplating his next move. He needed to pick Ethan up from Bailey's house, but he really didn't need to go there again. Walking away last time nearly killed him.

His mind drifted to the night before. She had felt so good with her body pressed against his. There was nothing more he wanted than to feel her move under him, to feel her body heat and catch her moans in a long, languid kiss. With Ethan already asleep, the temptation had been almost undeniable.

But he had managed to drag himself out the door before they crossed that line. It would be better from now on to meet in a more public place. He would still want her with every fabric of his being, but he would be less tempted to act on those feelings.

He pulled his phone out of his front pocket and pushed in her number. Brooke had pitched a massive fit when she discovered her sister's contact information in his phone. He tried to explain to her that it was necessary for Ethan's sake. She refused to let the matter drop, though, and eventually, he calmed her using a different means.

"Hello." The very sound of her voice made him smile.

"Hey, I need to pick up Ethan. Is there any way you can meet me at the burger place near Woburn?"

"The one with the playground?"

"That's the one. I'm almost finished at the job site. I'll buy, if you don't mind a burger for dinner."

"No, sounds good. I'll get Ethan from outside, and we'll head that way." They disconnected, and he sighed in relief. Avoiding Bailey's house wasn't going to solve the problem, but at least he had more time to come up with a solution.

He started the engine and pulled back onto the street. It

was only a ten-minute drive away, but he was anxious to see them both again.

He was sitting in a booth near the playscape when they arrived. Bailey climbed out of her car. Her legs swung out first, giving him a chance to take them in.

She looked only slightly similar to her sister. They both had blonde hair and blue eyes, but that was where it stopped. Where Brooke was waif thin, Bailey had soft round features. He liked soft more and more all the time.

"Fox!" Ethan called from across the restaurant the minute the little boy spotted him. Fox swept him into a hug when they met at the booth. "Can I go play?"

"Sure. I'll go order." He barely got the words out before Ethan disappeared behind the glassed play area. "Okay, then. What would you like?" he asked, turning to Bailey.

"A burger is fine. Whatever the meal is."

Fox walked to the counter to place their orders. A few minutes later, he scooped up a tray with their food. He added a couple different items from the service area before walking back to the table.

It took a couple of minutes to sort the items. He rapped on the glass to catch Ethan's attention, and the boy held up a finger in a plea to have one more minute. Fox nodded. Ethan would rather eat his burger cold on the way home, than give up any time on the playscape.

"How was work?" Bailey asked. He assumed there would be no discussion about last night.

"Long. I'm doing a remodel, and the owner is insisting I stay on the job the entire time," he said, popping a french fry in his mouth. "The owner's son actually. It's odd. He's odd."

"That's what you said before. Is it getting worse?"

"This time, he asked me if I've had any kids with the

barflies where I hang out with the boys. That was the gist anyway. He also suggested we go out for a drink sometime. I had to get out of there before I thumped him a good one."

"That's so weird. Why would anyone suggest you have multiple extra kids?"

"Yeah, no idea." They sat in silence while they worked on their meals. Finally, Fox felt like he had to say something more. "About last night."

"I get it," she said, cutting him off. "I really do. I think I'm going to head out." She sat her trash on the tray and stood. Fox stood also.

"Bailey."

"Tell Ethan bye for me. Call me anytime you need me to keep him, but I don't want to be in the middle of whatever problems you and my sister are having. Thanks for dinner." She turned before he could answer and walked quickly for the door.

He debated chasing after her, but knew he'd only make everything worse. She was right. He needed to get his shit together. Either he dug in and worked it out with Brooke, or he left.

He slumped back down in the booth. It had been tempting to change Bailey's mind in to staying, but that wasn't fair. He couldn't always fix the mess he was embroiled in by forcing a different outcome.

If there was one person he didn't want to alter their mood, it was Bailey. She was never anything but sweet and loving. In other words, she was already pretty perfect.

Standing back up, he collected the trash and dumped it in the trash can. He wrapped up the bag with Ethan's meal. Pushing into the playscape, he searched the tubes until he saw Ethan playing with a couple of other kids.

"Time to go, buddy."

"Awww," Ethan complained, but he slid down one of the slides to meet Fox. "I made some new friends."

"That's great." Fox held out his hand for Ethan to take. Together they walked out to the work truck.

"Where's Aunt Bailey?"

"She had to run. She said to tell you she had fun."

"I don't think she did," he answered. Fox stopped wrestling the seat belt that went over his seat.

"Why do you think that?"

"Because she was sad."

"Did she say why she was sad?"

"She said she wasn't when I asked, but I think that was a fib. She just acted sad." Fox finished buckling Ethan in and climbed into the front. He knew there was a good chance he was the reason she was sad. Why hadn't he picked up on it when she walked in? He heard Ethan open his food in the back seat.

He debated briefly about which direction he should go. Should he go to Bailey's? But he couldn't think of how the situation could be made any better. A simple conversation wasn't going to do it. Finally, he turned toward home. It was his only option.

CHAPTER 20

BROOKE STEPPED into the pub and looked around. She had some unfinished business to deal with during her lunch break. The last couple of days had been more than she could reasonably be expected to deal with.

First, she had rushed to the courthouse when her ex-husband was arrested. Then she got into a fight with Fox, though she still didn't get the whole blood gushing thing.

Demanding to know where Ethan was had almost been the last straw. Her sister asking really had been. Edmund had finally insisted she send Bailey the information on where he was so they would stop calling.

Edmund hadn't even acted excited to see her. It was the first time she had found an entitled jerk on her own. Except he had pointed out that the guy was just some useless schmuck right out of prison. He had been furious, but for the first time, he'd let her strap the man into the machine.

Soon, he would see her as a partner instead of just his assistant. His honeytrap, for lack of a better term. Perhaps he would even let her reverse their roles on occasion.

Then there was her sister, Bailey. She was positive Fox

was fucking her on the side. Normally, she wouldn't give two shits what her sister did. Sneaking around with her boyfriend, no matter how she felt about him, was unacceptable though.

Bailey would get hers in the end if Brooke had anything to do with it. The bitch should know better than to cross her.

Today, she just wanted to start setting things right again. Her life had been quiet, until Knox had arrived in town and begin interfering in her ex-husband's business.

Looking around again, she finally spotted him sitting in a booth toward the back with a mound of food in front of him. He had a notebook opened next to his plate and wrote something in it every few bites.

"Two pints of whatever you have that's good on draft," she said when the bartender stepped over to her. The pints arrived, and she took them over to the booth. She sat one in front of him as she slid into the seat opposite.

If he was surprised to see her, it didn't show. In fact, he kept writing in his notebook for several more seconds before looking up.

"Brooke," Knox said like it was simply a statement of fact. She took a long sip of her beer. It wasn't to her taste, but she doubted the Neanderthal sitting across from her drank anything else.

She watched him closely. Her shirt was carefully chosen this morning to present the best cleavage. If his eyes went straight to it, she knew she could charm him into doing what she wanted.

Unfortunately, his gaze never wavered from hers. It was a shame. She would much rather charm this man than press him. Then again, she still had some anger to work out. He would do as well as anyone. With a sigh, she set her beer back on the table and nodded at his notebook.

"Keeping a list of the lives you're trying to ruin?"

Slowly, his gaze left her to return to the opened notebook. He took his time clicking the button on his pen before setting it on the table. He reached over and closed the notebook. She wanted to tell him there wasn't anything in it she was interested in. She was only interested in one thing.

"That's a bit dramatic, even for you. I'm working on a lesson plan for a class on statistics and probability I'm teaching next year," he finally said.

She had dropped out of school at sixteen when it was discovered she was having an affair with one of her teachers. It was easier to leave on her terms than wait to be kicked out. Of course, the teacher only got a slap on the wrist. She found out later he was transferred to another school.

"Isn't that better done at home. I think I heard Chicago?"

They sat in silence for a moment while he seemed to size her up. She straightened in her chair slightly hoping to appear more in command of the conversation. The other brother, the cute one, would have been so much easier to deal with. He had been approachable. This one was not.

"What do you want, Brooke?"

"Are you this hostile to everyone? Your wife might get off on it, but I'm not going to put up with it," she said, pressing on. His eyebrow rose, she hoped in surprise. "Now that I have your attention, there's something we need to discuss."

"Please, lead on," he said, leaning back and crossing his arms over his chest. "I can't wait to hear this." She took a moment to admire the tree trunks he had for forearms. Even the worst male asshole had some decent qualities. There was no denying Knox had a few.

"Let me dumb this down for you," she finally continued.

"By all means, give it to me in simple terms so I can understand."

She sneered at him before she could stop herself. Edmund always told her that she would never be successful in life if she couldn't learn to control her emotions. But Knox's attitude was beginning to piss her off. She would give anything to strap him into the machine and watch the life slowly be choked out of him. It would be worth making Edmund angry to lure this man into the back alley. Emotions be damned.

"It's really very simple, you see. Pack up, go home, and stay out of my business."

"Mmm," he said after a few minutes. "Nah, I think I'll stick around for a while. I'm in the middle of a family reunion."

"You've seen them. Go home. Besides, I would hate for you to stay, and those babies grow up without a father. Bad things can happen in this city. Just ask your sister."

"Are you threatening my family?" he growled. If she wasn't so angry with him, she might be intimidated. His eyes shone brighter as he leaned forward in his seat. She decided to lean forward too, just to hammer her point home.

"You can call it a threat, warning, or whatever you want," she snarled back. "I don't care. Just stay away if you know what's good for you." She stood abruptly and stomped away from the booth.

It would take more than just a threat. She had known men like him her whole life. Thought they were God. She would teach him how wrong he was about that. He would pay one way or the other for not heeding her warning.

Now she just had to get Fox back in line. He would do whatever she told him to not lose Ethan. Her son made the perfect pawn. He guaranteed she had a decent place to live with all the bills paid. Fox would be easy.

Bailey, on the other hand, might be more of a problem. She was partial to Ethan also, though, one more well-placed threat might just warn her sister off.

She'd think about all that later. According to her phone, she was going to be back late from lunch. Her boss would be more than happy to dock her pay for it. Someday she would own her own place, then they could all go straight to hell. She'd show them she wasn't a woman to be messed with. She'd show them all.

━━━

Dover was bent over one of the tables in the incident room studying the latest autopsy report when Knox walked into the room. She had given up keeping him out of the investigation when Dex secured him a visitor's pass. Returning to her report, she waited for him to speak. She'd learned there was no use rushing him.

"I just had a very interesting lunch date," he finally said.

"Yeah?"

"Actually, I've had lunch dates two days in a row."

"Okay."

"Just FYI. Bailey knows about us. That was my first lunch date yesterday." Both Dex and Dover stopped what they were doing to stare at him. "She needed to know if she's joining this fight."

"What fight?" Dover asked, exasperated. When did whatever he was doing turn into all of their problem?

"That's what the second lunch today was about," he

continued. "Why would the girlfriend be so pissed off about her ex-husband being sent inside?"

"What are you talking about?" Dex asked. He sat across the room from them studying the crime scene reports.

"Just what I said." Knox gave a deep sigh when they both looked at him. "I was eating at the pub down the street working on a lesson plan when Brooke sat down across from me. I thought it might be civilized since she brought me a beer. But she then proceeded to threaten my family if I don't leave town. That was the general gist of it anyway."

"How did she even know where to find you?" Dover asked.

"Hell if I know. I'll tell you this, though. If she even looks at my family I'll kill the bitch."

"Okay. Calm down, Rambo. Did she actually threaten to hurt your family?"

"Not in so many words. She threatened me."

"Then I wouldn't worry about it too much. I'm pretty sure you can take care of yourself."

"Yeah, but I agree with Knox," Dex said, setting down his reports. "Why is she so worked up over a known drug trafficking ex-husband? You'd think she'd be relieved to have him out of her life. Something isn't right. First, she pulls a vanishing act when we tail her. Now, she's threatening Knox over something she should be relieved about."

"So, what do you suggest?" Dover asked. "I don't exactly have time to go chasing after my brother's girlfriend."

"I'm not sure, but you're right. This has us burning at both ends."

"Don't worry about her," Knox said. "I'll deal with her and your brother. What's happening with the case?"

"Bodies are stacking up, and we don't have anything that leads us to who's doing this. No trace, no prints, nothing. How is someone this good?" She shoved her chair back from the table in disgust. They had pored over everything.

"The only things these men had in common was the medallions, private school dump sites, and method of death," she continues. "We can't even count on a type now. The last guy was working class."

"No one is perfect forever," Dex assured her. "He'll make a mistake, and we'll catch him. This last guy might just be it. What happened to change his type?"

"I have an idea," Dover added looking out the door to make sure they wouldn't be overheard. "I hate this idea, but what if Knox comes to the next scene. If I can spot anyone in the crowd who looks like a possibility, like there's an aura that isn't right, I could point him out to be followed. I can't tell a patrolman or even another detective without throwing up red flags. Knox, however, could do it."

"Might be worth a try. Knox?"

"Yeah," he said, standing up. "Just let me know where and when. I'm heading back to the apartment to get the rest of this damn lesson plan done. The head of school wants it as soon as possible. I swear kids are getting too smart for their own good." He gave a small wave as he walked out of the room.

"Do you think my idea is nuts?" she asked when he was out of earshot.

"I think anything is worth a try. We have to get this person off the street. I believe nothing is off limits if it makes the world a safer place. Knox burned a warehouse down while in it to catch a killer. Following a person of interest is child's play for him."

"And until then?"

"Until then, we keep doing what we're doing. I guarantee he's made a mistake somewhere. We just have to find it."

"And if we don't?"

"We will," he said with conviction in his voice. "We will."

"Is this how every case is for you? Chasing your tail, biding your time until you get a lead? How do you stand it?"

"I remember that sometimes, we're all that stands between the monsters and the innocent. It's what your family is about. It's why Knox stayed. Why the rest of your siblings will drop everything to rush in when everyone else flees. Your family," he said, catching her gaze, "they are the monster slayers."

CHAPTER 21

FOX'S LIFE was spiraling apart. He knew it, he just didn't know how to stop it. The cat and mouse game over Ethan felt like it had taken years from his life. Brooke had saved her wrath for the night after. He had reached deep into his soul to calm her down, which resulted in another nosebleed he barely got under control.

Then, there was work. He worked a job he loved—until lately. Something about the Victorian was off, besides just the creepy-as-hell owner's son.

He had yet to meet the owner, and his wife hadn't returned from their vacation home since he'd first met her. None of that would matter if they hadn't left Edmund in control. He was turning into a serious problem.

His sister couldn't help him with any of it since she was on the trail of a killer. He had to admit that might be more important than his problems.

He guessed he could talk to his brother about it, but he still wasn't sure how he felt about his new instant family. Besides, as much as he liked the idea of Jimmy behind bars where he belonged, he didn't really approve of Knox's methods.

He put it all out of his mind as he trudged up the stairs to his apartment. Brooke was after him to upgrade to a building with an elevator.

He liked this one though. Only three floors and not too many tenants. The old walls were thick enough you couldn't hear your neighbors. Everyone minded their own business, which was an added bonus.

"Yay, Fox is home," he heard when he unlocked the door. He smiled when Ethan ran to him before he could even set his stuff down.

"How was your day?" Fox asked, hugging him.

"It was good. Jodie threw up all over the lunch table. She had to go home," Ethan answered. "It was awesome!"

"I bet it was. What else happened?" he asked with a laugh. Only a child would think someone barfing was cool.

"Hmm," the little boy said, thinking about it for a moment. "We made handprints with paint and learned a new song in music."

"Wow, that was a good day."

"I don't understand what was so important at work you couldn't pick him up. I had to leave early, and the boss doesn't like that," Brooke said, stepping out of the bedroom.

"There was a problem at one of the job sites like I told you." He didn't know how much longer this could go on. "Hey, buddy, why don't you go wash your hands. I brought home chicken."

"Chicken!" Ethan declared as he ran off to the bathroom.

"Can we just have a nice evening for a change?" he continued when he noticed Brooke had stopped with her fist on her hips. He was too exhausted for another fight. Was he asking too much to have a quiet evening with his family? Gazing at Brooke, he decided it must be.

"So you being late is my fault?" she sneered. "All I've asked is that you pick up Ethan for me three days a week. I don't think that's unreasonable."

"I didn't say it was. You know I never mind picking Ethan up, but on occasion, I have to work late. I can't always stop what I'm doing to leave. There haven't been but a handful of times I've had to ask you to pick him up. My job is what keeps the lights on."

"But I don't contribute anything. Is that what you're saying?" She rolled her eyes.

"Enough to keep yourself well entertained." He wished he could take back what he said the moment it left his mouth. "I'm sorry."

He hadn't even realized she was holding something until it hit him in the temple. There had been no time to duck. The coffee cup shattered when it hit the floor.

"Shit, Brooke," he said as he bent over, his hand pressing to the side of his face.

He felt where the heavy mug had hit both his temple and his cheek. Coffee soaked into his shirt and spread across the floor as he stared at the pieces of pottery now broken on the floor.

Out of the corner of his other eye, he saw Ethan hiding behind the corner of the bathroom door. Brooke just pushed past him and out the door. He didn't bother trying to stop her.

"Hey, little man. How about we get you some of that chicken?" he said, trying to lure Ethan from behind the door. He pulled everything from the bag and spread it across the table.

Slowly, Ethan walked over to his chair. "I got the crispy

stuff like you like." He picked out a drumstick for him. "I'll be right back, okay?" Ethan nodded, so Fox headed into the bedroom.

With a dry shirt on, he grabbed the broom and some paper towels from the kitchen. By the time Ethan finished, he had all the remnants of the cup cleaned up. He started one of Ethan's favorite movies on the television before going back into the kitchen. He stored the broom and found a bag of peas in the freezer. How would he explain the shiner at work the next morning?

What he really needed to do was go find Brooke. They should talk this out. He was tired of the back and forth. It was time to decide if they could work out the strife in their relationship or whether they should walk away.

He would offer to keep Ethan with him while she found somewhere else if it came to that. He would even offer to continue paying for his childcare. It might just convince her to let Ethan stay.

Except, he had no idea where to find her. It occurred to him that he really didn't know much about her at all. Their relationship had been a whirlwind. They met, and the next thing he knew she was moving in with a young boy in tow. He didn't know who her friends were or where she went when she went out. Now, all he could do was wait for her to cool off and return home.

It was several hours later before he heard her key in the lock. Ethan had been tucked into bed long ago, but Fox sat on the couch waiting for her. He wanted to be asleep also. The exhaustion from the week was weighing him down, but he needed to talk to Brooke first. She paused in the doorway when she saw him.

"What are you doing?" she hissed.

"Waiting for you."

"I'm too tired to deal with you," she said with an exaggerated sigh. He patted the couch next to him. "Why can't you just let anything go. Talk, talk, talk, that's all you do."

"I can't keep doing this, Brooke." He had planned to keep their conversation civil, but that looked like it was going to be easier said than done.

"This isn't okay," he added, pointing to the bruise on his face. "None of this is okay. I don't know what's been happening with you, but it has to stop."

"What do you mean what's happening with me? I don't ask anything from you except to pick up Ethan from daycare on occasion, and you can't even do that lately."

"I have to work," he snarled. It was the same argument from earlier. "I'll try to get away earlier from now on, but you can't come at me every time plans change. You go out more often than not now. Where are you? It's not a relationship if you're never here to be a part of it."

"You know what? I'm not doing this tonight. I'm tired, I'm going to bed." She stomped toward the bedroom. "You know I can do much better, right?" she said, stopping with her hand on the doorknob to the bedroom. "I get better offers all the time. It would be nothing for Ethan and me to move in with one of them."

"Brooke—"

"Just think about that tonight while you're sleeping on the couch."

"I'll go sleep at my sister's place," he said, following her into the bedroom.

"Good idea. You need some time to think over what you want."

He went to the closet and dragged out an overnight bag. She watched as he tossed a change of clothes inside. He added his toiletries before zipping the bag closed. He was on his way to the front door when he turned to find her watching him with a smirk from the bedroom doorway.

"We will talk about this tomorrow," he said.

"We'll see." She shrugged, and he opened the front door. Maybe by tomorrow he really would have a plan thought out for their future. He didn't see continuing the relationship with Brooke. That wouldn't even give him pause, except for Ethan.

He closed the door behind him. The walk down the stairs seemed to take him twice as long as normal. He climbed in his truck with his mind swirling over everything going on. It was probably why he drove past his sister's apartment and straight out the north side of Boston.

That's what he told himself anyway. He couldn't admit that he needed Bailey more than he ever had at that moment. She had become his safe place. The place where he could either work out his problems or leave them behind.

This time, he didn't even want to think about them. He simply wanted to lay in her arms until everything went away.

―

Bailey was sound asleep, dreaming about the new dog she planned on picking up from the shelter soon. In her dreams, she was trying to decide between an adorable black something-doodle and a fluffy retriever mix.

For some reason they kept banging on her door to be let in. She knew she needed to make a decision soon, but this seemed like a bit much.

Her eyes popped open right before she heard the banging again. Throwing the sheet off, she sat up in bed.

The banging started again. So, it wasn't two cute dogs begging to be let in. Shame.

She couldn't imagine who would be at her front door this hour. It was well after midnight. Grabbing a baseball bat she kept under her bed, she eased out of her bedroom.

She paused at the top of the stairs at the shadow behind the small glass windows to the side of the front door. Someone was still out there.

Careful to avoid the squeaky stairs, she slowly crept down them until she could look out the peephole. Quickly, she unlocked the door and pulled it open.

"Fox?" she rasped, looking through the slit she had allowed.

"Yeah."

"Do you know what time it is? Has something happened? Where's Ethan?" she asked, pulling the door a little further open. Then she saw the bruise on his face. Grabbing his wrist, she pulled him inside.

"Did she do this?" she whispered. Her fingertips brushed across the side of his face. "We should get some ice on that."

She turned to walk to the kitchen, but he caught her arm to stop her. When she turned around, his gaze finally found hers. It told her everything she needed to know. It spoke about how wounded he was, but also that she was the only one who could heal him. It wasn't about the physical pain, not really. It was all about what he felt inside.

He didn't say a word as his hand worked up from her arm to the back of her neck. She was pressed against the wall as his lips descended on her. He was gentle at first. His other hand rested on her hip as he took a tentative taste.

She didn't know if he was waiting to be granted permission or to be pushed away. She didn't care. All she knew was that she needed him as much as he did her.

She fisted his shirt in both hands and pulled him closer to her. His kiss became more frantic. His tongue swept through her mouth, then his lips were moving down her neck until they settled over her taut nipple.

A small gasp escaped her lips when he lifted her up to his hips. Her fingers played through his hair as he soaked the front of her tank top with his mouth.

His gaze landed back on hers when she moaned. She was in the middle of debating what to say to make him continue when he moved them to the stairs.

He carried her up like she was as light as a feather. It wasn't until he tossed her on the bed that she realized where he had carried her.

She lay back watching as he pulled his shirt over his head. It was a nice show. One she would never get tired of. Then it was her turn. He grabbed the front of her shirt and pulled her into a sitting position. He pulled it over her head before pressing his hand between her breasts to lower her back to the bed.

"I've dreamed about this," he said. His gaze roamed over her body. "So many times. Every day I think about the things I want to do to you."

"Like what?"

"Like this." He lowered himself until he was pressing her into the bed. Just the delicious weight of him made her want more.

He kissed the side of her breast before his lips skimmed back over her nipple. She wanted to scream, and almost did when he nipped the hard bud. Her hips bucked against his as he moved to the other one.

"Fox," she gasped as his teeth tugged. He stopped, and when their gazes met again, he was smiling.

"Like this," he said. He stood, reached over and slid her shorts from her hips. They were tossed over his shoulder to the floor. He lowered to his knees at the foot of the bed and tugged her to him. She bucked even harder when his tongue swept through her folds finding the perfect place.

"Please," she begged.

He growled and worked her harder. His tongue was perfect as she slowly lost track of time and space. Her senses were focused solely on him as she felt apart. He continued to lick and suck until she collapsed.

She could have fallen asleep except that she heard a zipper. Opening her eyes just in time, she watched as he pushed his jeans off. His black boxer briefs followed to give her a perfect view.

"And this," he said, climbing up the bed until he hovered over her. He sat back on his heels and rolled a condom down his length. Almost like it had a mind of its own, her hand reached out to follow the condom.

"Bailey," he groaned. Her fist tightened when it reached the root. He lowered over her as she guided him inside.

She had had sex before, but never like this. Most of the men she had been with were in a rush. It was all about getting there as quickly as possible. Fox took his time, however.

He watched her as he slid slowly inside her. She waited for the rush, but he kept the same languid pace for few minutes. If he continued, she was sure to lose her mind.

"You feel too good. I wish this could last forever," he said. Then he pulled out and slammed back inside her with a grunt. She felt something coil inside as he did it again. Was it even possible to have an orgasm this way? She never had before. It had always taken more than penetration to get the job done.

"Fox," she began to chant as his unrelenting pace washed over her. He pulled her onto his thighs which changed everything. She felt her muscles lock as wave after wave of ecstasy washed her away. When her body finally relaxed, she found him gazing down at her with a smile.

"Oh my god," she said in a panic. "Did you finish?" He laughed as he eased her back fully on the bed.

"I can just look at you and come. What do you think?" He settled between her legs for a minute. His hand lightly grazed her arm. "I guess I am that guy after all."

"Then I guess I'm that girl." He rolled off her to sit on the edge of the bed. His hand made circles over her stomach while his gaze followed it.

"I made the decision tonight before coming over here," he said without looking up. "I'm done. Brooke and I are over."

CHAPTER 22

FOX WAS GONE by the time Bailey rolled out of bed the next morning. He had said something about heading to work, but she wasn't much of a morning person, so she wasn't really listening. It didn't matter though. For the first time in a long time, she bounced out of bed with a grin on her face. The day was off to a great start.

There was a very good chance that multiple orgasms had something to do with her sunny mood. She couldn't think of a better way to spend a sleep deprived night than with Fox between her thighs.

Nothing could ruin her day. She had even decided to adopt the mostly Labrador from the shelter. Or maybe all three dogs and start her own herd.

"Hello?" she sing-songed into her phone when it rang next to the bed. She hadn't bothered to check the caller ID thinking it must be Fox calling to wish her a good morning. If she had, she would have just let it go to voicemail. Unfortunately, it was too late.

"We need to talk," Brooke snarled from the other end.

"We'll do lunch. I'll send you the details when I decide where I want to eat."

"Wonderful. It will be great to see you too," Bailey answered into the dead phone. Brooke had hung up the minute she was done speaking. "Said no one ever."

She tossed the phone on the bed. Nothing good ever came from meeting Brooke. If it wasn't for Ethan, she would have cut off contact with her years ago. So much for her perfect morning.

Walking into the bathroom, she turned her shower on as hot as she could stand. The soreness from last night came back to life as the water ran over her body.

She smiled at the memory of what caused it. At least her sister couldn't take that away from her. Then she went cold with a terrifying thought. *Did Brooke somehow know that Fox had spent the night? Was she about to walk into an ambush?*

She didn't think he would use it as ammunition to break up with her sister. He just wasn't that type of man. Sure, the guilt might gnaw at him, but he would never share something so intimate with someone else. She would even bet he had never participated in "locker room talk" in high school. No, he would keep their secret. But if Brooke wasn't wanting to meet over that, then what was it?

Finishing her shower, she dried off and moved into the closet to look at her clothes options. It didn't really matter what she wore. Brooke would look down her nose at whatever she chose. Still, she wanted to look like someone on a lunch outing rather than someone who worked alone at home.

She chose a simple wrap dress and a pair of strappy sandals. It was still miserably hot outside, so something cool was a must.

With her hair up in a ponytail and some light makeup, she deemed herself worthy of handling whatever Brooke was planning on springing on her. She just hoped Ethan wouldn't be caught in the middle of something nasty.

Her phone was still on the bed when it pinged. Brooke had sent a message with information about the pricey place near downtown where she wanted to meet. At least Bailey knew what she was going to pay for a salad her sister would push around the plate. It didn't leave her much time to get any work done this morning, though.

She was pulling out of her garage an hour before she was supposed to arrive. Between traffic and finding parking, she didn't want to leave anything to chance.

The drive in wasn't too bad. Finding a parking garage that didn't charge her an arm and a leg was a different matter, however. She finally settled on one that only required a two-block walk.

By the time she arrived at the restaurant, she was certain she looked like a sweaty mess. Slipping into the restroom, she worked feverishly to repair her makeup before Brooke saw her. Her sister would never let her get away with smeared mascara or faded lipstick.

She checked her hair in the mirror. Pulling the hairband out, she brushed until not a single hair dared to be out of place. She gave the ponytail one last tightening before returning to the lobby.

"Why do I always have to wait for you?" Brooke asked. Bailey froze for a moment in panic. She quickly adjusted her dress and plastered a smile on her face. Walking over, she went through the motions of hugging her sister. It was all for show. Neither one really wanted to touch the other one. "I swear you'll be late for your own funeral."

"Well, it's not like it can get started without me," she answered.

Brooke rolled her eyes in typical fashion. She gave her name to the hostess, and they followed the woman to their table. They both pretended to study the menu. Bailey knew Brooke would get what she always got. Heaven forbid she eat anything of substance.

"Caesar salad, dressing on the side, and I'll stay with water." She instructed the waitress.

"I'll have the grilled halibut, asparagus, and a diet soda, please." Bailey smiled at the harried-looking woman and handed her the menu. "It's good to see you. How's work?"

"How do you think?" Brooke snapped.

"I don't know, or I wouldn't be asking. I'm just trying to make conversation." The drinks arrived before they could descend into an argument. Bailey took a moment while she added her straw to the glass to regroup.

"Done anything exciting lately?" she asked trying again. A slow smile crept over Brooke's mouth. Bailey hadn't seen that smile since her sister admitted to sleeping with the basketball coach at the high school. It made her nervous.

"Oh, I've been doing a lot lately. Not so much exciting as time consuming," she answered. She took a sip of her water and set the glass down hard enough to slosh some on the tablecloth. "I spent a day sitting in a courthouse waiting to see if Jimmy would get bail. Know anything about that?"

Bailey almost sighed in relief. If this was all Brooke was here to bitch about, then she had nothing to worry about. She had plausible deniability on this. Knox had explained what happened, but that wasn't her fault. Besides, it had always been just a matter of time before her sister's sorry excuse of an ex-husband spent some serious time in prison.

"I knew he was arrested, but I had nothing to do with

it," she said. "The law of averages says it was only a matter of time. I think he's been pretty lucky to skirt the law as long as he has."

"Someone ratted him out, Bailey."

"Are you sure? The drug task force could have just gotten lucky."

Their lunch arrived which put the conversation on hold. Bailey had no doubt that Brooke would bring it back up the moment she had a chance. Hopefully, after they had a chance to eat. Bailey put a small piece of fish in her mouth. It really was quite good, even if it would cost her a fortune.

"I think it was that big asshole," Brooke said suddenly.

"That big asshole?"

"Yeah, turns out Fox has this whole other family." Bailey looked at her in feigned astonishment. There was no way she was going to let on that she already knew all about them. Had even met a couple of them. "There's an older brother who's just hanging around. He's staying with Fox's bitch of a sister."

"Brooke."

"Well, she is. Anyway, I'm almost positive he and Fox had something to do with Jimmy's trouble. Turns out, my idiot boyfriend has a pretty big tell." Brooke smiles again, this time in triumph. "It keeps happening more and more. The dumbass doesn't even try to hide it."

"A tell for what?" Bailey was already exhausted from dealing with her sister. Why was it impossible to have a normal, enjoyable conversation when they were together? She had always yearned for the kind of sibling bond that seemed to only exist in books. They had more of an adversarial relationship.

"For when he's lying to me," Brooke sighed in exasperation like her big sister was also an idiot. "I asked him about Jimmy the other day, and his nose started bleeding. Just spewed everywhere."

"That's awful," Bailey said, laying her fork on her plate. She was almost finished anyway.

"Right? Completely disgusting. I had to get out of there. But, anyway, I now know he's been lying to me." Brooke stabbed a piece of chicken off her plate and popped it into her mouth. She chewed it aggressively, cocking her head at Bailey. The look of satisfaction on her face reminded her of an evil manipulator more than a faithful girlfriend. "I mean he didn't do that before, but lately, it's happening more and more."

Knox had explained that with certain gifts, especially those that were mental, came physical repercussions. She knew if Memphis appeared as a hologram too many times, it made him sick. Knox told her about how bad it got looking for Thayer.

It only made sense that if Fox tried to change someone's emotions too hard, it made his nose bleed. Of course, she could say none of this to Brooke. Even if her sister believed her, she would find a way to turn it to her advantage.

As hard as it was to accept that there are people in this world with abilities that go beyond the rest of humanity, it was even harder to keep it their secret. She wondered how their significant others, like Dex, did it. She made a mental note to ask him when she had a chance. If she was going to stay with Fox, she had a lot to learn.

"Are you listening to me?" Brooke barked, pulling her from her thoughts.

"Yes. Nosebleed, got it. Are you sure you shouldn't have him checked for a brain tumor or something?"

"Fuck's sake, Bailey." Brooke rolled her eyes again. "To

be so book smart, you are such a moron when it comes to life stuff. He doesn't have a brain tumor."

"Hey, you don't always have to be nasty."

"It only hurts because it's the truth."

"Really?" Bailey's blood was starting to boil. She had driven all the way into the city, in a nice dress, only to be insulted. "He lies to you all the time? Is that why you threw the mug at him, because he's the one lying?"

She wished she could take the words back. There's no way she should know what happened last night unless Fox told her. And that would only happen if he had talked to her.

"Huh," Brooke said tossing her napkin on the table. "I knew it. I knew he's been fucking you on the side. Though why he'd be interested in that." She waved a hand at Bailey. "When he has all of this I can't fathom. I guess just the thrill of doing sisters. That'll pass of course. He'll realize you're nothing more than seconds at best."

"We haven't been—" she tried to argue. But what could she say. They had slept together.

"Save it," Brooke said, standing. The other diners were starting to take an interest in their conversation. "I knew you'd stab me in the back just like all the rest of them. I'm only going to tell you this once, so listen up. You come near my boyfriend, my son, or my ex-husband again, and I'll end you. Do you understand?" She didn't wait for a response. Spinning around on her impossibly high heels, she stalked out of the restaurant.

"Sorry," Bailey mumbled to her fellow diners.

"Is there anything else I can get you?" the server asked, hovering at the edge of the table. At least she waited until Brooke left before trying to hustle her out the door. She couldn't even fathom the fallout if she had approached when her sister was in mid-threat.

"Just the bill, please. I think I've done enough for today." The waitress squeezed her shoulder before returning to the kitchen. Bailey debated if she was going to cry but decided nothing her sister did could make her cry anymore.

She didn't worry about warning Fox that Brooke was on the warpath. He would have to deal with his own fallout over breaking up with her. No one broke up with Brooke. She was the one that left.

Ethan was another story though. It worried her how Brooke would use the little boy to get even with her. She would have no problem making her son part of the punishment. She had done it in the past. This time would be no different.

The server brought the check, which was impressive to say the least. Bailey looked at the barely touched salad on the other side of the table. "I'll take that to go," she said handing her credit card over. At least the lunch wasn't a complete loss. She would get two meals out of the experience.

Her thoughts turned to Knox. Had Brooke sunk her claws into him also? She doubted he could be intimidated by anyone. Still, she should talk to him. How did everything get so complicated? Life had begun to tangle the second Brooke caught Fox's eye. The woman should come with a caution sign.

She stood, taking her container of salad, and walked to the door. It really was a nice restaurant. Maybe next time she would bring Fox here for date night. The thought made her smile. Screw her sister and her threats. This was one war she intended to win.

CHAPTER 23

BROOKE STOOD at the end of the bar waiting for someone to buy her first drink. She had to ride the train all the way to the north end to find a bar Edmund approved of. He insisted that everything be done tonight to his strict instructions. They would see about that. If she was to be an equal partner, he needed to learn there was more than one way to skin a cat.

A few minutes later a pink drink was deposited in front of her. She took a long slow drink as she spun on her stool to smile at her mark for tonight when the bartender pointed him out. He was no more than forty with blond hair and pale brown eyes. His clothes screamed that he had money, but not obscene amounts. Perfect.

"May I join you?" he asked, sliding onto the stool next to her before she could answer.

"Of course and thank you," she said, holding her glass up. He clinked his to hers. If she had to guess, she would say he was a whiskey drinker. Typical. She actually preferred the beer drinkers. They were more fun. "How's your night going?"

"Much better now." He smiled, and she saw the perfect white teeth. They must have cost a fortune. She decided to test his vanity.

"You have a beautiful smile," she purred.

"It takes one to know one. I'm Peter. My friends call me Pete," he said, holding his hand out. She took it in hers with a coy smile.

"Cat," she answered.

"Hello, Cat. Can I refresh your drink?" he asked, nodding at her almost empty glass.

She nodded, and he motioned for the bartender to refill both drinks. She knew she had to nurse the next one until this was over. A few more whiskeys, and he would be good to stagger out the back door.

The drinks arrived, and he insisted on clinking them together again. She would roll her eyes, but that wouldn't send the right vibe by any means.

"So what do you do when you're not doting on a lonely barfly?" she asked. He laughed a little too loudly at her joke. Good, he was already tipsy.

"I'm a history professor at Cambridge. I know, you're wondering how I got that job so young. It was nepotism. My mother is the head of the Philosophy Department. I was raised by my dad over here, though. Hence the American accent. I'm here for a visit and some research on a book about the revolution. It's quite interesting really. You see—"

Brooke listened to him drone on about his research. She had become very good at acting interested while completely tuning out. Did she have a tell like Fox? Nothing as dramatic as his nose spewing of course. But could Pete see that she wasn't listening at all? Apparently not, or he wouldn't still be talking.

The bartender replaced Pete's drink without him noticing. He was now at least three whiskeys in and ready to start on the fourth. The man could hold his alcohol. She had to give him that.

"How long are you in town for?" she asked, cutting in to his rhetoric. He took a moment to drink more from his glass.

"Another week here, then I'll head west to visit my dad. He's firmly ensconced in the Berkshires." His voice was starting to slur, a very good sign. "I think I've finally discovered my favorite place to hang out too." He grinned at her. She winked back.

"I've never been there. Lived in Boston my whole life and have never ventured outside the city," she admitted.

"You should go. Better yet, you should go with me. I can show you all the finer points of the countryside. There's plenty of room too. Dad has loads of extra bedrooms."

For a moment, his enthusiasm was infectious. She wondered what life could be like if she just left with this man. Would living in England be better than this?

Then she came to her senses. Based on what she had heard, he would bore her to death quickly.

Edmund was more her cup of tea. She almost laughed at her own pun but schooled it at the last moment. Besides, Edmund would be waiting for her out back by now. She could never leave him. These men were too shallow to hold her interest. They were just like Fox, always trying to make her into a fantasy. Only Edmund saw the real her, the demon that lay underneath her skin. He was her soulmate.

"Maybe. How about we see how tonight goes first?"

"I think it's going amazingly so far." He finished his drink and set it back on the bar. No slamming down the glass for the college professor. There's absolutely nothing rowdy about the man. He was almost too easy.

"I feel the same way. Tell me more about your book

research." She listened to him drone on again. More importantly, his talking made him thirsty.

"You know what," he said, suddenly stopping his lecture on American history. "I need to make a quick trip to the gentleman's room." He stood from his chair on wobbly legs. "If you'll excuse me for a moment. Don't go anywhere."

She watched as he slowly wove through the crowd on the way to the back hallway. Taking one last sip of her watered-down drink, she followed him.

When he emerged from the bathroom, she was waiting for him. She leaned against the opposite wall with her clothes adjusted to present the best view.

"Here you are," he said. "Did you need to go also?"

She managed again not to roll her eyes. Fisting the front of his dress shirt, she pulled him against her. His first reaction when their lips met was surprise, but he quickly changed it to excitement when she slipped her tongue into his mouth. Then he was grinding against her when she grabbed his ass.

"Not here," she gasped. "Come on." Taking his hand, she pulled him through the back door into the alley.

He didn't notice the car sitting not more than two hundred feet down the alley. His only concern seemed to be how fast he could get his hand under her shirt. He barely let out a grunt when the needle plunged into his neck.

"About time," Edmund sneered as he dragged Pete's body to the car. "Do you have any idea how hot it still is out here? Even at this time of night, I've sweated through my clothes. It's disgusting."

"I'll trade with you anytime," she snapped back. "You can get pawed for a change."

He threw the body in the trunk and turned to glare at her. She knew he didn't like it when she talked back. He would just have to deal tonight, though. She had had a crap week.

Ignoring his gaze, she flopped down in the passenger seat. He didn't say another word as he drove them back through town. When they arrived at the warehouse, he unlocked the overhead door and pulled inside.

"You should give me a key to the warehouse," she said, climbing from the car. When he didn't answer, she continued. "It's only right if we're going to be equal partners." She helped him pull Peter from the trunk and drag him into the first room. They heaved him onto the table in the center of the room.

Edmund began undressing the man. He pulled everything from his pockets and set it aside. Peter's clothes, he folded neatly before loading them in a duffel bag. She had no idea what he did with them. He always took the clothes with him. She picked up Peter's wallet and walked to the mural.

"Put it back," Edmund snarled through his teeth.

"I'm just trying to help," she said, tossing the wallet back on the table. Suddenly, he was upon her. She found herself pressed against the wall with his hand squeezing her throat.

"You do nothing unless I tell you to," he hissed in her ear. "Do you understand?" All she could do was nod. His hand had made it impossible to speak. Releasing her, he moved back to the table. She waited by the wall until he'd finished stripping Peter. "You can help me strap him in this time."

Without speaking a word, she helped wrestle Peter into

the other room. They sat him on the floor, and Edmund wrapped the strap around his neck. She knew he would wake up soon. That's when the fun began.

She helped Edmund attach a cable to the back of the strap. He had explained several times how the contraption on the ceiling worked, but it still escaped her. All she knew was, the more the body struggled, the tighter the strap became. Eventually they were responsible for hanging themselves. That's how she saw it.

"Can I flip the switch this time?" she asked.

"Not until he wakes up."

"What do you want to do until then?"

"I have an errand to run. You can wait here until I return."

It was the first time he had ever trusted her to wait alone. In the past, he had always made her go home. Maybe he really was starting to see her as an equal. Her body buzzed at the thought. She would reward him when he returned by letting him do whatever he liked to her. She would do that now, but he was already leaving the room. Until he returned, she would just have to wait.

"Don't touch anything," he barked. She nodded once before he stepped through the outer door.

She wandered back into the outer room as the door slammed closed. How would she keep herself entertained until he returned? The clothes were gone, but everything else was still lying on the table. Even though she had agreed to leave everything where it was, she had a different idea.

She picked the wallet back up. She emptied everything from it and spread it across the table. Studying the mural, a pattern started to emerge. If she could copy it there was no reason for him to mind her adding her own touch. It would be another present for him when he returned. There was no reason he wouldn't see it as her complete devotion to him in her own artistic way.

Slowly, she began adding pieces to the mural. There was glue, tape, and everything else needed to attach something to the wall. It took her at least half an hour to get it just right. The cinderblock wall made it a challenge. It took several tries to find the best way to hang everything.

Stepping back, she was just admiring her finished work when she heard a cry from the other room. It seemed Pete was awake.

"Hello, Peter," she said, swaggering back into the room.

"Where am I?" They were always confused when they woke up. "Cat?" He tried to get up only to find himself too dizzy to stand. "Help me, Cat." He managed to make it to his feet and lunge toward her. His fingers grazed her face.

In a panic, she flipped the switch on the wall drawing the slack up in the cable attached to the ceiling. Peter was immediately jerked back against the wall.

She knew Edmund would be furious when he returned, but what else could she do? If Peter had managed to lay a hand on her she might have been hurt. It had been either him or her. She would choose herself every time.

"Now look what you've done," she screamed. Rushing to the outer room in fury, she looked around until she found the crop Edmund used on her occasionally. Taking it back into Peter, she began to whip him. "He's going to be so angry."

A red haze fell over her eyes as she continued to strike him. This was all his fault. Everything Edmund would do to her when he returned was because of this man. She struck him harder.

If she had only been listening, she would have heard

when he started to gasp for air. Even if she had, she was too angry to care.

He was dead, she realized suddenly. She had lost control and made him kill himself before Edmund was ready. Stepping closer, she poked him in the stomach. His body swayed slightly. She looked down to find his feet off the floor. There was nothing she could do to fix this problem.

Did she feel remorse? Not for Peter, he deserved what he got. But she knew there would be hell to pay from Edmund.

She needed to get out of there before he returned. He would calm down eventually, but not before he took his anger out on her. That was something she didn't plan to wait around for.

She would return home and make up with Fox. Edmund wouldn't dare go to her home. He would summon her when he was ready to see her again. She had no doubt that he would want her back. His urges didn't just go away, and he needed his partner to help him with them.

Tossing the crop back on the shelf, she pushed the outer door open. She didn't bother to check that it was closed before she was running across the warehouse. She didn't stop running until she made it to the nearest train platform. The T was just pulling in. Jumping on, she sank with a sigh onto a seat.

She would simply have to make it up to Edmund later. There was a man somewhere in one of the bars who would be her greatest mark. He would tick every box for Edmund, and she would be forgiven. Then she would convince him that they were still the perfect partners. One couldn't exist without the other.

The train finally made it to her stop. She walked the last

couple of blocks in exhaustion. What had started out as the perfect night had ended up in disaster.

Tomorrow would be better. At least she still had a roof over her head. Fox would never dare leave her. Edmund wasn't ready for her to move in with him yet, but he would be. Eventually. Until then, she just needed to bide her time. Everything would be fine.

CHAPTER 24

"HE'S ESCALATING," Dex said, staring at the body sprawled on the turf of the football field. "They're escalating."

"What's happened to make him lose control?" Dover wondered aloud.

This time, the victim wasn't lying relatively peacefully as if he fell asleep. The victim's throats were always abraded, but nothing else was disturbed. This was way beyond that. The body had been stabbed repeatedly, the genitals cut off, there were what looked like whip marks everywhere, and his intestines lay next to him.

"Something made him angry. This is extreme overkill. It could have been his partner, this particular victim, or even some situation that has no bearing on this that made him snap. It might just be the break we need. I would be very surprised if they don't find DNA on him this time."

"Christ! You could warn a guy," Sean said, stepping inside the tent.

"Why should you be the only one to get a warning?" she fired back.

"Fair enough," he answered. He knelt down next to the body and opened his bag. "I can get you an approximate time of death and then I say we let forensics process the scene. I'll stay in here while they work in case they need me."

"Let me know what you find out," she said. She and Dex stepped back out of the tent. They wrestled off their Tyvek suits and tossed them in a bin.

With any luck, the next time she saw the victim it would be in a clean autopsy room. Preferably one that was air-conditioned. It was going to be another scorcher today. She would rather be sitting by a pool.

"Lawn company found the body," Danny said. He had chosen to coordinate everything outside this time. "I have officers taking statements, but they don't know anything. The head of the school is on his way here. I'll have one of the other detectives interview him. I doubt he knows anything either."

"I'll pull prints," a crime scene tech said, stepping past them. "They should start running shortly. Hopefully something will pop on this one." He ducked inside the tent almost running into Sean on his way out.

"It's going to take a while. They've already swabbed a bagful. We'll put a rush on them," he said.

"I'm heading back to the office. If we can identify him, I'll start pulling everything we can find," Dover said. "I'll also ride the lab on those swabs and whatever else they can find. Here's hoping this is the one that busts this case open. We could use a break."

She started for her car with Dex beside her. He was texting something on his phone.

"I told my guys to be ready to run prints just to speed up the process," he informed her. "Looking at that crime scene, there has to be DNA somewhere. It was too chaotic for there not to be something. I can walk it through our labs if you need me too."

"Thanks, but I think everyone wants this guy caught. It's a top priority at our lab now." They reached the car, and she slid behind the wheel. "Jesus, I'm tired of chasing this guy. We have to get ahead of him." She rubbed her temples trying to will away the headache that had already started.

"We will," Dex assured her. They drove back to headquarters both lost in their separate thoughts. Dover hoped Dex was right.

The incident room was buzzing with activity when they arrived. It wasn't chaotic to the trained eye. Everyone knew their job and was carrying it out with efficiently. But to anyone else, it looked like a disturbed ant mound.

She was hit the moment she walked in with new information. Dex was being bombarded by his people, she guessed, with the same things. Unlike in the movies, the two groups worked very well with each other. Dex handed her a piece of paper.

"Listen up," she said loudly after reading through it. "We've got a name. Popped on the global entry registration list." She walked to the front of the room and picked up a dry-erase marker. They were starting to run out of room on the boards. More would have to be brought in if this continued much longer. "His name is Peter Hansen. He's a professor in England, here on a research trip."

"ME puts time of death at between ten and midnight," Dex continued as Dover wrote. "Initial examination states cause of death can't be determined due to trauma to the body. Visible marks on the neck strongly suggest strangulation, but there are also multiple stab wounds, and evisceration."

"I need to know everything there is to know about Mr. Hansen. Where he's staying, where he's been, about his research plans," she said. "Danny is tied up at the scene, so I need someone chasing down the bar. If our unsub held to the same pattern, he was picked up in one of the locals."

"Got it," someone in the room said. She didn't bother to find out who it was, assuming they would do a good job.

"If you find it, get down there and interview everyone." She pinned a recent photo of Peter Hansen to the board. "Someone saw this man. We need to know who he was with. With any luck there's camera footage this time. I'm going to head to the medical examiner's office and see if I can get them to move up the autopsy."

"Do you need me to go with you?" Dex asked when she stepped to the back of the room.

"No, I've got this. Can you see if you can speed up the lab?"

"I can handle that. I'll keep you updated on anything we get in."

"Thanks. I'll be back as soon as I can." She marched out of the building on a mission. Now, she just had to hope the sexy new examiner would find something she could use.

———

That morning Fox woke with a raging headache. They were becoming the norm instead of the exception. The stress he was under was closing in on unbearable.

He knew the person lightly snoring next to him was the main cause. Unfortunately, he couldn't put off dealing with the situation any longer. He needed to break up with her now, but he needed her to leave Ethan behind.

Quietly, he climbed out of bed. With any luck, a hot

shower would help his head. That and a cup of coffee should give him just enough energy to deal with Brooke.

He turned on the water as hot as he could stand and stepped under the spray. With the water pounding on his shoulders, he waited for it to relax his muscles. It didn't work. He was just as tense after the shower as he was before.

He tiptoed around the bedroom trying to dress without waking her yet. There was no reason to deal with her fallout until he had to.

The timer on the coffee maker had his cup ready when he walked into the kitchen. When his sister gave him the machine, he thought she was being ridiculous. What man couldn't make coffee? Turns out, she was right, it was the best gift he had ever gotten.

Sitting on the couch, he tried to frame the conversation he was about to have in his mind. He couldn't think of how to do this without drama involved. Hopefully, Ethan would sleep through the entire thing. He sighed as he pushed up from the couch. It was time to get this behind him.

"Hey, Brooke," he said as he stepped back into the bedroom. She grunted and rolled over away from him. He lowered to the edge of the bed. The coffee had been left in the kitchen this time. He didn't want another blackeye to explain. "Brooke."

"What," she whined, turning over to face him.

"We need to talk before I leave for work."

"Why? Can't it wait until later? That's all you ever think about now. Talking." Expecting her to roll back over, he was surprised when she sat up. "What? What is so important it can't wait until I'm awake?" She crossed her arms over her chest. "Well?"

"I wanted to talk about us. I think you'll agree that we

no longer work as a couple. You've been unhappy for some time, and if I'm to be honest, so have I. I just think we've run our course." It worried him that she wasn't fighting back. She simply remained glaring at him with her arms crossed.

"You have so many friends," he continued. "I thought you could move in with one of them until you found your own place. Of course, Ethan can stay here for now. I don't mind continuing to pay for his school. You can still spend time with him, and I can pick him up in the evenings or whenever. Just temporarily of course until you find something."

He knew that if she saw how much easier her life was without her son in tow, she would leave him with Fox permanently. But he didn't want her to think he was trying to steal Ethan away from her. He just wanted what was best for the little boy. Ethan stuck his head inside the bedroom with a grin on his face as if he had conjured him.

"Hey, buddy. Why don't you get dressed, and we'll get breakfast on the way to school?" Fox said.

"Yay!" Ethan shouted before slamming the door closed again.

"Okay, well, I think I said everything I needed to say. Is there anything you want to say?" He waited while she continued to glare at him. After a few minutes of silence, he stood from the bed. "Just find someone else to stay with tonight, and we can make arrangements to get your stuff moved."

He left the bedroom to find Ethan trying to tie his shoes in the living room. They had been practicing bunny ears, but he still hadn't mastered the skill. Fox ruffled his hair gently on the way to pack their stuff up for the day. Brooke still hadn't emerged when they left. Ethan shouted goodbye to responding silence.

"What would you like for breakfast?" Fox asked as they pulled away from the building.

"Pancakes!"

"Always pancakes. Okay, pancakes it is." He pulled into one of the fast-food restaurants that served breakfast. Ethan played on the playscape until their pancakes arrived.

Fox couldn't help but wonder what Brooke was doing as he cut her son's breakfast up. Would she be gone by the time he came home tonight? Would she take Ethan with her?

The thought that this might be the last time he saw Ethan was soul crushing. He had to hope that, for once, Brooke would put her son above herself. In the short time they had been together he had already begun to think of Ethan as his son.

"Are you not going to eat your pancakes?" Ethan asked.

"Oh, yeah, buddy. I just have a lot going on up here." He thumped the side of his head for emphasis.

"Is it about Momma?"

"Some of it." Ethan was always so perceptive. He debated trying to explain that his mom was moving out. That he hoped Ethan would get to stay, but it wasn't certain. Instead, he decided to let him enjoy what might be his last day in the school he had settled happily into. He would find out soon enough that life was often very unfair.

"You need a butterfly."

"Is that what my problem is?" He couldn't wait to see where this was going.

"Yeah. Ms. Wynn says sometimes you have to let your worries go. Just like a butterfly." He mimed setting a butterfly loose from his hands.

"Ms. Wynn sounds like a very smart person."

"She's very smart," Ethan agreed. "And pretty."

"Mmm, sounds like the perfect combination in a teacher."

"Yeah." Ethan giggled.

They finished their breakfast while Fox learned the other virtues of Ethan's teacher. He cleaned up their trash, and they walked back out to the truck. They sang along to all of the new songs the kids were learning at preschool on the way. When they arrived, Fox pulled over to the curb. It was policy that the four-year-olds were walked to class.

"Okay," he said, squatting to Ethan's level. "I want you to have the best day ever. Can you do that?" He pulled Ethan in for a tight squeeze. It took everything he had to finally pull back. "Bye, buddy." He watched from the hallway as the boy ran to greet his friends.

"Is everything all right?" Ms. Wynn asked.

"Not really."

"Oh no." Her gaze drifted to a happy Ethan before moving back to his. "Well, we're just going to wish for the best." With a nod, he left the building.

He returned to his truck but didn't drive away. Typing out a text to Bailey was next on his list before getting to work. He decided it made more sense to just call. Her voice would make everything better anyway.

"Hey," she answered.

"It's done. I broke up with Brooke this morning. She's supposed to find someone's couch to sleep on until she gets her own place. I can't spend another evening having things thrown at me or wondering where she is. I'm worried about Ethan, though."

"I know. I'm so sorry, but I think you did the right thing. Did you talk to her about letting you keep Ethan for a while?"

"I did, but I don't know. She wouldn't even talk to me

about any of it. We'll just have to see what she does. This is all such a fucking mess."

"It will get better," she answered. "Just give it time. I'll keep up with Ethan if nothing else. I don't think she'll cut me off. She still wants a free babysitter, and with Jimmy in jail, I'm it. This will all work out in the end. We just have to believe that."

"I hope you're right." He sighed. "I've got to go, or I'll be late to work. His majesty will never stand for that." He rolled his eyes even though he knew she couldn't see him.

"This too shall pass."

"From your lips to God's ears." They disconnected. This would have all been so much better if he had just met Bailey first. At least he was on the right path now.

CHAPTER 25

DOVER WAS EXHAUSTED. She had been running around for twelve hours now without much to show for it. Sean had prioritized the autopsy, but it didn't tell her anything she hadn't already figured out.

Death was caused by strangulation. He was also beat with a whip before death. The rest was caused after he was dead. That was at least a little good news in the middle of the horror.

The incident room was slowly emptying out as most of the extra support left for lives outside of the police station. She felt like she had been wearing the same clothes for days and wondered if anyone else felt the same. Knox had shown up around dinner time with an armload of sandwiches which he handed around to everyone staying on.

"I've got something!" Detective Jones burst in the room. She knew he had spent the day trying to run down the bar Mr. Hansen spent his last hours in. "The bartender remembers him. Said he was boring a woman to death at the bar half the night."

"Did you get a description?" Danny asked, moving to the boards.

"Blonde, thin, about five foot eight. He guessed her age between twenty-five and thirty. He said he remembered carding her just to be safe, but he can't remember her name," Jones continued. "I got a copy of the video from their cameras. I'll start going through it." He left the room for the video lab.

Dover stood at the back of the room looking at the boards in front. What was she missing? They had bodies, but no specific type. They had a matching means of death, but no answers on exactly what the strap was. They had staged dumps, but nothing that tied the scenes together other than they were all private schools.

If every school had been parochial, the saint medallions might make sense, but one was a science academy owned by one of the universities. There were a few things in common, however. All of the victims were men, they had been left on sports fields, and they were all last seen in a bar. Though never the same bar twice.

And then there were the medallions they wore. It was apparent that they were placed there by the killer, but what did they mean? Each one represented the business the men were in. No one, however, knew more than that.

Identifying where they came from had been a bust, as had finding any trace left behind on them. Were they simply a red herring to keep them chasing their tails?

"What am I missing?" she mumbled.

"Nothing," a deep voice said behind her.

"Where have you been hiding?" She checked her watch realizing it had been hours since she lost saw him.

"I've been in one of the empty incident rooms working on a theory."

"A theory about what?"

"I was studying the locations of the bars your people marked. I know they were looking for commonalities in them, but they're overloaded at the moment. So, I took that information and expanded on it. I just finished adding the most recent one. I think I've found something you and Dex should see."

"At this point, I'll look at anything."

"Okay, I'll find Dex and meet you next door." She watched for a moment as he headed down the hallway. It seemed like he now had the run of the building.

With a sigh, she walked to the room next door. Inside, maps were hung at the front of the room. There were lines drawn on them and a list of facts spread across the closest tables. He really had been working hard on something.

Next to the maps were a set of numbers in dry erase marker on a board. She had never been good at math, and they looked as familiar as Sanskrit. Staring at them for a few minutes, she tried to make sense out of what they were. The answers didn't line up with anything she knew.

"Those are probabilities," Knox said as he walked in the room. Dex followed on his heels. "Let me explain. I started by marking all of the bars based on what your people had already done. Then I began trying to triangulate them, but that didn't really work. So, I thought I'd try to determine how they were chosen."

"There's nothing we've found that link any of them together," she said.

"I focused on what would make them appealing to our killers. To begin, I wondered how transportation would play into it. I studied the option of driving to the bars.

"Parking around most of these is a nightmare. If you can find a garage, it costs a fortune and would require dragging someone several blocks. There are also cameras in front of most of the buildings and in the parking garages. I don't see that happening."

"So someone would have to wait in the car and pull up where the cameras didn't see them," Dex observed. "That shores up our two unsubs theory. I also don't see a woman being able to drag someone the size of Goodwin that far. Or any man for that matter."

"Right. I thought the same thing. I, then, went back to the bartenders who remembered a blonde woman, and none of them said she came in with anyone that they could see. Nor did any of the patrons I talked to."

"Damn. Have you considered changing professions?" Dover asked, truly impressed.

"Thanks, but I think I'd rather stick with teenage attitudes than serial killers. Though, they're not that different. Anyway, let's assume at least one of them has a vehicle, but they don't travel together to the bar. That leaves a cab, which is expensive and easy to trace. A rideshare is a possibility, but I'd argue it's also too expensive and traceable."

"That leaves only two other possibilities. A bus or the train," Dex said.

"These numbers show the likelihood of each mode of transportation. The one with the highest probability is the train. The bus has a lot more stops to navigate, but it's possible. The train makes more sense though. I traced it from each bar to the possible stops hunting for which stops they have in common. There is only one." He pointed to the train map. Both Dover and Dex leaned in for a better look.

"That station is down the street," she said after a few minutes. "It's the one someone coming to police headquarters would get off at. Shit, there are schools, businesses, and a ton of housing within that station service area."

"I didn't say it was going to close the case," Knox growled.

"But it will help build it when we catch the accomplice. Or partner? I don't know at this point," she admitted. "That is really good work. Thanks."

"If we get something on the camera at the last known for Hansen, we may be able match it to footage at that station," Dex added. "It would be much easier to find a needle in that haystack rather than all of the Boston area."

They stood in silence as they contemplated the map that centered around a T station not a block from where they stood now. Was it just possible that at least one of the unsubs had been right under their noses the entire time? If they could just get a hit off the video footage from the latest bar, they might have something to work with.

"If the medical examiner's times of death are correct for each victim, that should narrow the amount of train station footage we have to comb through," Dex finally said. "Especially based on any footage from the bar. We should be able to pin down the time in that station to within a twenty-four-hour period before each death."

"Let's wait to see what Jones and the tech guys find on those tapes first," she pointed out. "I don't want to spend more resources chasing something that we can't be sure of. It pisses me off, though, that she could be right under our feet, and we missed her all this time. If nothing turns up, you really might have to start tailing people from the crime scene."

"With any luck, Jones will find something we can use. Then you can have the pleasure of telling this unsub how pissed off you are in person."

"I'm looking forward to it."

"Hey," Danny said, sticking his head into the room.

"Damn, someone's been busy." He studied the maps and figures for a couple of minutes before shaking his head. "Looks like Greek to me. Tech found something."

Her gaze met Dex's gaze and then Knox's before it slipped away. Quickly, they followed Danny next door. Her heart was racing. What if this is what turned this case on its head?

"It's still grainy, but we've got your blonde. I followed up with the bartender. He verified that's who he saw. We're trying to clean up the image, but I didn't want to wait around," Jones said. He handed a photo to Dover. Dex and Knox crowded next to her as they stared at the image.

"Hmm," Dex mumbled almost to himself.

"Yeah, it does," Knox agreed. "But I can't be sure."

"Does what?" Dover asked. Knox pulled his phone out and flipped through the photos. Finally, he turned it around for her to see. She could only gasp at the image in front of her. "There's no way. He would know. Wouldn't he?"

"What is it they say? The wife is always the last one to know?"

"But this isn't just anyone's husband. This is my brother's girlfriend. You're wrong," she added for emphasis. But was he? Knox had shown her a photo of Brooke walking down a sidewalk while looking over her shoulder. It was timestamped the day they followed, and subsequently lost, her in an alley.

"Maybe," Dex agreed. "Let's see what we think after we get the enhanced image. It wouldn't hurt to check with Fox on her movements over the last couple of weeks anyway."

"All right, I'll give him a call. He should be off work by now."

Edmund had been waiting at the townhome when Fox arrived that morning. He couldn't begin to calculate the number of times he had counted to ten.

At least he was finishing the floors in the attic. After today, he should be done with the top floor. The crew was installing counters on the second floor. That only left a little finishing work that the site could handle without him.

He was ready to get on with his life. With any luck, Brooke was moving out at that moment. With any luck, she wasn't wrecking things on her way out. He wouldn't be surprised if she did, however. Her temper knew no bounds. But, if Ethan was waiting for him at the end of the day, it would all be worth it.

His life was slowly starting to rearrange itself back into something he recognized. Now if he could just get this remodel done, he was home free.

"It's not cool enough in here," Edmund complained suddenly dragging him from his thoughts. The man had sat most of the day in a soccer chair watching him. He was sullen today for some reason, which made him quieter than usual. Fox wasn't complaining. As creepy as the man was, he was much better when he wasn't talking.

"I haven't adjusted the air yet since I'm still finishing the floor. You can set it to whatever you're happy with once I'm done. I'm not leaving until this is finished." He leaned back over as he pounded the new wood floor into place.

"Is that the stain I picked out?"

"It is. I verified it with Heather before ordering and again once it arrived. She has the order you signed if you need to check."

Edmund made a dissatisfied grunt and sank deeper into his chair. Fox had a prepared answer for every problem the man could possibly perceive with the job.

Most of the answers involved the designer and her note-book of signed paperwork. Any change in design choices had to go through her first. For some reason, Edmund didn't seem to want much to do with her.

Fox could feel his glare trained on him as he worked his way across the room. It was a larger space than it had appeared to be originally. He would ask what it was going to be used for, but he wasn't sure he wanted to know. Edmund made his skin crawl enough as it was without delving into what he did for entertainment.

He was debating how to convince Edmund to return downstairs so he could finish when the man's phone rang. Looking up, Fox could only wonder who had made him scowl the way he was at the screen. It was the first time he could remember Edmund accepting a call.

"What do you want?" he snarled. After a few curt responses, he hung up. He stood and stared at Fox.

"Everything all right?" He sat back on his knees taking a break.

"It's nothing. Just something I need to take care of."

"Oh, okay. Well, I hope everything works out." Fox couldn't care less if things worked out for Edmund or not. It just sounded like the right thing to say.

"It will. Are you going to be here tomorrow?"

"No. I plan on staying tonight until this is finished. The crew can do any touch-ups before they clear out tomorrow. Heidi will be by in the afternoon to look at everything with Joey. As for me, I'll finally be out of your hair for good." He checked his watch. It was past quitting time and most of the crew would have already headed out.

Edmund made another of his disgruntled grunts and turned on his heel. Without saying another word, he stomped down the stairs. Fox listened until his footsteps could no longer be heard. With a sigh, he returned to the floors. Finally, he could work in peace. If he never ran into Edmund again, it would be too soon.

"Hey, bud," Joey said a few minutes later from the top of the stairs. "I think I'm going to call it a day. You coming? I saw his grace leave."

"Nah, I'm going to finish this up. The sooner I can be done with the job, the better."

"I hear you. This one's been a hell of a thing. I'll see you around."

"Thanks, Joey. Don't forget, I still owe you that beer."

"No chance of that." With a last wave, Fox turned his back on his foreman. Just a little bit more, and he could be done. Then he just had to run to Bailey's and pick up Ethan.

It had been a relief when she had agreed to pick him up. An even bigger one when she found him still at the school. He would convince her to join them for dinner before heading home. Yeah, his life was starting to shape up just fine.

CHAPTER 26

BROOKE STORMED around the apartment fit to be tied. Not only had Fox asked her to move out, but he had offered to take Ethan off her hands. She was supposed to be packing while he was out. That was a laugh.

She had no intention of giving up her living arrangements, though. He had no idea what he had. Not every woman would put up with him. He let her down time after time, but she never complained. And when she tried to have an occasional night out, he pitched a fit. He should be thanking his lucky starts that she had lowered her standards to be with him.

She also had no intention of giving him any leverage over her by keeping her son. It wasn't like Ethan was his. There would never be any children for him. She had made sure of that after Ethan was born. She was saddled with one brat. There would be no more.

Like it or not, Fox was stuck with them right where they were. He would go on paying for her needs until she said it was over. She broke up with men, not the other way around.

She stomped through the living room again. There must

be something she could do. She made another lap of the room and began to scheme.

The dream of strapping him into Edmund's contraption had been growing every day. She already knew he had enough money in his account for her to survive on her own for quite some time.

It wasn't hard to separate a man from his money. She had been doing it her entire adult life. And there were plenty of men left out there willing to roll over to make her happy. Maybe she wouldn't have to stay after all.

By the time she emptied his account, there would already be someone willing to do her bidding standing in the wings. Perhaps even Edmund would be ready to settle down. She just needed Fox to disappear for a while and to get her hands on the credit cards in his wallet. By the time she stopped pacing, she had the start of a plan put together.

Today seemed like as good a day as any to do something with him. With Ethan out of the way, nothing stood in her way. She would need help though. There was no way she could carry an unconscious man to the trunk of his car. She also had nothing to knock him out with that wouldn't kill him. Pulling out her phone, she made a call.

"What do you want?" Edmund said on the other end when he answered.

"I'm supposed to be moving out," she said, ignoring his attitude. "Fox tried to break up with me."

"What did you do?"

"Why do you think it was anything I did? That asshole is fucking my sister. He thinks he's breaking up with me," she raged. "He's a fool if he thinks I'm moving out. I need you to help me. Do you have a medallion for a builder? He's done tonight."

"Don't do anything stupid."

"I'm not the stupid one. Fox has pushed me one to many times. His time has come. Now, leave whatever it is you're doing and come help me. We can talk about our next steps when you get here. It's time I moved up in this world."

The phone was silent. So silent, she thought they had been disconnected. "Just don't do anything stupid until I get there," he finally said.

She heard the fury in his voice, but she didn't care. His anger was only matched by her own. It was time to do it her way for once. She wanted Fox gone now. Tonight. She wanted his body laid out in some anonymous private school field by the morning.

"Then hurry." She ended the call before he had a chance to.

She paced around the apartment waiting for Edmund to show up. He sounded like he was rushing over to help her, but where was he? Fox could be home at any moment, and they needed a plan before he arrived. Finally, she heard the buzzer at the door and pressed the button to let him up.

"What took you so long?" she hissed as she all but dragged him through the door.

"I was in the middle of something."

"Whatever. We don't have much time." She spun around and walked toward the couch. "I'm thinking we wait until he sits down. Then you can step out and—" She didn't get the chance to finish her sentence.

Her hand reached up brushing across the sting at her neck. Something warm trickled onto her blouse. She only had a moment to contemplate the red streaks on her fingers before her legs buckled. It felt like the world was rolling by in slow motion as she slumped toward the floor. Her gaze landed on the couch in front of her. Red was sprayed across the cushions.

She opened her mouth, but no words would come out. Then it occurred to her. Edmund had killed her. But why? She was the one who always came out on top. Not her drug-addled mother, not her backstabbing sister, not even her shit of a boyfriend. She was the winner. It was her last thought as her life bled from her.

———

Fox was exhausted, but for the first time in a long time, it was a good exhaustion. The work on the townhome was almost complete. He would soon be free of this nightmare and back to the job he loved.

He had broken up with Brooke. She should be out by now, and Bailey already had Ethan. His offer still stood to take care of the boy. He doubted she would agree at first, but he had some money set aside he could sweeten the deal with. He wasn't beyond bribing her to sign over her rights to him.

He rocked back on his knees to look at the new floor he had just finished installing in the attic. The house had settled into silence since the crew left for the day. The remodel was one of their best, and he wasn't bragging just because he was involved. The whole crew had done an outstanding job.

Standing, he quickly cleaned up what he had to. The rest could wait until tomorrow. With any luck, by the time he got home, his apartment would be just as silent.

He had no idea where Brooke would go, and if he was honest, he didn't care. The thought of relaxing in silence on the couch tonight after Ethan was in bed while nursing a beer, sounded like heaven.

He wasn't sure what he would do if she was still

there. Probably head to his sister's place to sleep on the couch. Anything would be better than being in the same room as Brooke. His fingertips brushed the remnants of the bruise on his face. How could two sisters be so different? He was really looking forward to getting to know Bailey better.

The smile on his face grew just thinking about her. His mind could already see the three of them, him, Bailey, and Ethan, spending holidays and weekends together. There were so many things he wanted to share with them.

He stepped out of the townhouse and locked the door. He would just run home for a minute to change and check the apartment. Traffic was already past rush hour, so it didn't take him long to get home.

He found a spot along the curb not far down the street and parked. Climbing the stairs to his apartment, he paused for a moment to take a deep breath. He needed to be prepared if Brooke was still inside. The key slid into the lock, and he stepped inside his living room.

His gaze landed on the couch first. There was something wrong with the upholstery. Parts of it were darker than normal like something had been spilled. His eyes moved down until they found Brooke lying on the floor in front of the coffee table. None of what he was seeing made any sense. *Why would she be lying there?*

"Brooke?" he asked, stepping forward. "What's going on?" His mind quickly moved on. "Ethan?" he called before remembering Bailey had picked him up.

A sharp prick bit into the side of his neck. His hand moved by instinct to protect the area but found nothing there. He took a step forward only to find his knee giving out. He just needed a place to lie down for a little while. He couldn't use the couch, since it was covered in something.

The floor would have to do. It rushed at him as if by invitation.

He could feel someone moving around him. His eyes couldn't focus enough to see who it was. Reaching out, he tried to touch Brooke. She was just too far for him to get to. He knew she would hate to know that her beautiful blonde hair was tinged pink. His mind floated, unable to put together what was happening.

His eyes had closed when he heard a knock at the door. A familiar voice called his name. He tried to warn away whoever was there or maybe he was going to beg for help, but he couldn't form the words. Then he heard the thud of something large hitting the floor before he was wrestled off of it.

He fought to open his eyes only to find himself being carried over someone's shoulder down the stairs. His eyes fell closed once again. Finally, he felt himself rolled onto a solid surface, but it was the last thing he knew before he lost consciousness.

―

Dover felt frantic when she pressed the number for her brother's phone again. Just like the last five times, it went right to voicemail. She didn't bother to leave a message this time. If he was going to hear it, he would have already responded to the first four.

"No luck?" Dex asked. He was studying the video from the bar where Peter Hansen was last seen. "Hand me the photo again." He held out his hand, and Knox handed him his phone.

Pulled up on it was the photo he had taken of Brooke earlier. At the time, he told them he took it so he would remember who they were following. Little did he know it would be used to compare to a grainy video.

"Why don't I go to his apartment to check on him," Knox offered.

"That's probably a good idea. Until we can say for sure that's who it is, I'd hate to get everyone else involved," Dover agreed. She watched as he walked out of the incident room before turning back to Dex. "Anything?"

"I'm pretty sure it's her. We should take that photo to the bar to be sure."

"Let's go then. Danny, can you see if they can get us a better copy? We also need someone to go back over all the other video and see if she shows up."

"Got it," Danny said before walking out of the room.

"I need to let the captain know about this on the way," she said.

"I'll meet you at the car."

She felt almost giddy following Dex out the door. Finally, they had a break. It might be a small, blurry break, but it was one nonetheless. She didn't even stop when she was waved directly toward the boss's office. It only took her a few minutes to update him before heading outside to join Dex.

"Knox sent me the photo," he said as she slid into the driver's seat. "I forwarded it to Danny."

"This is it. I can just feel us getting closer," she said almost vibrating in her seat. Adrenaline coursed through her at the thought of someone identifying her brother's girl-friend as a person of interest. Hell, she was possibly even an accomplice. "I can't believe she was under our noses all this time."

"Hopefully she doesn't suspect us of knowing anything.

That would be dangerous for Fox, not to mention Ethan," Dex answered.

"Jesus, I didn't even think of Ethan. See if Knox is there yet."

"I told him to call the second he found out anything. They'll be fine. We just need to focus on identifying who's in that video. If she can just lead us to her partner, we can stop them both."

It felt like it took years to drive to the bar. The place was in the middle of serving the after-work crowd when she pulled up in front of the door.

A large man standing at the door started to wave her away when Dex pulled out his credentials. They moved through the crowd until they found the back office. A manager met them at the door.

"We need to ask if any of your staff recognizes this woman," Dex said pulling the photo up on his phone.

"Of course," he answered. They followed him around the room asking servers until they made it to the bartenders.

"Yeah, she was in here the other night," the man said.

"Can you be more specific?" Dover asked.

"Like I told the other guy. It was two nights ago. She left with some guy she met at the bar. I remember her as quite the looker. Turned down several guys before she settled on the one, she went home with. I didn't really see them leave though. I just know they were there one moment and gone the next. Anything else?" There were patrons waving their hands for his attention.

"No, thank you. You've been very helpful." They thanked the manager and headed back to the car. "Son-of-a-bitch, we got her!" Dover exclaimed once the car doors were closed.

"I think so, but we might have another problem," Dex

answered. "Knox never called, and his phone goes straight to voicemail now."

"Shit. Send a patrol car to Fox's apartment." She started the car and pulled back out into traffic. They raced back across Boston. There were already several patrol cars parked in the middle of the street when they finally slid to a stop. She was out of the car in a heartbeat racing up the stairs behind Dex.

"Oh, shit!" she cried out when she stepped up to the tape marking off the apartment entrance. Her gaze took in the mayhem. Blood was everywhere. Brooke lay prone on the floor. Knox was sitting to the side with a medic holding a bandage to the back of his head. She flashed her badge and covered her shoes before stepping carefully under the tape.

"What happened?" she heard Dex ask behind her.

"I don't know. The door was open when I got here. I barely stepped inside before I was hit over the head. Brooke had her throat slit, and Fox is gone. So is Ethan," Knox answered.

"Call Bailey. Let's pray she has Ethan. Maybe Fox is there too," she ordered.

Dex stepped back out of the room with his phone already held to his ear. She knelt next to Knox. The cut on top of his head looked like it needed stitches. What had happened here, and where was her brother?

"She has Ethan," Dex announced from the door. "But she hasn't heard from Fox."

"We have to find him," she whispered. Looking at Knox, she found him gazing back at her with fire dancing in his eyes.

"We will. Dex, get Memphis on the phone."

CHAPTER 27

FOX'S WORLD returned a little at a time. The first thing he knew was that at least he was still alive. He hadn't opened his eyes, nor could he hear anything. But he was hot, and if he could feel heat, then he must still be among the living. For how long, he had no idea.

Slowly, he opened his eyes. Everything was blurry at first. Then he saw his legs, then his feet, and finally the concrete floor. Pain shot through his head as he gently lifted it to look around his surroundings. Closing his eyes again, he leaned his head against a wall behind him until the worst of it passed.

He was in a room with concrete walls and floor. In front of him was a wall of glass that looked into some kind of office. Except it wasn't really an office; it was more of a meeting room with a table in the center. His gaze found a large mural on one side of the meeting room. There was a piece of art in the center with stuff attached to the wall around it. He couldn't quite make out what any of it was.

His tailbone felt numb from sitting on the floor. That's when he realized that he no longer had on any clothes. He could see them piled on the table in the other room in a neat stack. He moved to retrieve them, but something stopped him.

Tracing his body with his hands, he realized he was tethered to the wall. He was free to move his arms and legs, but something around his neck held him in place.

His fingers probed the leather strap at his throat. It had a lock on the side that he couldn't break no matter how hard he pulled on it. He couldn't even get a finger between the strap and his neck it fit so snuggly. Looking up, he found a series of pulleys across the ceiling with cables running through them.

There was a part of him that wanted to scream for help, but there was another part of him that dreaded what the screams would bring.

As hard as he searched his memory, he couldn't remember how he got here. The last thing he remembered was walking into his apartment after leaving the townhome later than normal. He had been finishing the flooring in attic after the rest of the crew left.

Something had been wrong at the apartment. He remembered seeing red before everything went dark. His mind fought to bring it up, but it was no use. His memories were murky at best. The harder he worked to remember, the more his head throbbed.

"Hello?" he croaked. His throat was so dry. How long had he been out? Was it hours or days? "Tell me what you want. I'm sure we can work out something." The room remained silent.

The glass in front of him looked thick. He wondered, even if anyone was in that room, if they could hear him. His hands reached up to wrestle with the strap again and brushed against something lying on his chest.

"What the hell?" he mumbled. It was something hung around his neck. He lifted it as far as he could but couldn't quite make it out. He knew it was oblong with a relief etched into the surface of the disk. It hung on a chain that was around his neck under the strap. He tried to pull it over his head with no luck.

"Not important right now," he said, dropping the necklace. "What's important is getting out of here. There has to be something I can use." His gaze took in the room again. "The only thing in here is me." He checked every inch of what he could reach of the cable connected to the wall. Nothing.

"Help me," he screamed. Still nothing.

He gave up, letting his hands flop back onto his lap. Never had he felt so helpless. Though he suspected once whoever took him showed up, that feeling would reach a new level.

The only thing that would save him now was his sister finding him. But how would she even know he was missing? They had never thought about communicating when they weren't in the same room, but this seemed like a good time to try.

He took a deep breath and closed his eyes. Focusing on just two words, help me, he started chanting them over and over. Chances were that wasn't how it worked, but it was worth a try. It was all he had left. If no one ever came, he would soon die of dehydration. It would be a nasty way to die.

The heat must have helped lull him to sleep, along with the chanting. He woke up with his head slumped toward his chest. His neck felt like it was on fire from the angle.

Something caught his attention in the other room. A man sat in a chair on the other side of the glass. Slowly, he got up and walked to a door cut into the glass. As the man came into focus, Fox was shocked to realize he knew him.

"Edmund?" he rasped. "Holy shit, I'm glad to see you. Help me out of this. How did you find me?" He had a million other questions. All that mattered right now, though, was that someone was here to rescue him.

Edmund casually walked over until he was just out of reach. Then he crouched on his heels with a smile. Fox watched him trying to understand what was happening.

None of this made any sense. Where had Edmund come from? What had happened to him? He struggled again in an effort to put the pieces from earlier together.

"I think there's a lock on the side. If you can find something to break it with or maybe there's a key in the other room," he added, more confused than ever. "At least call for help. My phone should be in my pants pocket in the corner. You can call my sister."

Edmund simply watched him with interest. He made no move to help Fox in any way. He didn't even look at the strap around his neck.

Slowly, Fox began to see that Edmund wasn't a savior sweeping in to rescue him. He was the devil come to torture. Edmund must have recognized the moment Fox realized how much trouble he was in because he laughed.

"You know," Edmund said. "I think I finally understand what Brooke saw in you. I've spent weeks trying to understand. Not that I wanted her, but I always wondered why she set the bar so low. I mean, a construction worker? What was she thinking? But now I get it. Free room and board were a plus, but not enough. Free babysitting was also a perk. But I think she just wanted something pretty on her arm that she could control."

"You're probably right," Fox admitted. He couldn't

remember what his sister told him about psychopaths. Did he humor them or push back against them. He was gambling on the former.

"I know she was seeing other men behind my back. I can only assume she needs more than I can give her." He would say anything if it would get Edmund to loosen the strap.

"From what I heard, she wasn't the only one sneaking around. Best of both worlds, huh? Exciting, crazy Brooke in one bed. Her sweet, soft sister in the other. Well, you won't have to worry about choosing which sister anymore. Let's just say I took care of that little problem for you."

"What did you do?" Fox whispered.

"Nothing you haven't dreamed about. Put it this way, nothing should stand in the way of that delectable older sister getting the brat. But that's neither here nor there. I have to meet my decorator to pick out furniture for my new loft in," he checked his watch. "About fifteen minutes. I'm sorry you won't get to see how it turned out."

The two men stared at each other. One with contempt, the other with amused arrogance. Finally, Edmund pulled something out of his suit pocket. Fox couldn't help but grab at the bottle of water held out to him. Edmund let out another laugh before standing.

"We'll talk more in a little while," Edmund said. "I hope you'll look forward to it as much as I will." He walked to the glass door before stopping. "No, perhaps not as much as me. I'm afraid you might be a little too...choked up." With another laugh, he walked out of the room. Fox barely watched him leave the outer office as he took a long swallow of water.

After drinking half the bottle, he recapped it and set it

on the floor. Without knowing how long Edmund would wait until he returned, he needed to conserve it.

He tried to adjust his seat with no luck. The strap around his neck wouldn't budge. His sister hadn't mysteriously appeared, so he doubted his attempt at telepathy had done anything.

A shimmer in the far corner caught his eye. The shimmer quickly morphed into a person. He should have been more surprised when Memphis appeared in the room. He was so happy to see him, though, that he forgot everything else.

He should have known they would have noticed when he went missing. Hadn't Knox said that they always took care of their own. But how did Memphis find him?

"Oh hell," Memphis said. "What have you gotten into? Is there anyone else in here?" Fox shook his head. "Okay. Let's see what we have then." He moved across the room to investigate the neck restraint.

"That's a nasty lock. Let me go see if I can find a key." Fox watched as he walked through the glass wall into the other room. He could tell there was no key since there was nowhere to hide one. Still, Memphis combed the room before returning.

"I think I know where the evidence your sister is missing turned up. That wall is an ode to past victims. We just have to figure out how to release his current one right now, however." He walked through the wall Fox was restrained against.

"Okay, I at least have a name on the side of the building. Don't know if that will help," he continued once he popped back inside. Fox would have jumped had he not been tethered to the wall.

"I think it belongs to an Anderson family. It looks like a

warehouse. The sign was old, so who knows," Memphis added.

"Edmund Anderson," he said. "It was Edmund. He was just here. He said he'll be back later."

"Now that's something they can use. Will you be okay if I go back for long enough to get this information to Knox?"

"Yeah, I'm not going anywhere. He said he was meeting a new decorator to pick out furniture."

"Do you know who that is?"

"No. I only met the designer his mother hired. She might know. Her card is in my truck."

"I'll pass that on. I'll be back when I can. Don't give up."

"I won't. And, Memphis," he said before Memphis could shimmer away. "You don't have to come back. I know the toll it takes on you firsthand."

"Psst. Piece of cake," Memphis answered with a smile as he disappeared.

Fox wanted to scream for him to come back, so he wouldn't be alone. But he was already gone. Besides, without help there was no way he was escaping this.

He tried to relax, but his mind turned to Brooke. What did he mean when he said he took care of the obstacle blocking Bailey from gaining custody of Ethan? That was basically what Edmund said wasn't it?

Had he been one of the men Brooke was seeing behind his back? He wouldn't put it past her. He knew she had always been scheming to land a rich man. He was just a stepping-stone on her way up.

Thoughts of what could have happened to Ethan if he had been there swept through his mind. He quickly pushed them away though. Those thoughts would drive him mad if he wasn't careful.

If only Memphis would return, he wouldn't have to wait

to die alone. No, he couldn't think like that. Dover would find him in time. He just had to keep telling himself that.

His eyes were slipping closed again, he guessed from whatever drugs were still in his system, when the outer door opened. Edmund stepped inside and walked quickly to the glass door.

"Unfortunately, our time has to be cut short. It seems someone is putting ideas into your sister's brain. She called our office asking about properties near the wharf. I don't know how she found out, but I have to leave immediately on an extended vacation."

He walked over to a box on the wall. Taking out a key, he opened a panel on the front and flipped a switch inside. Then he slammed the panel closed. Fox felt the strap around his neck tug upward.

"It's a shame. I was really looking forward to our time together. I'll just have to see your demise in my dreams now. What delicious dreams they will be. Now," he said, squatting in front of Fox again. "Try not to struggle. It will be better that way." With a final laugh, he left the room.

Fox used his hands to pull against the cable over his head. It responded by tightening a little more lifting him off the floor slightly. He managed to get his knees under him before he was strangled, but that just made the cable inch upward again. Before he knew it, he was having to stand to take the pressure off.

"Stop," Memphis said, appearing out of the corner again. He quickly moved until he stood eye to eye with Fox. "I know it's hard but stop moving. I think this thing has some sort of system that reacts to movement. The more you fight, the tighter it will get."

Fox stopped fighting and became completely still. He felt a tear roll down his cheek.

"I know, but I'm with you. I'm not going anywhere until they get here. Trust me, Dover is running every lead to find you. There are cops swarming all over this city looking for this building. She'll find you."

Fox didn't dare nod that he understood.

"All we have to worry about right now is if Knox will burn Boston to the ground to find you. He's got a pretty impressive knot on the back of his head, but a bleeding head wound has never stopped him in the past."

CHAPTER 28

"MEMPHIS," Dover barked into the phone the moment it rang. She had been holding her cell phone as she wove back through traffic toward her office.

Dex sat in the passenger side relaying information to Danny. They sent a patrol car to Bailey's home until they knew what was happening. The crime scene team was finishing up at her brother's apartment, and Knox had sent Memphis to find Fox.

"He's in a warehouse of some kind. He's not good, but he's still alive," he said.

Dover felt her grip on the steering wheel loosen slightly. Alive was good. She could deal with the rest.

"There's some kind of contraption that is attached to his neck with a strap," Memphis continued. "He said something about one of the Andersons being there? Edmund? I guess you know who they are. The outside of the building said 'import/export,' but I couldn't see much more."

"The Andersons are in the import/export business. Shit, they own half this city."

"Sorry, I'll try to get more. I need to go. Thayer has my

phone if you need to find me before I call you again. I don't want to scare you, but hurry. Fox said he was coming back." She heard the phone disconnect as she pulled back up to her office. She left the car in a no parking zone and told the desk sergeant to threaten anyone who wanted to move it.

"We need the tax rolls for any property owned by the Anderson family or their companies," she called to one of the tech people on the way by. "And we need a building map of Boston."

She continued into the incident room where no less than twenty law officers worked. They spanned from Boston police to FBI. It looked like a beehive, and she couldn't help but feel like the queen bee.

"Here's what we know," she said, walking to the white-boards. "One Brooke Sullivan was found dead. Time of death is estimated to be less than an hour ago.

"Also found at the scene was Knox Monroe with a head wound. Not found was Fox Addams who is now believed to have been taken by an unknown perpetrator." She wasn't sure how you explained information like Memphis had without sending red flags up everywhere.

"The bartender verified that Brooke Sullivan was the woman at the bar. Further intel has led us to believe she has been in contact with a man with the last name of Anderson. We're led to believe it is Edmund Anderson," Dex continued.

"We will be treating this individual as a person of interest at this time. I already have tech combing the footage around the latest bar and the others for this individual."

She nodded at him gratefully as a man with an armful of papers and a rolled-up map came rushing through the door.

"I have the records you requested," he said breathlessly.

A table was cleared so he could lay everything on it. Dover and Dex leaned over the map unrolled across the table.

"Dom, you take the south side," Danny said, ripping off a stapled sheet. "Kyle, you've got north." He continued to divide up the town records. "You two, get this up on a board so we can mark it," he instructed two junior officers. "Blue for personal, red for business." He snatched up a box of magnetic flags and followed the map to the front.

"Thanks, Danny. I'll go update the captain," Dover said.

"And I'll check on how the CCTV stuff is going," Dex said, following her from the room. "I'll also see if Thayer has heard anything more," he added quietly. She reached out and squeezed his arm before moving down the hallway. She had never been more grateful for family than right now.

Knox was stomping across the foyer when she turned the corner. He looked like he'd gone three rounds with a bear. There was a large patch on the back of his head. He wore a pair of sunglasses betraying the status of his concussion. His jeans still had blood on them where he landed at the edge of the blood pool when he hit the ground.

"What are you doing here?" she asked, coming to a stop in front of him. "You should be at the hospital."

"Hospitals are bullshit. What have you heard from Memphis?"

"They're not bullshit. It's obvious you have a concussion. I don't need you dying on me." He simply gave her a glare, or so she imagined he did. It was hard to tell through the sunglasses. "He's in a warehouse hooked up to some sort of machine. I would guess it's the same one that strangled all of our other victims."

"Do you know which one?"

"Do you think I'd be standing here talking to you if I did?"

He crossed his arms over his chest and stood silently staring at her. Or looking over her head. She had no idea. He stood there long enough, she moved to go around him. She had only taken a step when one of his hands wrapped around her upper arm. For a second, before he started talking, she had a fleeting thought about how his hand dwarfed her arm.

"I might have an idea of where he could be," he said.

"Then why are we still here?" Breaking his grip, she broke into a brisk walk to the front doors. Knox followed behind, climbing into the passenger seat of the car still parked on the curb. She would call Dex or Danny in a little while to explain where they were as soon as she knew.

"That time Dex and I followed Brooke, we think she ducked into a warehouse near the water," Knox continued. "It didn't look like they were used much anymore, but the doors were locked. That's why we thought it was so strange that she could just disappear like that."

She parked near the bar they had followed her from. Knox needed to retrace his steps from that night. They wove several blocks over to where the streets looked more abandoned.

"This is the one. I'm almost positive," he said. Looking up, she saw an old sign that had once read Anderson Import/Export. Several letters were now lost to the weather and time, but there was no mistaking who it belonged to. They climbed from the car, and Knox tried the door. "It's still locked solid. But these tire tracks going inside aren't that old."

"There should be several dock height doors around the other side," she said. "This one would have been the tradesman side. They would have unloaded on the other side." They jogged to the end of the block and around the

back. There were doors, but they were all covered in corru-
gated metal and locked tight.

"Here, help me get some of the metal off. I just need a
hole," Knox said. He climbed up to the loading dock and
started pulling on the loose panels. She joined him and soon
they had a sizable piece removed. Unfortunately, there were
large solid wood doors standing behind the metal. "Move
back." She stepped back and watched as he started to rub
his hands together.

"Don't burn the block down," she warned.

He smirked and threw a large fireball at the wood part
of the door. "Just the door this time," he said as he began
building another one.

"We should wait for a warrant."

"I mean, we were, but then we found this door missing,"
he said as the door caught fire. "We were afraid someone
one inside was hurt." He threw one more fireball for good
measure. "Did you hear that? Sounds like someone in
distress."

"You're a little too good at this." But she didn't argue
anymore. She wanted to find Fox more than anyone. If she
had to commit breaking and entering to do it, so be it.

The second loading door caught on fire as they
watched. She didn't worry too much about burning the
building down. These old warehouses were made of stone
and had survived worse than they could dish out.

"About damn time you showed up," Memphis yelled
the moment the doors were cool enough for them to step
inside. "He's behind this wall. There has to be some hidden
door in it." He popped back through the wall.

"His gift is much better than mine," Dover grumbled as
she felt along the wall searching for a hidden door. "Wait, I
might have found something." Her hand traced a groove in

the stone. She found a small depression in the rock that a key could fit in.

"We need a sledgehammer or something to get through this door," Knox said. "Do you have anything in your car? Something big enough to blow a hole in the door lock."

"A shotgun?"

"That would work. Go get it while I look around for a key."

Dover raced back through the burned-out doors. She didn't stop running until she was back to her car. Jumping inside, she squealed away from the curb while pressing numbers on her phone. When it began to ring, she put it on speaker phone and tossed it onto the seat.

"Dex," she yelled when he answered. "We've found him. Get everybody to the warehouse you followed Brooke to. He's trapped behind a hidden door in the stone. The back freight doors are open. Hurry."

She didn't wait for him to respond before jumping from her car next to the burned doors. Grabbing the shotgun from the safe in the trunk, she raced back inside.

"They're on the other side of the room," Knox said when she joined him. "They won't be hit."

She pulled two shells from the box of ammunition and chambered the rounds. There was no time to even consider the damage that might be done to their ears. She just aimed at the depression and pulled the trigger. The gun sounded like a cannon going off, but it did the job. Using his shoulder, Knox managed to push the door in.

"Over here," Memphis called.

Dover's gaze swept over the room. There was some kind of mural on one wall behind a table. A glass wall separated the room in half. It had a glass door that was propped open with a chair.

Inside the chamber was her brother. He was standing on a chair with a leather strap wrapped around his neck. Blood poured out of his nose and down his naked body.

"He's been trying to self-soothe, I think. Hence the blood," Memphis said.

"I'm sorry." Their gazes met as her brother stood on a stool trembling still at the hands of a madman. *"I didn't know."*

"He can't move, or this thing tightens. I can't see how to stop it. Knox, do you see anything. You're better at physics. Hang in there, Fox. We'll figure it out." They moved to the box in the wall. Their voices were too quiet for her to hear as they tried to find a solution to the contraption.

"I'm right here." She brushed his arm gently. *"Everyone is rushing over here. Someone will know how to stop this. In the meantime, we can hoist you on Knox's shoulders."*

"He's bound to be good for something." Fox smiled.

"You know I would say something," Knox said from the other corner. "But this time we'll let it slide."

"I was just telling him he can always stand on your shoulders if he needs," she said.

"Hell, yeah, he can. Anytime, brother."

Fox swayed, and they all rushed at him when the strap tightened another notch.

"Hey, hey. I said not to move," Memphis chastised gently. He moved to the wall and stuck his head outside. "I think I hear the cavalry. Hear the sirens, Fox? You'll be out of here soon. Just hang on a little more, buddy." The sirens grew louder. "Well, this is where I leave you. There's no way I can explain this. Call me first chance." He slowly shimmered away.

"I'm not sure I'll ever get used to that," Dover said.

"Wait until he starts doing it just to jack with you," Knox grumbled.

"Dover?" she heard from somewhere in the main part of the warehouse. She gave a sigh of relief as Dex stepped inside the outer room. He took one look at the situation and turned around to start barking orders. A perimeter was set up outside the room which limited the number of people rushing inside.

"You. We need bolt cutters. Let's go," he barked. Two firemen rushed into the room carrying their gear. Two more EMTs followed behind.

"We need to be careful," Knox snarled. "Every time he moves, it tightens."

"We need a ladder," one of the men shouted. Soon a large one appeared through the door. "We'll get above it and sever the cable. I need to make sure we can cut it with one go just to make sure." They set up the extension ladder against the wall and climbed up to survey the cable.

"Go get Moose." A few minutes later a man easily as big as Knox walked through the door. "We need that cable cut in one go. Can you do it?" Moose climbed up and studied it.

"If he can't, I will," Knox responded.

"I've got it," Moose said. He took the cutters and eased them toward the cable. Knox positioned himself next to Fox. Dover wondered if the man would really lift her brother higher with his bare hands if he had to. "I'm going to count to three. Are you ready."

Dover's gaze met Fox's gaze once more. His nose was still bleeding, but he looked calm. *"Ready?"*

"I love you."

"Shut up and tell me that when this is over." She nodded at him. "He's ready."

"Here we go. One. Two. Three." On three, the fireman

gave a huge grunt and cut through the cable. Fox fell from the top of the chair, but Knox was there to catch him. The cable whipped across the ceiling as it unspooled on the other side of the room. "Watch out!"

Knox somehow managed to block both Dover and her brother from the cable until the firemen could get it under control.

"Sir," one of the EMTs said, stepping into the room. "We need to get in there."

"Where's the ambulance?" Knox followed them out of the room with Fox cradled in his arms. Dover debated between following and making sure the room was processed.

"Go," Dex said, ushering her out. "I've got this, and Danny is on his way." With a grateful nod, she hurried to the ambulance. She found it to be crowded with Fox stretched out on one of the gurneys. An IV was already taped to his hand, and Knox was arguing about the gash that had reopened on his head.

"We're heading to Mass Gen," the EMT said.

"I'll meet you there. I need to talk to him as soon as possible." She turned and snapped at one of the patrolmen. He immediately jogged over to her. "I need a ride. And I need lights and siren."

CHAPTER 29

DOVER MADE it halfway to the hospital before remembering she had left her phone in the front seat of her car. "After you drop me at the front door," she said to the patrol officer. "Go back and get my phone off the front seat and bring it to me wherever I am in the hospital. Can you do that?"

"Yes, ma'am," he answered. They rode the rest of the way in silence. Finally, he pulled up to the emergency entrance of the hospital.

"Thank you," she said, jumping out. She swung the car door closed and jogged through the automatic door of the emergency lobby.

"Fox Addams," she barked at the harried-looking receptionist. The woman opened her mouth to say something only to find a gold shield waved in her face. With a scowl she picked up a phone and paged someone behind the swinging doors.

"You're asking about Foxworth Addams," a young doctor said, stepping through the doors. "Ms. —?"

"Detective Addams," she corrected.

"Detective. Let's step over here." He led her to the side of the room that wasn't as crowded. "He's being evaluated. As you can imagine, his throat is badly abraded. He needs to rest before he's interrogated."

"There is a serial killer out there, and I'm losing time finding him because I'm dealing with you. I will be talking to him, so you can either take me, or I'll find him myself. Your choice." She cocked a hip as she stared at him. His face morphed through several emotions before it finally settled on one.

"Follow me." Turning, he quickly walked through the doors. She followed him down a hallway to a triage room. There, she found Fox dozing on a bed covered in blankets. "The less he speaks, the better," the doctor said before disappearing.

"Thank you, I'll keep that in mind." Her gaze moved back to her brother. He was paler than normal, and his throat was a deep purple from where the strap had been. An IV line ran to the back of the hand that lay across his stomach. She watched as his chest rose with each breath he took. She had come so close to losing him.

Her attention shifted as the door to the room slowly opened. The gun on her hip was in her hands before she had time to even think. She felt her shoulders relax when Knox slid inside. His hands immediately flew up when he saw her.

"Are you planning on shooting anyone who comes through the door?" he asked.

"Maybe."

"Okay. Well, there's a cop standing outside who almost wrestled me to the ground. I think he's safe for now." He put his arms down and walked to the other side of the bed. "How's our boy doing?" He took the untethered hand in his.

"He's good. He's a fighter." She knew he said it as much for his own benefit as hers.

"I need to ask him some questions, but I can't bear to wake him."

"Except there's a killer on the loose," he said, completing her thought. "I think he'll understand. Hey, buddy." Knox gently tapped Fox on the chest. Fox's eyes flickered open and he looked first at his brother, then over at Dover.

"Did you see who kidnapped you? Was it Edmund Anderson?" she asked.

"He was waiting for me. He killed Brooke, didn't he? Where's Ethan?"

"With Bailey. He's fine."

"What's he saying?" Knox asked.

"Shit, I need something for him to write on. I'll need to get an officer in here to take his statement."

"I'll get it." Knox left the room in search of paper.

"You scared the shit out of me, you know that?" she snapped. A tear rolled down her cheek. "You've got the entire Boston PD chasing a phantom around town. All Memphis could tell us was that it was one of the Andersons' warehouses. Danny's trying to get the employee records now. I'll let him know to focus on Edmund."

"Here we go," Knox announced, stepping back into the room. "Also, some terrified looking rookie gave me your phone." He handed Fox a clipboard with several sheets of paper and a pen.

"For sure it was Edmund?" Dover asked. She watched as Fox scratched something on the paper. "You were working for him?" she asked, reading the scrawl. "On a project?"

"Yes," Fox whispered. "Edmund."

"Edmund Anderson? How is that possible?"

"Who's Edmund Anderson?" Knox asked.

"Only the son of one of the wealthiest families on the East Coast."

"I've known some wealthy assholes in my day."

"Point taken," she agreed. "I've got to get back to the office. I'll get Danny to put out a BOLO on the way in. We need to get his passport pulled." She was almost to the room door when it was shoved open. Bailey rushed in looking like the devil was on her tail. Her gaze landed on the bed, and she froze.

"Fox," she whispered. Quickly, she moved to the bed. "Please tell me you're all right. He's all right, isn't he?" She met Dover's gaze then her head swiveled to meet Knox's gaze. "Tell me he's going to be fine."

"He's going to be fine," Knox answered. "He's a little worse for wear, but nothing that won't heal." He moved toward her when she swayed slightly. Finally, she sat on the edge of the bed taking Fox's hand.

"Two cops showed up at my door saying Brooke was dead, and Fox was missing. They couldn't tell me anything else. We weren't allowed to leave. Your phone went right to voicemail," she said to Dover.

"I'm so sorry. I didn't have my phone with me, and everything moved so fast. I wouldn't have been able to answer anyway."

Fox whispered something, and they all leaned in to hear him better. "Ethan?" he said, trying again to be understood.

"We ran into Dex outside. He took him to get something to eat in the café downstairs," Bailey said. "We were so worried about you." She turned to face Fox again with tears beginning to roll down her face. He pulled her down until she was snuggled against him.

"I really do need to get back," Dover said.

"I'll walk with you to the door and then go find Ethan. Give them a second," Knox added. They quietly slipped out the door into the hallway. "We need to get them into a safe house. This guy could be anywhere."

"At least we have a lead on him. I'll get a warrant to search every damn piece of property they own if I have to. Forensics should have that room processed soon. I'll see what they found. Can you stay with Bailey and Ethan until I can get them moved?"

"Absolutely. Would you have a problem if I squirreled them away in Connecticut? I know a guy with a well-protected house all three can stay at." They reached the elevators right as one opened, and Dex stepped out carrying Ethan. "Hey, buddy," Knox said reaching for him. The little boy wrapped his arms around Knox and buried his head in his shoulder.

"Back to the office?" Dex asked.

"Yeah, we've got work to do," Dover agreed.

"So, is it good if I whisk this group a state over?" Knox asked.

"That's a good idea. They'll be safe there. The fewer people who know where they are, the safer, I say," Dex added. With a nod, they parted company. Knox headed back to the hospital room while Dex and Dover entered the elevator. "Don't worry about them. Knox will make sure they're safe."

"I'm just going to have to take your word for that. I don't have time to second-guess that decision. Fox said it was the son, Edmund Anderson, who abducted him."

"Do you think that's also who killed Brooke? I'm thinking it would have to be. There are simply too many coincidences to discount that they're connected."

"I agree it has to be. Right now, our priority is finding Anderson. Have you heard from anyone about either scene?"

"I was just hanging up from talking to Danny when I saw Bailey. He was still waiting for the reports to come in—said he'd crack a whip if he had to."

"He will too. Grab one of these patrol officers to take us back to the office while I start the BOLO for Edmund Anderson." Dex headed toward a patrol car while she dialed her phone. "Danny, we need warrants for anywhere Edmund Anderson lives, works, or breathes. We also need to put out an all-points for him. I'll explain when I get back."

She hung up and walked to where Dex was waving at her. Even her bones felt weary as she slid into the passenger side of the car. It was a struggle to even remember the last time she slept. Now she was gearing up for a manhunt of a serial killer. But only if Fox's memory could be trusted.

Laying her head back on the headrest, she closed her eyes. She needed to collect her thoughts. Was it possible that the other half of this killer team had been under their noses all this time? Or was Brooke just another fatality of one killer? None of it made any sense. They would need to make a timeline of her movements over the past months.

There was a list of things to do forming in her head. She needed to check with Sean about Brooke's autopsy. The murder board needed to be updated with Fox's information. There was a timeline one of the other officers started that would need to be added to. She could rely on Danny harassing forensics, so that was off her plate.

"Detective?" she heard. Opening her eyes, she found herself outside the police department.

"Right. Thank you," she said as she opened her door.

She was heading inside when she remembered Dex was locked in the back of the cruiser. "Sorry," she said when the officer opened the back door for him.

The incident room was packed and loud when they entered a few minutes later. "Okay, listen up." She crossed to the front of the room as it drew silent. Picking up a marker, she wrote the name "Edmund Anderson" at the top.

"This is our focus now." Danny handed her a photo to attach to the board. "We need to find this man as soon as possible. He is considered to be armed and dangerous. I need people tracing his steps over the last couple of days. I also need his friends interviewed. Find his parents. See if they know where he is. He is very well connected and considered a flight risk."

"The warrants to search his home and any properties he owns have just come in," Danny broke in. She set the marker down and walked to his laptop. "Special Agent Tanaka will head up the search for Mr. Anderson while I lead the search of his home. Anything comes in, I want to know about it immediately. Let's go." Danny stood and followed her out. They picked up the warrants down the hall.

"Hey," Dex said, catching up. "One of the nurses handed this to me. I thought you might want to see it before I take it to trace." He held out a plastic bag. Inside was a medallion of a man holding one arm up and a book of script in the other. "St. Vincent Ferrer. Patron saint of carpenters."

"Does that mean he targeted my brother?" Her thoughts went back to Fox hanging from the strap around his neck. She had been too busy trying to free him to notice something under the strap. What she had noticed, though, was the fear in his eyes as he fought to stand as still as possible. She would never forget how he fell into Knox's arms in exhaustion.

"I don't know, but I thought you needed to see it."

She nodded and continued through the building toward the parking lot with Danny on her heels. If he planned to take her brother instead of it just having been bad happenstance, it was a completely different problem. It meant Fox was still in danger. The killer could still finish the job.

With renewed determination, she pushed through the doors. It was time to hunt down a killer. And if he didn't make it to the jail cell? Well, that was fine by her. It was time he reaped what he sowed.

CHAPTER 30

FOX SAT in a hospital chair in a pair of borrowed scrubs watching Ethan play with the dinosaur he had packed in his small backpack. Bailey had only agreed to leave him there because there was a policeman stationed outside the room. There had been a rotation of them for the last two days while he recovered from being strangled.

The doctor assured him that his voice would recover in time, he just needed to rest it for now. Ethan thought it was great fun drawing on the small whiteboard Knox found for him to communicate with.

His brother had hovered around like an old woman the entire time. He had explained that they would be met at a private airport and whisked away the second he was well enough to leave the hospital. No one told him where they were going.

Knox was currently running Bailey to her house to gather them some clothes. He had already packed a bag from Fox's apartment. He wasn't too worried about them even though Edmund was still on the loose. Dover had regaled him with the story of Knox burning the warehouse doors down to get inside. If anyone could protect Bailey, it was his overgrown brother.

"I'm hungry," Ethan complained. Fox rubbed his stomach and nodded. The whiteboard was great with adults, but the four-year-old couldn't quite read sentences yet.

"What do you want?" Fox croaked out instead.

"Pizza!" His grin was so infectious that Fox grinned back. Then Ethan's grin turned into a frown. "Aunt Bailey said you're not supposed to talk."

Fox held up his fingers like he was locking his mouth, then he crossed his heart. Holding up a finger, he snatched up the whiteboard. Quickly, he wrote a message while Ethan watched.

Slowly, he opened the room door. The officer quickly turned to see what was happening. Fox held up the whiteboard so he could read it.

"I can have some sent up to you from the café," the man said. Fox scribbled another line on the board and turned it around. "No, you're not leaving this room, even for the café, without authorization from Detective Addams. She'd have my head."

Fox wrote one more time on the board. Turning it back around, the officer read it with a smile. "Call me what you want, but that's the best I can do." Fox nodded. The officer motioned for a nurse and asked that some cheese pizza sent up.

Fox closed the door. He wouldn't be eating any of the pizza. His throat still hurt too much to swallow anything but soft food. At least he could smell it while Ethan ate.

He was so ready to leave the hospital, he could scream.

Not that he would ever return to his apartment again. Knox was making arrangements to pack everything up and move it to storage. He would deal with that when they returned.

The future was such a crapshoot now anyway. Dover had mentioned him moving in with her, but he would much rather relocate farther north. He didn't know if Bailey would even want him around after all of this. Somehow, he had managed to get her sister killed and her pulled out of her home and into hiding.

The pizza arrived, so Ethan sat on the bed eating it on the rolling table. Fox searched the room for something to do. He had no idea what had happened to his phone, and the television was set to cartoons. They had agreed the last thing Ethan needed was news coverage of his mother's death. Fox had watched more cartoons in the last two days than in all his life prior.

"Hey," Knox said, pushing the room door open. "Pizza? How did you get pizza?" Ethan giggled. "Man, someone's getting spoiled." Ethan giggled again. "You about ready?" he asked Fox. Fox nodded, so Knox gathered up Ethan and his pizza. "Bailey is waiting with Dover in the lobby. The bags are already in the car. We're getting an escort."

"What's that?" Ethan asked.

"The police are going to take us to the airport. Isn't that exciting?!"

"Yay!"

They rode the elevator with two police officers to the ground floor. In the lobby, they not only met Dover and Bailey, but Memphis stood next to them. A pretty woman and a little girl completed the group.

"Hey, you look a tad better than last time I saw you," Memphis said. "I mean, as much as your ugly face can." He pulled Fox into a bear hug. Turning him lose, he turned to the woman. "I'm staying in Boston to help with the hunt. This is my wife, Thayer. She thought Ethan might enjoy someone to play with for a little while." He squatted to his knees. "Ethan, this is Blue. She wanted to meet you. Is that okay?"

Blue waved, and Ethan smiled. "I like dinosaurs," he announced.

"Me too," she answered. "Daddy said were cousins."

"Okay," he agreed.

"Thayer will show you around and make sure you're settled," Memphis said, pushing back up to his feet. "If you need anything, you just have to ask. Or in your case," he added, turning to Fox, "grunt."

"We need to get you out of here," Dover said. She pulled Fox in for a hug. "Take care of yourself." She handed him a phone. "It's encrypted so you can get a hold of me whenever."

"Let's go." Knox took the hands of both kids and herded them through the door. There was a large SUV waiting just outside with what looked like undercover agents standing at the ready.

"Be careful," Memphis said when Fox shook his hand.

He nodded before joining Knox next to the car. He slid into one of the seats next to Bailey. Her hand found his. A police car pulled away from the hospital with their car following. He turned to look out the back to find a second police cruiser following.

"Are you doing okay?" she asked quietly. He nodded and moved his arm around her shoulders. She leaned against him the entire way to the airport. He decided that moving north of the city might not be such a stretch anymore.

When they got settled wherever they were going, he did need to email his boss though. Hopefully, he would still have a job when all of this was over.

The kids chatted in the back seat, both bent over some game Blue had brought. Knox sat next to them dozing with his head against the window. Thayer sat on the other side of Bailey. He hoped she would be the comfort Bailey needed to mourn her sister if he wasn't enough.

They pulled through a private gate onto the tarmac of a private airport. The SUV stopped next to a private jet.

"Exactly who did you make arrangements with?" Bailey asked.

"It belongs to Thayer's father. I used to work for him. He does me a favor from time to time," Knox answered.

"Some favor." They opened the doors and climbed out. Blue ran up the steps into the airplane as if she did it every day. Ethan waited at the bottom until Bailey nodded at him to follow. By the time Fox managed to climb aboard, they were sitting in the back with a box of colored pencils between them on a table.

Fox dropped into a seat, leaned his head back, and closed his eyes. It had been impossible to sleep in the hospital with the staff coming into his room every few hours. Fatigue was finally catching up to him.

"Is there anything I can get you before we take off," Thayer asked quietly. "It's a short flight. The drive after is only half an hour, then you can rest."

"Thank you for doing all of this," Bailey answered.

He listened to them visit as he slowly fell asleep. His dreams were brief but filled with a faceless man torturing him as he swung from the ceiling in a cell. The face slowly morphed into a man he had spent days ignoring while he worked on the townhouse. The cell became the attic with the new floors he had painstakingly laid and the deep blue paint Edmund had chosen.

The dreams continued until he was jolted awake by the wheels touching down on the runway.

They were ushered into another large SUV. It wound through the countryside until it reached an intimidating set of gates. There was a guard who stepped out to nod as they drove by. The driveway ended at a house that landed just under what would be considered a mansion. It could easily accommodate all of them with room to spare.

"Dad sent his regrets that he couldn't be here to welcome you himself. He's busy arguing about the military budget on Capitol Hill this week," Thayer said as she led them up the front steps. The kids pushed past her and barreled up the stairs into the foyer. "They're fine. There's a room full of toys upstairs. We probably won't hear from them for hours."

"I'm sorry. He usually acts better than this," Bailey began.

"He's had a lot to deal with this week. It will be good for him to forget for a little while. Now, let me show you to your rooms." Thayer led them up the stairs. "The kids have adjoining rooms at the end of the hall, and yours are this way." They followed her down the hallway to a suite of rooms at the other end. "I'll sleep in the room next to the kids in case they need anything."

"This is beautiful. Thank you."

"Just let me know if you need anything. We'll have dinner about six. I'll be downstairs or checking on the kids. We might go for a walk after a while." Thayer pulled Bailey into a hug. Fox watched as Bailey seemed to melt against her. Finally they parted.

"Get some rest and don't worry about a thing." Thayer

turned and walked to the other end of the long hallway before disappearing into one of the rooms.

"Which room do you want?" Bailey asked. In answer he took her hand and led her into one of the rooms. He didn't care where he was as long as he was with her. "Okay, I can take the other one." He pulled her around him until the back of her knees touched the bed.

"Stay with me," he whispered. She sank to sit on the bed. Her bright blue gaze looked up into his. She nodded, and he pressed her back onto the bed. He followed her down until he lay over her with his arms taking his weight. His lips met the hollow where her neck met her shoulder. Her moan urged him on. "I need to be inside you."

"Yes," she begged.

He stood and moved to lock the door, so they wouldn't take a chance on any young children walking in on them. Returning to the bed, he pulled her blouse over her head. It was tossed to the floor. She arched her back so he could slide a hand up her back to unhook her bra. It was added to the growing pile of clothes.

"You're so beautiful." He bent until he could pull a hard nipple between his teeth.

"Fox," she gasped. Her hands stroked through his hair. He continued to worry her breasts with his tongue, flicking until she gripped his hair in her fist. His hands slid inside the waistband of her pants and pulled them down. Sinking to his knees, he pulled them over her feet and tossed them out of the way.

He spread her legs wide taking in the dampness of her panties. His nose pressed against them as he took a breath. Nothing was better than being pressed between her thighs.

Sliding her panties to the side, his tongue reached for its

first taste. She began to squirm, and he pressed an arm over her abdomen to hold her in place.

"Be a good girl," he snarled before returning to where he left off. She fought against his arm as her moans grew louder. Without warning, he felt her contract against his tongue as he thrust it inside her. He wrung every ounce of her orgasm from her, leaving her replete on the bed, before standing.

He expected her to remain down as he undressed. Instead, she sat up quickly and began tearing at his clothes. Her hands plunged into his pants as she worried the tie at his waist loose. Then his pants and underwear were around his ankles.

Her mouth quickly closed over his hardness. For a moment, he worried he'd finish before he could press inside her the way he wanted. But she stopped at the last moment to lay back on the bed.

"Turn over," he growled. He helped her roll onto her knees. Grabbing her hips, he climbed onto the bed and slammed into her. She groaned loudly like a reward only he understood. He held her shoulder in his hand to keep her steady as he plowed into her over and over.

Nothing he could remember in this life had ever felt so good. It wasn't just about the sex. It was knowing the woman he'd always meant to be with was finally his.

There was a second of guilt over Brooke that rushed through his mind. He would never have wished the fate of a violent death on her, but it had happened nonetheless.

He felt Bailey tighten again, and he was done. Lava rushed up his spine, spilling into her. She collapsed under him, with him following her down. He rolled off quickly to prevent hurting her, but he pulled her into his arms.

"I know we're in hiding," she said quietly. "And there's a

part of my heart that will always miss Brooke." She rolled over so they were facing each other. Her hand carefully brushed his cheek. "But I can't help feeling happy. I know it's early, but I think I fell in love with you the first time I met you. In lust anyway."

"I understand," he whispered. Softly, he kissed her nose. "And this is only the beginning."

EPILOGUE

"I'M SORRY, Detective, but we can't waste any more time or resources on this." Dover heard the words her captain was saying, she just didn't believe them. "We're turning the files over to the feds and letting them run with it. I'm sure SAC Tanaka will contact you if he has any questions."

The captain turned back to his reports. She would have argued with him, but it wouldn't do any good. Once the boss made up his mind, there was no persuading him otherwise.

"What did he say?" Danny asked when she walked back into their office.

"No dice."

"I really am sorry," Dex added. He was perched on the edge of Danny's desk. "This wasn't my call."

"We know," Danny answered. "It's how things work. The bastard has been running for two weeks now. The chances of him even being in the country still are slim. We've got other things to move on to."

"Do we?" she wanted to scream. What was more important than finding a killer? Her brother, Bailey, and Ethan

were still in hiding. Though they had moved on to Minnesota with Thayer to meet more family. She was a little jealous of that. Knox had given up and returned home as well. He had to get ready for the new school year.

Everyone went on with their lives like nothing had happened—except her anyway. Even Dex was putting together a team to continue the job. In his world, it was just another workday. She was the only one left hanging with nothing to show for her hard work. There had to be something she could do.

"You should think about taking some time off," Danny said. "When was the last time you got any sleep?" The bags under her eyes must be more pronounced than she thought.

"I don't know. Months? Years?"

"That's what I'm saying. You'll burn out early if you don't take some downtime occasionally. Go join your brother on vacation. I can hold down the fort here."

"I don't know. I'll think about it." She signed some paperwork that Dex handed her. This would be one of the smoothest transitions of a case ever. It still rankled her though. "I'll head over to the medical examiner's office and let them know to start pulling their files. See you later."

"Take care. Get some rest." Danny waved as she walked out the door. He would make sure Dex had everything he needed. She just wanted to clear her head for a while. The morgue seemed as good a place as any. Besides, she would much rather sit in a room and whine with Sean than Danny. Not that Danny wasn't a good guy, but he didn't hold a candle to Sean in the looks department.

She took her car this time instead of one of the cars in the detective pool. There was a very good chance she would head home after talking to Sean. She didn't want to have to return to police headquarters just for her car. It would be time for dinner when she was done anyway. She just wished someone was left in town to eat with. It looked like it would be a heat-and-serve on the couch again tonight.

Finding parking in a civilian car was always a lot harder than in a city-owned one. She finally managed to wedge her car along the curb a block from the ME's office. It was still hot as Hades outside, but there was already a whisper of fall beginning in the evenings. Just a whisper though, no verbose yelling.

"Hey, Detective," Sean said as she walked into the building. He was leaning over the reception counter visiting with the woman who had worked there as long as Dover had been on the force. She was smiling widely and twirling her hair as she flirted with him. All fifty-plus years were working it hard enough for Dover to be impressed.

"Got a minute?" she asked.

"Yeah. I was just going to give you a call." He motioned for her to join him as he walked to his office. The receptionist gave her a conspiratorial wink on the way by. "I was wondering if you have any plans for dinner tonight? Nothing crazy. I just thought we could grab a burger somewhere and talk. I heard the saint killer case is going to the feds."

"The saint killer?"

"No?" He grinned at her. "I was trying it on for size."

"Keep working at it."

"Noted. Anyway," he continued, ushering her into his office. "What about dinner?"

She had to think for a second about how to answer the question. What she wanted to do was jump up and down clapping her hands. No self-respecting police detective would do that, however. "Why not," is what she finally settled on without looking too interested.

"Perfect. It's the start of the weekend, but we should be able to squeeze in somewhere." His voice drifted off as he started searching for open tables on a phone app.

"I have a better idea," she said. A brilliant thought had suddenly struck her. "How about a weekend date. You have a bike, right? A mountain bike?"

"Yes?"

"Great. I'll pick you up at your place in an hour. Pack for the weekend, and we'll get some biking in somewhere in New Hampshire. What do you think?" She hadn't biked in years, but it shouldn't take long to pick it back up. She was still in decent shape.

"Umm. Sure, I guess."

"Send me your address. I'll see you in an hour." Without waiting for him to come up with a reason to back out, she walked out of his office. She would heed Danny's advice to get some rest.

A little mountain air would do her good, and if she just happened to check out a couple of abandoned cabins for a madman, so much the better. Especially if there had been sightings in the area.

An hour later she was pulling up to one of the many apartment buildings near the university area. She had wrestled her bike rack onto the top of her SUV and thrown some extra clothes into a bag. She had even managed to run through the shower. Sean stood waiting for her with his bike and a large backpack.

"I honestly didn't know if you were serious or not," he said. "I figured if you didn't show in half an hour, I would just go back inside. Chalk it up to some twisted prank to get out of dinner." He picked his bike up like it weighed nothing and slid it into the rack. "I've heard there are a couple of good trails in the White Mountains, but I've never ridden them myself. There's just never enough time."

"We can grab something to eat outside of the city. I made room reservations at a place my brother and I have stayed at in the past. It's nothing fancy, but it does the job." She climbed back into the driver's seat. He stored his pack in the back and climbed in next to her.

"This is going to be great. I can't believe I'm finally getting away for the weekend. Thanks for asking. I can't wait to see what we do," he added with a grin.

"Me too," she answered, glad she had remembered to pack her ankle holster.

———

Sean wasn't sure how the weekend, which had been full of promise, had turned out the way it had. He had finally gotten up the nerve to ask Dover on a date. It had been her idea to make it an entire weekend, though he didn't hate the idea. Who wouldn't want to spend two days with a gorgeous woman in the mountain air.

This wasn't what he had in mind when he agreed, though. It had started out okay. They found a small diner that sold hamburgers and hand-cut fries somewhere between Boston and the New Hampshire border. He'd watched as she slowly relaxed in his company. It was a heady feeling knowing he could have that effect on her.

She was right about the hotel. It wasn't going to win any awards, but the bed was soft, and the water was hot. They started out the next morning on a ten-mile easy trail just to get back into the mountain biking groove.

They moved on to a harder one before lunch. Then they transitioned to a remote trail that went deep into the woods later that afternoon. Where they had passed several bikers on the other trails, no one was on this one.

By nightfall, they found themselves at the very back of the trail near an old abandoned cabin. Dover stepped off her bike half a mile from the cabin and watched it for a few minutes. He leaned his bike against a tree. Fishing his water bottle out, he took a long drink.

"Need some?" he asked.

"Shh," she answered. She was still staring at the cabin. To his amazement, she pulled a pair of high-powered binoculars out of her daypack.

"What are you looking at?" He was quieter this time when he spoke.

"There was a sighting of Edmund Anderson in this area."

"Are you kidding me? Is this what all this weekend thing was about? Catching the very person you were told to let the FBI handle?" He shoved the bottle back in his pack.

"Shh. I'm just going to take a look." She eased toward the cabin. He shook his head and followed her. "Get down. I don't want to alert him that we're here, just in case he's in there."

Sean found himself walking from tree to tree in an awkward squat. He guessed if this got it out of her system, then it wouldn't hurt.

Slowly, they approached the cabin in a hunch. Several times he found himself shoved onto his stomach in the dirt until she decided they could continue forward.

By the time they made it to the cabin, his once just sweaty biking clothes were covered in dirt. They made a round peeking in windows until she was satisfied no one was inside.

"Damn it!" she exclaimed before kicking in the front door.

"Christ, what are you doing?"

"Memphis thought he was here," she mumbled. "He was so sure this time."

"Who's Memphis? What are you talking about? Did he see Anderson around here?" Sean couldn't help but peer into the darkening woods around them. There were shadows everywhere. If Edmund Anderson was one of them, he'd never know it. The thought made him nervous.

"Sort of."

"Sort of. What does that mean? Did he see him or not?" He stood in the doorway as she sifted through the contents of the interior. As far as he could see, no one had been here in a while. Perhaps, whoever Memphis was, just thought he saw someone who resembled the killer. "Probably just a crank or something. You know how unreliable witnesses are."

"This guy is different." She finally gave up her search and brushed past him. Pausing on the porch, she began brushing the dirt off her own clothes. She hadn't elaborated on her statement before she started down the steps.

"What do you mean he's different? What's so special about him?" He watched as she stopped on the top step and turned to face him. "Is there something you're not telling me? I deserve to know what it is you've got me up here for. Was it on false pretenses so you could continue your chase of a serial killer? I'm all for doing my civic duty, but this might be a bit too—"

He didn't get a chance to finish his sentence before she had stepped up to him and pressed her lips to his. Nothing could have taken him more by surprise.

She pulled back and gazed at him as if she was going to

confess all of her sins. That could wait. He wrapped a hand around the back of neck. Pulling her back to him, he kissed her again.

This time he wasn't surprised. There was no ambush involved. He felt her melt against his chest as his tongue swept across hers. Somehow, he forgot to be indignant about how he got to this place. If this was the result, the why didn't matter. Neither did the how, or the who, or the when. Since he met her, this was all he had thought about. All he had fantasized about.

Unfortunately, they were human and had to break for air. He wanted to stand on this porch forever doing exactly what he was doing at that moment. Dover had other ideas though. She placed a hand on his chest pressing him back slightly.

"You wanted to know why Memphis was different."

"I mean, yeah."

"Memphis is my brother," she continued.

"Okay. I didn't know that, but I can't see why that matters."

"Because we're all different in my family."

"I'm not following."

"You'd better sit down." They sat next to each other on the rickety steps. She turned her warm gaze to his. "How good are you at keeping secrets? Because I've got a real doozie."

———

Thank you for reading Fox and Bailey's story. Looking for more? Don't miss out on book six, Dover and Sean's story, coming soon.

Until then, have you ever wondered how the family got

its powers? Find out in Irreversible, free just for signing up for my monthly newsletter. Just don't expect a happy ending.

https://BookHip.com/QPQHKJK

Ashur is no ordinary man; he's a god. The council tasked him with one mission. To save humanity one person at a time. Either that, or he'll be forgotten for eternity.

Sunny is an ordinary woman. She's just finished high school and is working to save for college. Life isn't perfect, and when a beautiful man seems to appear from nowhere with her in his sights, she's hooked.

It's he beginning of a legacy that will save mankind from its own destruction. Even if there's no happily-ever-after for them this time around.

ALSO BY A. SAMSON

Hers to Forget

Hers Always

The New England Romance Series

College Contemporary

Nothing Ventured

Best Laid Schemes

In For a Penny

Actions Speak Louder

The Dansboro Crossing Series

Small-town Contemporary

Overdue

Upshot

Brazen

Harmony for Christmas

Falling

ACKNOWLEDGMENTS

I hope you enjoyed my first attempt at a serial killer story. As you're now aware, Dover's book will continue with the hunt of the man who tried to kill her brother.

I've always loved a good mystery or thriller. Now, I have a whole new level of respect for those authors. These things are hard! Thankfully, I had a lot of good people to help.

When I mentioned the idea for book five in this series, Rachel was right there with me. I think her exact words were, "fun." She didn't just create the gorgeous cover, she also both alpha and beta read it for me. She was the voice that told me to keep going every time I questioned what the heck I was doing. She also has my biggest thanks for everything she does.

Thanks to Meredith at Anessa Books for hunting down the plot holes and inconsistencies. The edits weren't too bad this time which means I must be getting better.

As always, thanks to Ellie at My Brother's Editor for evicerating my manuscript and then helping me put it back together better than before. This is our fifth year working together and I wouldn't trust anyone else. I lost count at our twenty-fifth book.

As always, my family jumped in to suggest names, plot points, and even how to build the machine used in the kill room. They are the best for giving me the time and space to do what I love. I wouldn't trade them for anyone.

Finally, thank you to all of the readers, ARC readers, influencers, and everyone else who picked up this book. In a world with so many books, choosing mine warms my heart. I am eternally grateful for each and every one of you.

- Avery

ABOUT THE AUTHOR

Avery Samson grew up on a ranch outside of a small west Texas town. Since she could remember, she's had her face stuck in a book. High School graduation found her leaving ranch life for the big city.

After living all over the state of Texas, she now finds herself back on one of the family ranches near Dallas with her husband surrounded by cattle. A lot of them. They're everywhere! When not traveling or reading, she spends her time writing.

Avery would love for you to follow her. She's everywhere (just like those damn cows.)

Join my newsletter for all the latest news.
averysamsonbooks.com/newsletter

Visit my website for my current book list.
averysamsonbooks.com

Like me on Facebook.
https://www.facebook.com/averysamsonauthor

Follow me on Instagram.
https://www.instagram.com/averysamson91/

Watch my videos on TikTok.
https://www.tiktok.com/@averysamson91

Check out my Pinterest page.
https://www.pinterest.com/averysamson91/

www.ingramcontent.com/pod-product-compliance
Lightning Source LLC
Chambersburg PA
CBHW020416260626
47156CB00007B/2411